KISSING THE CAPTAIN

"Stop talking."

Juliette was so taken aback by his command that she ceased speaking. He stepped closer to her. Losing all sense of what they had been arguing about, she stared up at Captain Harrison Fleming.

He leaned in toward her and tore the straw hat from her head, her long black hair spilling around her. Stunned, it seemed her heart stopped for a second and she could not draw a breath. As she suddenly sensed what he was about to do, a ripple of exhilaration raced through her. In a quick movement, Harrison pulled her against his chest, lowered his mouth over hers, and kissed her.

For the first time in her life, it seemed she could do nothing. Nothing except kiss him back. In an instant, she lost herself completely in the feel of his warm lips upon hers. It was like nothing she had ever known or expected. Juliette had been kissed before, certainly. Many times, in fact. But this . . .

Kissing Captain Harrison Fleming was something else altogether . . .

Books by Kaitlin O'Riley

SECRETS OF A DUCHESS

ONE SINFUL NIGHT

WHEN HIS KISS IS WICKED

DESIRE IN HIS EYES

Published by Kensington Publishing Corporation

Desire In His Eyes

Kaitlin O'Riley

ZEBRA BOOKS
Kensington Publishing Corp.
http://www.kensingtonbooks.com

ZEBRA BOOKS are published by

Kensington Publishing Corp.
119 West 40th Street
New York, NY 10018

All Kensington titles, imprints, and distributed lines are available at special quantity discounts for bulk purchases for sales promotion, premiums, fund-raising, educational, or institutional use.

Special book excerpts or customized printings can also be created to fit specific needs. For details, write or phone the office of the Kensington Special Sales Manager: Attn.: Special Sales Department. Kensington Publishing Corp., 119 West 40th Street, New York, NY 10018. Phone: 1-800-221-2647.

Zebra and the Z logo Reg. U.S. Pat. & TM Off.

ISBN-13: 978-1-4201-0447-9
ISBN-10: 1-4201-0447-0

First Printing: March 2010

10 9 8 7 6 5 4 3 2 1

Printed in the United States of America

*To Yvonne TC La Brecque Deane
for being like another sister to me since the fourth grade,
and for those novels we started*

Acknowledgments

Oh, there are so many people to thank! Thank you to my wonderful agent, Jane Dystel, and my fantastic editor at Kensington, John Scognamiglio. I couldn't possibly write in French without help from my very own French connection—my cousin Laurence Maurin Cogger. *Merci beaucoup!* Thank you to Billy Van Zandt and Adrienne Barbeau for their sage advice and unending support. Thank you to my incredible network of aunts, uncles, and cousins who buy my books and come to all my book signings! A note of thanks to Yvonne Deane, Kim McCafferty, Michele Wiener, Cela Lim, Melanie Carlisle, Gretchen Kempf, Jeff Babey, Lynn Kroll, Eric Anderson, and Jaime Merz.

Since I'm in the middle of a series about sisters, I want to thank *my* sisters—Jane, Maureen, Janet, and Jennifer—without whom I would not have the inspiration. My life would be empty without these four amazing women, who just happen to be my best friends. (And special thanks to Jane, as always, for her expertise in editing and for giving me a home away from home.) Of course I have to thank the best brothers-in-law in the world: Richard Vaczy, Scott Wheeler, and Greg Malins. I also want to thank my father, John Milmore, who is my biggest fan and will even research elusive historical facts for me.

By the way, my books are works of fiction—any similarities to members of my family are purely coincidental!

Note to Riley:
Thank you for all those pajama days.
I love you more than you know.
(Now go get your homework done!)

∾ 1 ∾

What a Way to Go

London, England
Summer, 1871

The evening Captain Harrison Fleming came to supper at Devon House was the night Juliette Hamilton finally made up her mind to run away.

That had been three weeks ago.

Now Juliette held her breath, her heart pounding an erratic rhythm against her chest, waiting silently in the shadows as a small group of sailors, laughing and talking in boisterous tones, walked by oblivious to her presence. *Oh, God, she was really doing this.* She was actually leaving. Leaving her sisters. Her family. Her home.

A strange thrill coursed through her and she took a deep breath of the briny night air to fortify her shaking legs. She peered cautiously from her hiding space on the dock behind a stack of large oak barrels filled with she knew not what. The moonlit water glistened as still as glass beside the dock.

All her planning had come to this moment.

There was the *Sea Minx*, docked just where Captain Fleming had said it would be. For some reason, it looked smaller than she had imagined.

When the last sailor had disappeared up the gangway, Juliette pulled the black cap down over her head to heighten her boyish disguise and took another deep breath, before scurrying on silent feet, up the ramp onto the deck of the *Sea Minx*.

Juliette had somehow managed a minor miracle by reaching the dock and boarding the ship without being detected. Now began the more challenging aspect of her plan. She needed to remain hidden until they were well out to sea, when it would be too late for Captain Fleming to turn back and bring her home. Unsure where to go next, she hesitated before she ducked through a low doorway and climbed down into a narrow and dimly lit passageway. Suddenly hearing male voices and heavy footsteps approaching, she opened the nearest door in a blind panic and found herself inside what appeared to be some sort of small storage room.

Once again she held her breath, not daring to move until the voices passed by, as her eyes slowly adjusted to the dimness. When the passageway quieted and she no longer heard voices, Juliette softly exhaled before daring to draw another breath. *Now what?*

Her plan had not been so detailed as to exactly what she would do once she finally boarded the ship, aside from keeping out of sight until they had set sail. Now she fumbled about in the cramped, dark space awash in briny smells until she found a small wooden crate upon which to sit. Thrilled with this bit of good fortune, she sat and nervously patted the little satchel she had managed to bring with her. She had packed enough food to sustain her for a few days if she ate sparingly, a photographic card of her family which was taken at her sister Colette's wedding last fall, letters with her friend Christina Dunbar's address, a change of clothes, and money. She had more than enough funds to last her quite a while. Her brother-in-law had settled a rather large amount of money on her and she had gone to the bank that afternoon and, not sure how much she would need, she had withdrawn much of it. Once she reached New York City she would seek out her friend at her house on Fifth Avenue.

Then her adventure would really begin.

She had finally done it! She had successfully boarded Captain Fleming's ship! She hugged herself in disbelief, stunned that she had actually accomplished her goal.

A rather strong pang of regret filled her at the thought of her four sisters. When they discovered the note of explanation she had left in her bedroom her sisters would undoubtedly be overcome with worry and panic at her unexpected departure, but there was no help for it. It was time. Juliette had had to seize this opportunity to leave. She simply had no choice. She wished to be free and independent and this was the only way.

As she sat in the dank and brine-scented gloom, she felt the ship begin to rock beneath her and pitch forward. Loud shouts and excited cries could be heard above deck. Her heart lurched. *This was it!* There was no turning back now. The *Sea Minx* was sailing out across the Atlantic Ocean to America. Her fate was sealed, for better or for worse. For a fraction of a second she regretted her crazy desire to venture out and see the world, but then she held up her chin and grinned to herself in the dark.

She had always longed to break free, to have an exciting

adventure, for a chance to visit exotic locales, to meet new people. However, she had not envisioned doing so in such furtive secrecy.

But that night at Devon House three weeks earlier she knew within an instant that Captain Harrison Fleming had unwittingly presented her with an advantageous opportunity to escape her stultifying existence.

Perhaps it was while he described his beautiful clipper ship, the *Sea Minx*. The color of his eyes seemed the exact shade of the ocean on a stormy gray afternoon. Or maybe it was when he regaled them all with tales of his life at sea and his adventures in ports around the globe. He had actually *been* to exotic and foreign lands. India. China. Africa. The Caribbean. America. Captain Fleming was living the life she had only dared to dream of and it fascinated her to hear him speak.

Juliette's brilliant scheme had come to her in bits and pieces throughout the lengthy eight-course meal. She could not quite pinpoint the exact moment that the idea to stow away on his ship popped into her head, but by the end of that intimate supper party at Devon House, the beginnings of her plan had everything to do with the charismatic Captain Fleming. As soon as she learned that he planned to return to New York shortly, Juliette knew just what she had to do. She might never have this chance again.

He was her only means of getting to New York. She had to sail with him.

She had barely been able to finish her dessert for containing her excitement at this revolutionary idea.

"Look at Juliette, would you? She looks like the cat that ate the canary," Lord Jeffrey Eddington had remarked to everyone gathered around the dinner table, an amused smile lurking on his boyishly handsome face, his merry eyes dancing. "Tell us now what is going on in that pretty head of yours, Juliette. Whatever are you scheming about now?"

Juliette had flashed him an irritated glance while trying to maintain an innocent expression. Leave it to Jeffrey to notice the slightest bit of change in her. In spite of being her dearest friend, he could be quite exasperating. If Jeffrey even suspected what she was plotting to do he would see to it that Lucien had Juliette locked in her bedchamber and under twenty-four-hour guard for the rest of her life.

She had to be very careful with Jeffrey. He could easily spoil everything.

"It's exciting listening to Captain Fleming's adventures of life at sea," Juliette had answered Jeffrey coolly, glancing toward the tall and rugged looking man who sat to the right of her sister Colette. They had all just been introduced to Captain Fleming that evening, because her brother-in-law, Lucien Sinclair, the Earl of Waverly, had invited him to stay at Devon House while he was conducting business in London. Apparently the two men were good friends, although Juliette had a difficult time imagining her staid and very proper brother-in-law fostering a friendship with the rather daring sea captain.

At her remark to Jeffrey, Captain Fleming questioned her across the long and elaborately set table. "Is that so, Miss Hamilton? And just what part of my story did you find so exciting?"

His exotic accent added to his charm, Juliette acknowledged. He sounded very American, which, of course, was only natural considering he was born in New York, but she found it intriguing nonetheless. He was vastly different from any man she had ever met in London, and Juliette found herself staring boldly into his silver gray eyes. "I believe it was the part where you described your journey from New York to San Francisco. It was as though I were on your ship. I could hear the waves. I could feel the excitement and the freedom of sailing on the ocean."

Captain Fleming smiled at her, and Juliette felt her heart flutter erratically. How peculiar! She had never met a man who made her heart race. Nor had she ever expected to. At least not here at Devon House.

But she had always held out a vain hope that she would meet one. All through the Season last year, when her Uncle Randall had forced her and Colette to find husbands, every man she had met had bored her to tears. While Colette had been fortunate enough to fall in love with the handsome and wealthy Lucien Sinclair, and rescue the family from financial ruin and save the family bookshop, Juliette had had a more difficult time. Aside from becoming fast friends with Jeffrey Eddington, she had not met a single gentleman who held her interest for more than a minute. To be completely honest with herself, she knew she scared the trousers off most of the men who met her and she took a perverse delight in doing just that. All she had to do was say something even remotely opinionated or slightly out of the ordinary and they did not know what to do with her. Despite her behavior, most of them became besotted with her anyway, declaring their love in the most embarrassing manner. The rest saw her as a challenge, something that they could tame or subdue. Juliette despaired of ever meeting a man who lived up to her expectations. Not even her darling Jeffrey.

No. She had to leave London. If she didn't get away from London, away from the tightly bound rules of society, even away from her family as much as she loved them, she knew she would go mad. Stark, raving mad.

So she had left.

Now she found herself aboard a ship captained by a

man she barely knew. What would Harrison Fleming do when he discovered her, which at some point he undoubtedly would? Would he be angry with her? Most likely. Would he punish her somehow? Perhaps, but she doubted it. Most men were full of bluster but would never dare to lay a finger on her. Would he immediately turn the ship around and drag her back in humiliation to face Colette and Lucien? Perhaps. She could bear almost anything rather than that. She had come so far. She could not return now. She also knew that Captain Fleming had a schedule to keep and needed to arrive in New York before the end of the month, so she had doubted he would lose valuable time by sailing back to London simply to return her.

At least Juliette fervently hoped he would not.

She presumed he would be forced to keep her until they arrived in America with a plan to send her back on another ship, but by then she would have arranged to stay with her friend Christina Dunbar. It was a good plan. In fact, it was the most daring she had ever come up with. Now she only hoped that it worked.

She sighed heavily wondering how long she would have to remain in this dark, cramped space, but she would stay there a month if she had to. If that was what it took to get her to America, she would gladly do it. Her legs were slowly falling asleep and her lower back was beginning to ache. With some rearranging, she managed to lean her satchel behind her as a sort of makeshift cushion for her back. That helped a bit. With nothing else to do but to sit there in the dark, she closed her eyes. Allowing the gentle sway of the ship to lull her, she drifted asleep, dreaming of her new life in New York.

Startled from her sleep by the door being flung open, Juliette screamed, covering her mouth with her hand in a belated attempt to silence herself. She could not be found yet! It seemed too soon, but she had no idea how long she had slept. Were they far out to sea by now? Filled with bitter disappointment, and fear, she glanced up at the person responsible for exposing her hiding space.

A young man, his freckled face awash with disbelief, stood in the dim lantern light of the passageway, startled speechless by her presence in the storage room. They stared mutely at each other for a moment before he recovered his senses. With a disapproving scowl, he cried in outrage, "Hey now there, lad! We don't allow stowaways on board the *Sea Minx*."

Juliette did not dare to move, but she was pleased that she had fooled him with her disguise. Having sweet-talked one of the shorter stable boys from Devon House into giving her his old clothes, she had donned trousers, a shirt, and a tweed cap. She had even smudged her face with ashes. And wearing trousers was most freeing, making her feel even more reckless and independent. No wonder men wore them! She thought she looked quite passable as a young boy, and just as she had planned, this sailor naturally assumed she was one.

"You'll have to come with me to see the captain." The young man grabbed Juliette's arm and yanked her roughly to her feet.

Instinctively, Juliette resisted him, pulling her arm away and retreating further into the storage room.

"Hey!" he cried, reaching for her once more. Angry, he grabbed her tighter and pulled her forcefully into the passageway.

As they tussled, Juliette stumbled forward and her cap fell off her head. Her long dark hair fell in soft waves to her waist.

As the light fell across her face, he shouted, "Bloody hell!"

"Let go of me!" she cried, taking advantage of his stunned state and breaking free of his hold on her.

"You're a girl!" He stepped back from her in astonishment, his eyes round.

"Of course, I'm a girl, you simpleton," she snapped at him, irritated that she should be found out so soon by this mere slip of a boy. She snatched up her cap from the floor in a swift movement, but did not bother to put it back on.

"Wait until the captain sees you," he whispered, shaking his head in disbelief.

Reaching down to grab her tapestry-embroidered satchel, she thought to herself, "*Yes, just wait until the captain sees me.*" Juliette cringed inwardly at the thought of facing Captain Fleming, but there was no help for it. Besides, he was merely a man. Like all the other men she had ever known, she could handle him easily enough. There wasn't a man yet that she hadn't been able to control.

With a remarkable shift in his attitude toward her, the young man said, "You'd better come with me, miss."

Juliette squared her shoulders and followed the young sailor down the narrow passageway toward the captain's cabin.

The door opened into a gorgeous anteroom with wood-paneled walls and gilt-framed maps. A round table with six leather-backed chairs dominated the room. Another door opened partially to reveal the captain's private quarters. She could see a large bed within. Her eyes flashed back quickly to the oak desk, behind which sat Captain Harrison Fleming.

In an excited and incredulous tone, the young cabin boy explained Juliette's presence. "Captain, I found a stowaway aboard, hiding in the storage room with the oilskins. A *girl* stowaway."

"Yes, so I see."

Ignoring her rapidly beating heart, she stared at the imposing figure who was in charge of the *Sea Minx* and now apparently Juliette's fate as well.

"Thank you for bringing our unexpected visitor to my attention," Captain Fleming said with an even-toned voice, although his intent silver colored eyes never left Juliette's face. If he were surprised by Juliette's presence on his ship, he hid it well. "You may leave us now, Robbie."

As the young boy nodded his head and quit the room, Juliette was left alone with Captain Fleming. She had been in his company on many occasions during the past few weeks while he visited her home in London, but never had she been with him alone. Each time she had thought him quiet and somewhat disinterested in her, which had been surprising. Every man she had ever met could not seem to help but lavish her with attention, even the painfully shy ones. Now it seemed that the aloof Captain Fleming was finally giving her his undivided attention.

And that made her uncharacteristically nervous.

He continued to stare at her. His stormy silver gray eyes, with startlingly long lashes, bored into her. She waited in silence, a strange tingling sensation building within her.

Juliette suddenly came to the realization that he was made of sterner stuff than she was accustomed to seeing in most men. He had the bearing of a pirate and beneath his cool surface he seemed to possess a sense of tightly leashed desire as if he kept his emotions on a close rein. With a high forehead, aquiline nose and rakish mouth, he exuded a rugged, very masculine handsomeness. He was quite taller than average, with broad shoulders, sun-streaked blond hair and those amazing eyes. His bronzed skin declared boldly that he spent much of his days out of doors. Yet for all his commanding presence, there was nothing aristocratic about him.

"Well, Juliette, it seems you have put me in an awkward position."

She raised one eyebrow at him for stating the obvious while noting he had dispensed with any formality by not addressing her as Miss Hamilton. Being that she had brazenly stowed away on his ship, she supposed the need for propriety had passed.

"I merely wish to go to New York to visit a friend."

"Then why didn't you simply ask me to take you?"

"My family would never allow me to go. In fact, my mother expressly forbade my going to New York under any circumstances."

"Ahh, I see," he nodded his head, crossing his arms across his broad chest.

His white shirt was partially unbuttoned and Juliette could not help but notice the bare expanse of tanned skin. She swallowed and forced herself to focus on his face. But that also was dangerous. He was a very handsome man. Yes, he was. Definitely.

"I should take you home directly."

"I wish you wouldn't," she managed to respond. If he took her back now, she would die of disappointment. She could not go home.

"Your family must be sick with worry about you by now."

Once again guilt surged within her at the thought of leaving her sisters in such a manner. But truly, she had no other recourse. "I wrote them a letter, explaining what I was doing and telling them not to worry. They won't find it until the morning when I don't appear at breakfast."

"Well, it seems as though you have thought of almost everything."

She challenged him. "Almost?"

"Everything except one."

They waited in tense silence, regarding each other with undisguised wariness. Her heart hammered erratically in her chest. Oh, she had *definitely* underestimated Captain Fleming. Of course he would never harm her. He was a friend of her brother-in-law and had been a guest in their house. Still, a strange sense of nervousness engulfed her at his masculine presence and she trembled. Odd, she had never felt nervous with a man before.

Standing up and stepping from behind his desk, Captain Fleming moved closer to her and she sucked in her breath at his nearness. He loomed over her and the mysterious scent of him made her weak-kneed.

"It seems you overlooked something important in your little scheme to flee to New York," he breathed. He leaned in closer to her face.

Unconsciously she inched away from him. He pressed closer, his intense gray eyes on her, his lips hovering near her cheek. The heat of his breath made her shiver and his whispered words left her speechless. She had backed up against the table and could retreat no farther. She had no choice but to face him.

"You did not factor me into your plan, Juliette."

She stared helplessly at him, this handsome sea captain who held her fate in his hands. This man who embodied all the adventurousness she harbored in her soul. He was close enough to kiss her and for a wild, panicked moment Juliette hoped he would.

His whispered words brushed her lips, causing her to stop breathing altogether.

"Or what I plan to do with you."

∽ 2 ∽

The Best Laid Plans

What the hell *was* he going to do with her?

Harrison Fleming could not believe the woman standing in front of him, close enough that he could kiss her. How had she managed to stow away on his ship? It was unthinkable! Unbelievable. And just what was he going to do with her now that Robbie had found her? Harrison had had grown men flogged for just such an offense. He couldn't very well whip Juliette Hamilton, although the idea held a certain amount of temptation. She stood before him with her hands on her hips and a determined gleam in her heavenly blue eyes, her every movement challenging him to do something about her presence.

He had met Juliette at Lucien Sinclair's home and he knew the moment he first laid eyes on his newly married friend's sister-in-law that she was trouble. Trouble in an enticing package, but aggravation none-the-less. Miss Juliette Hamilton was the very essence of trouble all right. With her audacious manner, flashing eyes, and impudent wit, she was no timid English miss. And he had wisely kept his distance from her while staying at Devon House, not because he was afraid of her, but because Juliette was exactly the kind of trouble a man didn't need in his life.

"And just what do you plan to do with me?" she asked, her voice rising slightly.

He inched closer, sensing her fear increase as she held her breath. She should very well be scared. Needed to be scared. Did she have no concept of what could have happened to her? Of just how dangerous her actions were? Was she completely unbalanced? How dare this slip of a girl sneak aboard his ship? Which brought him back to his initial problem.

What the hell was he going to do with her now?

Logic and good sense dictated that he turn the ship around and haul her back to Lucien Sinclair and let him deal with her. He had heard Jeffrey Eddington make a not very veiled reference to the fact that Juliette was hell-bent on getting everything she wanted. Well, Harrison would be damned if he would be the one to help her get to New York. He should drag her right back home.

Juliette Hamilton was not his problem.

Unfortunately, this little not-his-problem being on his boat was very much his problem at the moment.

Taking Juliette home would seriously delay his journey to New York. He had already postponed his return by a week to wait for a shipment of wine from France to arrive in London and be loaded onto his ship. He had to be back in New York by the end of the month. He had been gone too long as it was. Melissa would be frantic if he were delayed any longer. The last letter he received from home conveyed a sense of urgency at his return.

Melissa needed him desperately and he could not disappoint her. Not again.

Now he had Juliette Hamilton on his ship! How dare this little upstart inconvenience him and his plans with her reckless behavior. He ought to teach her a lesson.

Yes, that was it!

She needed to be taught a lesson. And he would be the teacher. The twit obviously had no idea how dangerous it had been for her to run away. She could have been hurt or lost or accosted by strangers a dozen times over just getting to his ship. Yes, the high-handed miss deserved to be given a lesson she would never forget. And no doubt her brother-in-law would thank him for helping out.

Harrison stared at her, his eyes locked with hers. Good God, but she had the bluest eyes he had ever seen. Eyes filled with intelligence, humor, and something else he could not yet define . . . restlessness . . . impatience . . . resilience . . . defiance? He could not be sure. In any case they were not traits he generally cared for in women.

"You have trespassed on my property and should be punished."

Those blue eyes widened slightly at his words but she did not so much as flinch. He had to give her credit for her bravado if nothing else.

"And just how do you propose to punish me?" One delicate eyebrow arched as she questioned him.

Harrison grinned wickedly.

Juliette rolled her eyes in exasperation and pushed her way past him, startling him. He had meant to intimidate her, but apparently that did not work. He turned around to face her. She had crossed her arms across her chest. He could not help but notice that she looked extremely enticing, even dressed in men's trousers and a shirt that was entirely too large for her small frame.

"Surely you can come up with something more original than ravishing me!"

He laughed at her. "Don't flatter yourself, Juliette."

"Isn't that what men do when they want to intimidate a woman?"

He shook his head at her sarcasm. She was not an easy woman to rattle. "Not always."

"Well then? What shall it be, Captain Fleming? Am I to walk the plank? Shall I be tossed overboard? Will you tie me to a mast and flog me?" She glared at him, her eyes flashing with something between anger and amusement.

He fought the urge to wipe the condescending look off her beautiful face. "Any one of those punishments would suffice."

"You wouldn't dare," she held his gaze. "Lucien would kill you."

She had him there. Harrison would never do any of those things to any woman, let alone the sister-in-law of his good friend and business associate. He could not harm a hair on Juliette's reckless head. But lord knew she needed to be taught a lesson.

"I should turn the ship around and let your family deal with you."

She did not utter a word or move a muscle, but her quickly downcast eyes told him more than enough. *What? No challenging remark? No sarcastic retort?* Harrison had finally hit his mark with her. She truly did not wish to go home. Her desire to go to New York was strong enough to curb her tongue. Who or what awaited her in New York that was compelling enough to lure her away from her family and risk her pretty neck and more simply getting there?

"Yes, that would be best," he said nonchalantly, nodding his head. "I should inform my crew that we will be delayed because we need to return an errant young lady back to her home."

"Please don't do that, Captain Fleming."

He barely heard her whispered plea. Ah, he was finally getting through to her. He walked closer.

She glanced up. "Please don't take me home. I've come so far. I can't go back now. I would rather you flogged me. Or even ravished me instead."

Stunned by her words, he stood speechless for a moment. "It is quite gratifying to know that you would prefer my charms over a flogging, Miss Hamilton." He considered her carefully. "However, before I make any decision, I must ask. What on earth is so important to you in New York?"

She shook her head, causing her long dark hair to swing seductively around her shoulders. "You're a man. You wouldn't understand."

Harrison eyed her with keen skepticism. Her transparency was obvious to him. "You must be madly in love with him."

Again she shook her head, her eyes rolling in derision at his question. But Harrison was not so sure. What else could drive a woman to take such a reckless chance with her life and endanger herself but love for a man? He would lay odds there was a handsome young man, probably deemed unfit by her family for whatever reason, waiting for her somewhere in New York City.

"You men all truly believe the world only revolves around you, don't you?"

The bitterness in her tone surprised him. Dumbfounded by her comment, he stared at her. "What are you babbling about?"

"Not a thing." Again she shook her head as if she

thought he wasn't worth the effort of explaining her opinion to.

Harrison clenched his teeth, fighting the urge to wipe the smug expression off her face. That little act of derision and her air of complete condescension infuriated him. Harrison felt outraged at this untamed girl who just upset his ship, his plans, and his schedule by saddling him with the responsibility of dealing with her well being, and who then had the audacity to challenge him while looking down her nose at him at the same time.

"I have plenty of money with me," she declared. "I can pay for my passage."

"That might work if this were a passenger ship and not a private vessel."

Juliette folded her arms across her chest again, distracting him. The loose men's shirt she wore hid what he knew to be a very womanly figure. He'd seen her in lavish and stylish gowns at Devon House which had showed off her ample charms and feminine curves quite well, but for some reason she appeared even more beautiful and appealing in her plain men's attire than when he first met her. *Lord, but she was trouble.* He held his breath and counted to ten. Then he counted to twenty.

"So just what is it, Captain Fleming, that you intend to do with me?" she glanced up at him, a curiously challenging look on her pretty face. "Are you going to take me home?"

Harrison smiled at her exultantly, as an idea occurred to him. He shook his head. "No, I won't take you home, Juliette. Not yet anyway." He gazed at her pointedly. "I'm already late returning home as it is, myself. And I refuse to be inconvenienced by your little whims any more than necessary. So, yes, for now you get your trip to New York. But rest assured, my dear, as soon as we dock I'm sending you on the first ship back to London." As he stalked toward her, he took pleasure in watching her look discomfited. He leaned over and whispered in her ear most threateningly, "In the meantime, you will be treated just like any other stowaway would be treated."

"Fine." She shrugged and stepped away from him. "I wouldn't expect anything less from you, just as long as you take me to New York."

He had to hand it to her. She had courage.

"You may sleep in my bed tonight." He stifled a laugh as a hint of fear flickered in her eyes. Good. The little vixen deserved to be scared. "I shall bunk elsewhere until we can make other arrangements. Sleep well, Juliette. You'll need plenty of rest for tomorrow."

He taunted her with that thought as he left her alone in his cabin.

∞ 3 ∞

Finally

Sitting in the beautiful Devon House library, Colette Sinclair heard an anguished cry and glanced up from her book, her hand instinctively covering her rounded stomach. Yvette's dramatic ways would wear her down one of these days. Wondering what had upset her youngest sister now, she debated whether it was worth hoisting herself from her comfortable seat to find out. Colette shook her head and remained where she was. Yvette would come to her eventually if it were anything of importance. And even if it were not, more was the pity.

Returning to the pages of Louisa May Alcott's *Little Women*, Colette found the American author's tale of the lives of four sisters to be quite amusing. She well knew that life with five sisters was never dull either. She continued reading for a minute before she heard footsteps outside the library. She waited for the rush of words that she knew would come. What terrible calamity had befallen Yvette this morning? Did she tear her best gown or lose her favorite gloves? Could she not get her hair styled just the way she wanted it? Was Juliette tormenting her yet again?

Colette's look of surprise changed to concern when her sister Paulette entered the room, not Yvette. The ashen expression on her face caused Colette to place her hand over her heart. Of all her sisters, Paulette was the least prone to dramatics. Something was terribly amiss.

"What is it?" she asked, placing the book on the end table beside her chair.

"Juliette is gone." Paulette's voice quivered as she waved a sheet of paper. "She left a note for us."

Colette felt the room spin a little and grasped the edge of the table. Surely she had misheard. "What did you say?"

Paulette took a shaky breath. "I said Juliette has run away. To New York. Oh, Colette, what should we do?"

Colette's heart pounded and again she placed her hand protectively over the baby growing within her. *Oh God.* She did it. Juliette had finally done what she had always vowed she would do. She finally ran off and did something wild and reckless . . . and typically Juliette.

"Give the note to me." She snatched the letter from her sister's hand, while her own hand trembled as she read the words written in Juliette's bold and careless style.

> *If you are reading this note, then you have discovered by now that I have gone. I have finally decided to go to New York. I am truly sorry to cause any of you pain at my leaving, but please do not worry about me. I have everything well planned. I will write as soon as I arrive at Christina Dunbar's house. I am sure you think that I have completely lost all good sense, but please try to understand that this is*

something I need to do. I will be quite safe, I assure you, so do not worry. I love you—

Unable to bear reading any more, Colette closed her eyes, as tears welled up. Wherever Juliette was at this moment, Colette knew with a sickening certainty that she had just lost her sister and her best friend in one fell swoop.

Familiar footsteps caused her to open her eyes to see Lucien stride into the room with a purposeful air, followed by a panic-stricken Yvette and a very anxious Lisette. Colette glanced up at her husband, relieved by his very presence. Tall and commanding, Lucien had a way of taking care of things. He would get to the bottom of this and make sure her sister was safe.

"Juliette is gone?" he asked, obviously unsure whether to believe the news he had been told by her younger sisters.

Remaining tight-lipped in an attempt to control her tears, Colette handed him the note. He read it quickly while Yvette sobbed and wailed with her usual dramatic flair. Colette watched a grim expression appear on Lucien's handsome face.

"How is she getting to New York?" Lisette asked, her brows creased with worry.

"The only person I know going to New York is Captain Fleming," Colette murmured in somewhat of a daze.

Lucien nodded in agreement. "I know he intended to sail for New York last night."

Colette's heart pounded with fear. "Do you think Juliette has gone with him?"

"I would not put it past her," Lucien said grimly.

"How could Captain Fleming do such a thing?" Yvette cried in outrage, her face awash with tears. "How could he just take her from us?"

"If Harrison Fleming had any indication that Juliette was leaving home without our knowledge or permission, especially by way of one of his ships, he would have informed me immediately." Lucien staunchly defended his friend. "There is not a chance that he assisted her in this ridiculous scheme."

"You believe Juliette hid herself on his ship then?" Colette asked. She could barely catch her breath. How did Juliette manage to get to the docks by herself? Where was she now? Was she in any danger? And the question that hammered her heart above the rest: why had her sister not confided in her? Filled with a pain she could not describe, she wiped the tears from her eyes.

"Knowing Juliette, yes," Lucien began. "Somehow your sister managed to slip onto his ship. If they set sail only last night it's quite possible they aren't even aware that she's aboard."

Paulette added, "Oh they'll know she's aboard soon enough for Juliette can never keep quiet for very long!"

Colette gave her a frown before turning to Lucien. "Do you think she's safe?"

"Unquestionably. Harrison would never allow anyone to harm her."

"Oh, Lucien!" Colette's heart skipped a beat as a dreadful thought occurred to her. She could barely utter the words. "What if she never even made it as far as the ship? What if she were lost, or hurt, or accosted on the docks—"

An anguished gasp interrupted Colette.

"Don't even think such things!" Lisette cried out in horror, wrapping her arms protectively around Yvette, whose eyes were wide with fear.

Colette stared at her husband. Lucien's grim expression

showed that he obviously considered her words a distinct possibility.

Before the awkward silence became too unbearable, Lucien declared, "I'll go down to the docks now to search for her and see what I can find out."

"I'm coming with you!" Colette cried, attempting to rise from her chair, which was not an easy feat given her thickening girth.

"You are not going anywhere," Lucien said in a definitive tone. Then his voice softened. "You cannot go traipsing around the docks with me in your condition. It's best for you and our unborn child if you remain at home."

Colette wisely, but reluctantly, sank back down into the leather armchair, her hand on her swollen belly once again. Her husband was right. She certainly had not the energy to do much of anything lately. The baby would be arriving in only a few weeks time and its weight made it more difficult for her to move around as it was. She had not even visited the bookshop lately due to her discomfort in getting in and out of the carriage. She would not be of any use to Lucien on the docks. As much as she worried over Juliette's whereabouts, Colette did not possess the strength to physically search for her.

Now in his element, Lucien took charge of the situation, his tall handsome form full of authority and confidence. Colette loved him more than she did the day she married him almost a year ago. And she loved how he took care of her family.

"Lisette, would you please help Colette upstairs so she can rest," Lucien asked. "She must not become overexcited. Yvette, you must go back to your studies as usual, and Paulette—"

"I'm coming with you!" Paulette stared at Lucien, her pretty face set with determination.

Colette watched the interplay between Lucien and Paulette, knowing Lucien would not win this battle with her little sister. The two of them shared a special bond of friendship and Lucien was not one to deny Paulette anything, especially not when Paulette had that look.

Lucien grimaced, but nodded. "Fine. You must remain in the carriage though. We'll stop and pick up Jeffrey as well."

Lucien leaned down and kissed Colette. She pulled him close to her, holding him tight. She whispered in his ear, "Oh, Lucien, what are we going to do?"

"We're going to find Juliette and bring her home safely."

The surety of his words calmed her and again she realized how much she loved him and how much he meant to her.

Now if only they could be sure Juliette was safe.

Wherever she was.

∽ 4 ∽

*Sailing, Sailing
Over the Bounding Main*

Juliette gritted her teeth and bit back the urge to scream. *That self-centered, egotistical tyrant. How dare he treat her this way!* Tossing the scrub brush back into the bucket with a splash, she arched her aching back and rubbed her sore neck. She never expected to have to scrub her away across the Atlantic.

Treat her like a stowaway, indeed.

After a fitful night's sleep in Captain Fleming's bed, he had awakened her before dawn and explained that she needed to begin to earn her keep. He ordered, yes, *ordered her*, to get herself above deck in less than ten minutes or he would drag her up himself. Bleary-eyed and nervous, still wearing the same men's clothes she had worn the night before, she staggered on deck, sleepy and cold, with the pale sunrise illuminating the planking. Captain Fleming handed her a wooden bucket and a scrub brush and told her to get down on her knees and wash until breakfast was ready.

Which she had done, without even the slightest grumbling, even though she had a few choice words in mind for him. Then he escorted her back down to his cabin for a quick breakfast and returned her to her work immediately after. She had been scrubbing the yellow pine deck for what seemed like hours now and her entire body ached, from the tips of her wrinkled fingers to her throbbing knees.

Other members of the crew were busy coiling ropes and lines, raising and lowering the canvas sails, polishing the brass-works, swabbing other areas of the deck, and all the while singing strange and somewhat bawdy songs. They steered clear of her, acting as if she were not working alongside of them. She had to say that Captain Fleming ran a tight ship, for it seemed quite clean, organized, and efficient.

She sighed and squinted at the glittering waves. She had heard of people becoming seasick, but the swaying of the ship did not bother her in the least. Glancing upward, the huge white sails of the *Sea Minx* billowed gracefully against the cerulean sky. Admittedly, Captain Fleming's ship was beautiful, as far as ships went, of which she knew relatively little. In fact, she had never even set foot on a ship before in her life.

Now apparently, she was expected to clean the entire thing!

Last night, thrilled that he had not taken her directly home, Juliette would have done anything to remain on board. However, since dawn she had begun to rethink her easy acceptance of the situation. The man was batty if he expected her to clean his blasted ship for the entire journey.

Her boast of letting Captain Fleming ravish her had not been that much of a lie.

For a fleeting instant she thought she would have preferred being taken to his bed than perform the labor she had been subjected to thus far. Captain Fleming was an attractive male and being ravished by him seemed much more exciting than scrubbing the deck with sandy saltwater all morning, at least judging from what precious little information her sister Colette had divulged to her on the matter of sex. Her friend Jeffrey Eddington had also alluded to the great pleasures of the act on more than one occasion but refused to share any details, no matter how much Juliette cajoled him. How bad could it be if everyone did it all the time? At the very least her curiosity would have finally been appeased. That would be something.

But not now! She would never consider Captain Harrison Fleming's bed! Now she would gleefully push him overboard and sail away laughing without a single regret.

She would not give up or give in to him. As much as she loathed scrubbing his wretched deck, the triumph she felt at having gotten her way more than made up for the discomfort. She was going to have her great traveling adventure and there was nothing to stop her now. The *Sea Minx* was sailing across the Atlantic Ocean.

So she would scrub his moldy old boat and do anything else he asked.

"Excuse me," a hesitant voice began. "But you're in need of a hat, miss."

Glancing up, Juliette looked into the face of a young man. Realizing immediately that it was he who had discovered her hiding place the night before, she scowled. Then her hand touched the tweed cap that sat upon her head, containing her mass of black hair. *What did he mean?*

"I am already wearing a hat, thank you," she said, unable to keep the sarcasm from her voice.

Shaking his head, he held up a wide-brimmed straw hat. "That little cap won't keep you cool when the sun hits noon, and you'll need more shade around your face or you will burn to a crisp. The captain sent me to give you this."

Ah, so it was the captain, still giving his orders, was it? This time he sent a minion to do his bidding. Juliette studied the young man standing before her. She sensed that he possessed an innate kindness, evident by his easily readable expression. "What is your name?"

"Robbie Deane."

"I am Juliette Hamilton."

"Yes, Miss Hamilton, I knew that already. I think you should heed my advice." He handed her the hat. "Although I reckon that's not something you do easily."

"That's the truth." Juliette smiled ruefully. She stood up and removed the tweed cap from her head, her dark hair falling in heavy waves around her face. She swept it up again, and taking the straw hat from him, she placed it upon her head, securing a few stray tendrils beneath the wide brim. She had to admit she felt cooler already. "Well, please thank the captain for me. And thank you, Mr. Deane."

"You're welcome. You can call me Robbie." He grinned at her, his boyish face alight. "Everyone else does."

"Then you can call me Juliette." She cast him a brilliant smile, knowing she already had an ardent admirer and an ally. He had reddish hair and a sweet face, covered in a generous sprinkling of freckles. She had never seen so many freckles on a face before! "You were the one who found me last night, were you not?"

"Yes. That was me." He eyed her carefully. "You gave me a quite a scare. It's not often we have stowaways on the *Sea Minx*."

"That's not too surprising."

He gave her a shy smile. "But even the few we've had, they've never been girls."

"Never?" she asked with feigned innocence. "Not even once?"

"Not once." Robbie shook his head. "You're the first girl stowaway I've ever seen. And by far the prettiest stowaway we've ever had. Why, you're the talk of the ship!"

"Am I now?" she exclaimed with a light laugh. She had seen a few of the crew this morning giving her a furtive glance or two, but not one of them had uttered a single word to her. The captain must have given them orders not to speak to her. "If you don't mind my asking, what are they saying about me, Robbie?"

To her surprise he blushed beneath his freckles. "Most of it I can't repeat in front of you, miss."

Juliette smiled kindly at him. "You certainly do not need to tell me anything you don't wish to, Robbie."

"Well, we—I mean they—were all wondering why a lady like you would hide on a ship in the first place."

"I'm certain they were wondering why, but I have my reasons." She nodded decisively. "Very good reasons."

Robbie paused briefly before blurting out, "We—They think it's because you're in love with the captain."

Juliette laughed aloud, so loud that she drew the attention from a few of the other sailors on deck. The laughter flowed from her too easily and she could not contain her amusement. Robbie stared at her in surprise, his brown eyes full of confusion. Tears trickled down her cheeks and she swiped at them with the back of her hand. It was too funny. Men were all alike.

When she could finally catch her breath, she responded. "Let me assure you—and them—that I am *not* in love with Captain Fleming. The thought has never even entered my mind."

"I see," Robbie said, but clearly he did not. His expression appeared quite puzzled, his young brow furrowed.

"What else are they saying about me?"

"They are saying you should get back to work."

Startled, both Juliette and Robbie turned to see Captain Fleming looming over them, looking decidedly displeased.

Robbie straightened up, the sweet smile disappearing from his face. "Yes, Captain." He fled to the opposite end of the deck, leaving Juliette alone with Harrison. Folding her arms across her chest, she sighed.

"Well?" he said.

Their eyes held a moment longer than necessary and Juliette felt her stomach flip over.

"Well, what?" Juliette asked, looking up at him from beneath the brim of the straw hat. He seemed more handsome today. More rugged. His hair glinted like pure gold in the sun, almost blinding her with its brightness. "Am I supposed to say, 'Aye, aye, Captain' and hurry back to my scrubbing?"

"Yes."

She stared at him, trying to decide if he was serious. Deciding he was not, she remained standing, her arms crossed.

"Come with me," he barked. Turning on his heel, he strode away, expecting her to follow. She hated being ordered about. But she was no one's fool either. If following him got her out of scrubbing the deck for a while, she would follow him to the bowels of his infernal ship if he wanted.

In the end, she merely followed him back to his cabin. As she entered his quarters, he closed the door behind them. They stood quietly, facing each other.

"Listen to me very carefully, Juliette, for I only intend to say this once."

The edge in his voice caused her heart to beat faster than usual. She ignored it. "You have my undivided attention."

Harrison eyed her skeptically. "The ship and my crew are not here for your amusement, Juliette. You have inconvenienced me beyond all measure, but I will not have you causing any trouble or inconvenience to my crew as well. They have a great deal of work to do and cannot be sidetracked from it. And the last thing they need is to be distracted by the likes of you."

She bristled at his attitude. "What have I done?"

"Don't play the innocent miss with me. You know entirely well the effect you have upon men, and you should leave poor Robbie alone. By the look on that boy's face, he's already half in love with you."

Juliette laughed at his presumptuousness. "Pardon me," she paused before adding, "Captain . . ." She gave him a pointed look. "But were you not the one who ordered him to bring me this hat?"

"Yes, I did. That tweed cap of yours is entirely unsuitable to protect you from the sun."

"Then I don't see why you are laying the blame at my door. A young man is smitten with me. I cannot be faulted for that, now can I?"

"Yes you can, damn it!"

Juliette stepped back without thinking. Captain Fleming's

eyes had turned a cold and dark gray, like the color of a storm-threatened sky.

"You are disrupting my entire ship."

Again Juliette laughed at his overstating of the situation. "Your entire ship? Is such exaggeration truly necessary, Captain Fleming? I spoke to one young boy, at your request."

"Yes, but you were distracting him from his duties. This ship requires the constant attention of my crew. You cannot be a diversion for them."

"It was not my intention to be." She placed her hands on her hips. "I was simply scrubbing the deck, as you ordered me to. You were the one who told Robbie to bring me this hat in the first place. We were merely having a civil conversation as people tend to do when they—"

"Stop talking."

Juliette was so taken aback by his command that she ceased speaking in midsentence. He stepped closer to her. Losing all sense of what they had been arguing about, she stared up at Captain Harrison Fleming.

He leaned in toward her and tore the straw hat from her head, her long black hair spilling around her. Stunned, it seemed her heart stopped and she could not draw a breath. As she sensed what he was about to do, a ripple of exhilaration raced through her entire body. In a quick movement, Harrison pulled her against his chest, lowered his mouth over hers, and kissed her.

Juliette could not breathe. She could not think. She did not laugh. She did not wriggle away, nor could she. His arms were wrapped around her like a vice. For the first time in her life it seemed she could do nothing. Nothing except kiss him back. In an instant, she lost herself completely in the feel of his warm lips upon hers. It was like nothing she had ever known or expected. Juliette had been kissed before, certainly. Many times, in fact. But this . . .

Kissing Captain Harrison Fleming was something else altogether.

She felt herself spinning, her pulse racing, her world careening around her. His lips were insistent, pressing against her, playing with hers. There was the faintest hint of sea salt on his lips. His tongue ran across her lips sending a shiver through her. Her head tilted back and her mouth opened, and he slipped his tongue within her mouth. All reason fled from her. Her tongue met with his and the intimacy shocked her to her toes.

Perhaps she had never truly been kissed after all.

Perhaps those stolen kisses with eager young gentlemen were not real kisses. They had seemed impersonal and well, *inconsequential*, in comparison to the magnitude and intensity of this kiss with Captain Fleming. Those kisses had not made her feel hot and shivery and full of longing for something she could not name.

Without consciously being aware of it, Juliette found that her arms had reached up and encircled his neck, and she drew him closer to her. The hard muscles of his chest pressed against her. Harrison groaned and kissed her harder, taking more from her. She gave it willingly, surprised by the force of her own desire. She liked the feel of him close to her, smelling of the sea air and sunlight.

The stubble on his face scratched her cheeks, but she didn't care. She had never felt so alive, as if every nerve in her body were on fire. She only wanted more. More kissing. More of him. A passionate thrill coursed through her entire being. Whatever Harrison Fleming wanted to do, wherever he wanted to take her, she would go willingly. Gladly. Eagerly. She kissed him without the slightest bit of hesitation, for it was quite the most exciting experience she had ever had. She never wanted it to end.

Suddenly he released her, stepping back from her. She stood there feeling bereft and dazed, her knees weak and wobbly, and her breath uneven. Their eyes met and held for a long moment. He had the most spectacular eyes. They changed color to reflect his mood. Sometimes they seemed smoky gray, sometimes a dark slate. Looking at her right now they were intense silver.

Slowly she smiled up at him.

"Eat your lunch," he ordered her, his voice hoarse, his expression unreadable.

The smile vanished from her face. "Excuse me?"

"Your lunch is on the table. Make sure you eat before you get back to work." With that, he abruptly left the cabin.

Speechless, Juliette stood still, battling bewildering senses of humiliation and exhilaration. What had just happened between them? He had kissed her quite intimately, quite passionately. And then he left her alone. Without saying a single word about it.

What was she to make of *that?*

After men had kissed Juliette in the past, they immediately declared their love and devotion to her and she could make them do whatever she wanted or needed them to do. And she had never kissed anyone the way she had just kissed Harrison Fleming. She certainly hadn't expected a declaration of love from him, but she *had* expected—well, she wasn't quite sure what.

But definitely something more than "Eat your lunch" and a curt dismissal.

For the first time she had thoroughly enjoyed kissing a man and being kissed in return. Running her tongue across her lips, they seemed fuller, softer. They felt different. *She* felt different.

Apparently Captain Harrison Fleming felt nothing after kissing her.

Oddly put out, somewhat embarrassed by her own behavior, and more hurt than she cared to admit, she turned and glanced impatiently around the cabin. The captain's cabin. *His cabin.* Yes, a midday meal of bread and cheese had been set for her on the table. She had been starving earlier, but now she had no appetite at all.

What was she to do with herself? Go back out on deck? To continue scrubbing? Not bloody likely! Not after kissing him, she wouldn't. She'd stay in here all day and do absolutely nothing to help on his ship.

How dare he treat her like that? Thinking he could take liberties with her person and then . . . and then . . . leave! As if she were of no consequence.

For the first time in her life Juliette felt a little frightened and truly at a loss as what to do about it. She had left the security and love of her family to sail on this ship across the ocean to an unknown city with a man she did not understand and, to a certain extent, now feared. What had she been thinking? What had possessed her? Stinging tears sprung to her eyes, but she blinked them back in a valiant effort to not crumble to pieces.

She would not cry. She dared not cry. She had gotten herself into this mess and she would get herself out of it.

Just how she was going to do that, she wasn't entirely sure.

If only she could talk to Colette.

Colette was her best friend and would know what to do, and together they would figure everything out. In fact, Juliette would be happy to talk to any of her sisters. Of course, Lisette would be kind and consoling, as was her way. She would understand why Juliette had left London, even though Lisette could not even contemplate such an action herself. She would commiserate with her over her unusual situation. Oh, but how Paulette would tease and mock her! She would call her a fool for leaving in the first place and tell her that she had gotten exactly what she had deserved. And Yvette would be full of awe and admiration at her dramatic escapade. Lucien would be disapproving, no doubt, and would scold her for her recklessness, while Jeffrey would smile and congratulate her for finally doing what she had always wanted to do. At this point Juliette would even settle for talking to her mother, Genevieve, even though their relationship had always been a turbulent one.

But she could not talk to any of them. And probably would not be able to for a long time to come.

The enormity of what she had done suddenly dawned upon her. The unexpected and intense longing for home and her sisters overwhelmed her. Hot tears threatened once more.

Juliette looked up at the small rectangular windows. Staring out at the blue sky, knowing there was not a speck of land in sight, she felt small and insignificant. The endless expanse of sea made her wonder just how many more days she had to survive on this ship with Captain Fleming before they reached America.

What had she gotten herself into? And more importantly, just how would she get herself out of it?

~ 5 ~

Can't Live With Them

Standing on the forecastle of the *Sea Minx*, Harrison stared out at the horizon, that elusive thin line where the sky met the ocean. One never actually arrived at the horizon, for it was always just out of reach until land took its place. Yet one always looked toward it. The fresh sea air washed over his skin, bracing him. He felt more at home at sea than he did on land. He knew it from the first time he set foot aboard a ship in New York harbor when he was thirteen. The freedom, the constant challenge, the danger, and the mystery of the sea, as well as its ever-changing beauty, invigorated him like nothing else in his life ever had.

Now that he owned the *Sea Minx*, he did not wish to be anywhere else.

This beautiful, elegant clipper was the ship of his heart. One of the fastest ships in the world, with her sleek, jet black hull, elegant lines, billowing snow-white canvas sails, and superior craftsmanship, she sliced through the water like a razor and could reach speeds of up to 18 knots. The bowsprit extended regally and held an intricately carved figurehead of a buxom woman wearing flowing robes, his Sea Minx. The red, white, and blue vertical striped burgee house flag of his company, H.G. Fleming & Company, waved on the masthead. Harrison had the *Sea Minx* custom built to his exact specifications. All the talk was of the new *Cutty Sark*, but Harrison knew his *Sea Minx* could outrun her if given the chance.

His other ships were cargo steamers. It was the logical choice for sea trade and the wave of the future, and Harrison had built H.G. Fleming & Company to be the best fleet in the world. Soon he would sell it for an incredible profit, which would add to his ever-increasing fortune.

But the *Sea Minx* was his personal pride. The first trip he ever made to China was on a clipper ship, and he had fallen in love with the speed and beauty of the craft.

Now if the winds held and they made good time, Harrison knew they could dock in New York in less than two weeks.

He sighed heavily and rubbed his forehead.

Almost two weeks with Juliette Hamilton on his ship. Staying in his cabin. Tempting him. Sleeping in his bed, for God's sake! She hadn't been aboard even twenty-four hours and he had already kissed her! He had thought to teach the impudent woman a lesson, but he felt the tables had somehow been turned on him. Her response to his kiss shocked him. She had been incredibly sensual and passionate, arousing him so thoroughly that he had to force himself to leave her before the situation got out of hand.

He shouldn't have kissed her and he knew it. Lucien Sinclair was a trusted friend and business associate. He would expect Harrison to keep his wayward and dangerously beautiful sister-in-law safe, even if she did sneak aboard the *Sea Minx*. Lucien would not expect his friend to take advantage of her. If the situation were reversed, Harrison would demand nothing less than the same of his friend.

Yet Harrison did not have a sister-in-law to worry about. No, he had other issues on his mind.

As usual, his thoughts turned to Melissa.

She would be overly anxious to see him at this point and worried over his late return. He hoped Annie would be able to calm her. A pang of guilt ran through him. Harrison always avoided situations which might cause Melissa strain or grief and he regretted that he was surely causing her heartache now. But there was no help for it this time.

If not for Melissa, he would have turned the ship around directly to return Juliette Hamilton to her family to deal with, but he could not in good conscience delay his trip home any longer than he already had.

Melissa had been more distraught than usual at his departure and he promised her that he would return as quickly as possible. He had curtailed most of his frequent business trips as it was. And he had already decided that this was his last trip to London for a while. He even said as much to Lucien Sinclair and Jeffrey Eddington.

As much as he tried to help her, her emotional state seemed more fragile than ever. She was more tearful, more petulant, more demanding of him and, God help him, he could not deny her. Melissa was the only person in his life who could bring him to his knees with a mere look. For all he had accomplished in his life: his business, his ships, his houses, none of it meant anything without Melissa.

If only she weren't so fragile and unstable. If only she

wcre stronger, healthier. How different would their lives be if Melissa had even a fraction of the spirit that Juliette Hamilton possessed?

Surprised by that thought, Harrison shook himself back to reality. Yes, he had to admit that Juliette had an unusual amount of spirit and as hard as he tried, he could not imagine Melissa ever doing any of the things that Juliette had done.

Juliette was too much of a temptation.

Why the hell had he kissed her earlier? He should never have even touched her. *What in blazes was he thinking?*

That was just it.

He had not been thinking at all. He had simply wanted her to stop talking. She had stood there with her beautiful mouth and pouty lips beckoning him and he could not help himself. He had to taste her. Which was a mistake, because now having kissed her once, he only wanted to kiss her again. And again.

He needed to stay away from her.

"It looks like we'll have clear weather tomorrow."

Harrison turned to his first mate, Charlie Forrester. Charlie was a good-natured man, always quick with a smile. He had been sailing with Harrison for years and was a good friend as well. They had known each other as children, growing up wild in the streets of New York City. Together they worked their way out of the slums and onto the decks of a ship. Charlie had stuck by Harrison through some of the toughest times of his life.

Harrison nodded in agreement. "Yes, it looks fine. Even though we're against the trade winds, we should make good time. Is Dowling at the wheel?"

"Yes, he just took over for me. How is our pretty

stowaway holding up?" Charlie asked with a wide grin. "She's sure the talk of the ship, that one."

"What's sure is that she needs someone to keep her in line. She's a dangerous creature."

"She's a real beauty."

Harrison's expression became grim. Beauty didn't even begin to scratch the surface in describing Juliette Hamilton. Irritated that she seemed to have gotten under his skin so quickly, he kept his mouth shut.

"Did you find out what she's after in New York?"

Harrison shook his head. "She won't admit it, but it has to be a man."

"The crew thinks she's here because she met you in London and fancies herself in love with you," Charlie muttered, failing to hold back the awe in his voice.

Harrison scoffed at his first mate's remark. "No, it's definitely not me she's in love with, I promise you that. Besides, I hardly saw her in London."

Charlie gave him a questioning glance, one bushy eyebrow arched high. "You stayed at her family's house though, didn't you? Perhaps more happened than you realized."

Harrison stared at Charlie. "You really think that's the truth? That I somehow bewitched this poor girl and led her on and now she's set on following me across the ocean? Is that what you truly believe?"

"No. No, of course not." Charlie had the good grace to look chagrined. "They were all saying it, but to hear you tell it, it doesn't sound very feasible after all."

"Well, believe me, I had absolutely nothing to do with Juliette Hamilton's decision to leave London, except for the fact that I unwittingly provided her with an opportunity to escape. Which it seems I now must pay for," he grumbled.

"Are you going to keep her in your cabin?"

"Where else would you suggest I put her, Charlie? In with the rest of the crew?"

Charlie laughed, a big booming laugh. "The fellas wouldn't mind that at all, I'll tell you."

"No, I imagine they wouldn't at that. If she weren't Lucien Sinclair's sister-in-law, I'd do it. Or I swear I would have tossed her shapely bottom overboard by now."

"If I know nothing else about you, Harrison, I know you would never do something like that to a lady!" Charlie challenged him.

"You're right," Harrison admitted without hesitation. "But I've thought about it enough." He'd recently thought about doing other things to her as well, but those were better left unmentioned in front of his first mate.

"Why isn't she cleaning the deck?"

"She's having her lunch in the privacy of my cabin." Harrison thought for a moment. "But I'm not sure it was a good idea to have her scrubbing the deck anyway. She was too much of a distraction for the men." *And for me*, he admitted to himself. The sight of Juliette Hamilton's pert derriere swaying in those men's breeches as she was on her hands and knees was a little too much for any man to bear.

"Aww, they need a little fun, Harrison. Let 'em enjoy the view for a while. No one was bothering her."

Harrison felt oddly put out at the thought of his men enjoying the view of Juliette's rear end, even though he had quite enjoyed the sight himself. And he did not even want to think about just how much he had enjoyed kissing her.

Juliette was trouble all right.

"No, Charlie." He shook his head. "I was trying to teach her a lesson, but it was a bad idea to begin with.

Though she should have something to occupy her time and to keep her from distracting the men. I need to find something else for her to do to earn her keep."

"Well, you had better find it quick." Charlie pointed toward the stern of the ship. "There she is now."

Harrison was stunned to see Juliette Hamilton climbing the rigging of the mizzenmast with Robbie Deane and a few of the other men helping her along. God help him, but she was a sight to behold. With her black hair whipping in the breeze, her elegant arms and long legs in her men's trousers moved gracefully up the length of rigging. She was incredible, moving quickly and easily, higher and higher. What did she think she was doing? How high up was she planning to go? Had the woman no fear? Or good sense?

And how the hell did she get up there in the first place?

Torn between wanting to haul her back to his cabin and give her the spanking of her life and watching her climb the rigging in mute fascination, Harrison remained rooted to the spot. He could not take his eyes off her. She reached the mizzen topsail and glanced below her with the brightest smile he had ever seen. The force of her smile almost knocked him senseless. The men clapped and cheered her on from below. Juliette waved in response, while clinging to the rope with only one arm. Harrison caught his breath. If she fell he would never forgive himself.

In an instant, he raced to the other end of the ship, his heart pounding. She was so slight; a strong and sudden gust of wind could knock her clean off the rigging and send her plummeting into the ocean. He yelled up to her.

"Juliette, get down from there right now!"

"Hello, Captain Fleming!" She called to him cheerily and gave another little wave with her hand.

"Hold on with both hands!" he cried, his heart filled with a wrenching fear. Good lord! The woman was completely unpredictable and her capricious ways would get her killed.

Her rich laughter floated down around him, infuriating him. Terrifying him. Harrison turned to the group of sailors standing around, looking up at the wild show Juliette was providing for them. These were his sailors. His men. His crew. Some of them had been with him for years. Yet here they stood, not doing their jobs, staring in fascination at their beautiful little stowaway. They were caught in the spell of the minx on his mizzenmast.

He lifted his head up to her. "Come down now, Juliette," he ordered in an authoritative tone. "You've had your fun."

She had the audacity to stick out her tongue at him. His men roared with laughter and cheered raucously. It was complete insubordination from a woman in front of his own crew. A mixture of anger and fear filled him at the sight of her dangling so dangerously high above him.

He eyed the men carefully and demanded, "Who the hell let her get up there in the first place?"

Robbie hung his head in embarrassment. "I did, Captain."

"It wasn't Robbie's fault though, Captain," Frank Hastings spoke up. "He warned her not to go up there. We all did. Short of holding her down, there wasn't anything we could do to stop her."

Even knowing as little about Juliette Hamilton as he did, Harrison reasoned that they were more than likely right. That willful, headstrong woman did just as she pleased. Aggravated nonetheless, he glanced back up at Juliette, still atop her perch on the mizzenmast. He turned his attention to his men, who knew him well enough not to question the look he gave them now. "Get back to work all of you. I'll get her down myself."

They scurried away attempting to look busy, but he knew they kept an eye on the drama that was about to unfold. What would Captain Fleming do with their pretty stowaway after she deliberately defied an order?

Harrison leaned against the wall of the coach house, below which were his quarters, crossed his arms over his chest, and waited. He would not go up after her for fear his presence would prompt her to do something even more reckless and foolish, causing her to lose her balance and fall. Unless she called for his help, he would not go up. She had to come down some time. And he would be waiting for her when she did. Then he would teach her a lesson about obeying orders that she would never forget. First however, he gave a silent prayer that she would not fall.

Finally realizing that her adoring audience had fled and there was no one left below her but him, she flashed a smile. It was not a victorious smile, but one of genuine joy and it occurred to Harrison that she truly was not afraid. She waved again, and brushed the hair from her eyes. She turned her face toward the sea and looked toward the horizon.

She was beautiful.

Obviously she loved being up there, which stunned Harrison. At last, he saw her sigh and slowly make her way down the rigging. With his heart in his mouth as she descended, he felt an odd swell of pride at her fearlessness and her sense of ease aboard the ship. He couldn't think of one single woman he knew who would have done what Juliette had just done. Lord knew Melissa would not even set foot on his ship, let alone do something as outrageously daring as to climb the rigging lines.

When Juliette came within arm's length of him, he grabbed her around the waist. She flung her arms about his shoulders and he held her tightly. He could feel her heart racing. She let out a delighted squeal.

"That was the most thrilling, most exhilarating thing I have ever done in my entire life!" she cried with such joy that Harrison couldn't help but smile at her. "The view is incredible from up there. I felt like I was flying, with the wind and sky above me and the sea all around! Just endless blue everywhere. No wonder you love sailing so much! It was heavenly! I could have stayed up there all afternoon." She gave a little laugh. "But my arms got too tired."

The smile gone from his face, Harrison looked her directly in the eyes. "If you ever do anything so reckless again while on my ship, I will beat you within an inch of your life. Do you know how easily you could have been killed?"

He still held her in his arms; her feet did not touch the ground. She felt as light as a feather.

Juliette laughed, her beautiful face alight with happiness. "But I wasn't killed or hurt, was I, Captain Fleming?"

"But you could have been," he muttered angrily.

"But I wasn't," she persisted with a smile. "Now put me down."

"No." He didn't trust her.

"No?" she echoed in disbelief, her expression turning to one of suspicion.

"No." With that he continued to hold her tightly as he made his way back to his cabin. Aware that his crew was watching, he determinedly ignored them.

"Put me down this instant!" Juliette ordered, outraged

at his treatment of her. She struggled in his arms, but she was no match for his size and strength.

He held tight and did not let go of her until they reached his private quarters. He marched through his outer office directly into his bedchamber, where he proceeded to dump her unceremoniously on his bed.

"Just what do you think you are doing?" she sputtered angrily, scrambling to sit up. Kneeling on the edge of the bed she placed her hands on her hips, her appearance beautifully irate. She looked for all the world like an angry angel, if such a thing were possible.

He took her face in his hands, determined to get his point across. Juliette immediately put her hands on top of his in a defiant effort to break free from him. Unable to remove his secure hold on her, she glared angrily at him. If he were not so angry himself, he might have admired her courage.

Leaning in close, so she would not miss a single word, he uttered in a low, steady voice, "Listen to me very carefully, Juliette Hamilton, because this is the last time I am going to explain it to you. I am the captain of this ship and what I say goes. Everyone on board my ship abides by my orders, because this is *my* ship. Their safety is in my hands and so they obey me. You could have been killed up there today and I will not have you taking chances like that on my watch again. Be as reckless as you like when you get to New York and you are no longer my responsibility. But like it or not, my pretty miss, when you stowed away on the *Sea Minx* you made yourself part of my crew, which means you have to obey me too. And when I tell you to do something, you will do it or you will not like the consequences. Do you understand me?"

She stared up at him, her eyes the color of the sky fringed by thick, black lashes. God, but she was beautiful.

Her delicate bone structure, her fair skin, the adorable tip of her nose, the fullness of her lips could cause any man to lose his head. She possessed the face of an angel, but not the personality to match. That was the most deceptive part about Juliette Hamilton. She looked like an angel but she certainly was not angelic.

Harrison was so captivated by her sweet face that he didn't see the blow coming. In one swift movement, Juliette slapped him across the cheek with a stinging crack.

∾6∾

Can't Live Without Them

Juliette stared angrily at Harrison, her handprint clearly visible on his face. His stormy eyes narrowed and she swallowed. Resisting the temptation to wring her hands, she kept her arms at her sides. The slap probably hurt her more than it hurt him, but she'd never let him know that.

For a split second she feared he was going to hit her back.

But he didn't. He wouldn't. Yet he still held her face in his hands.

Neither of them moved.

They stared at each other for an endless moment. Something tangible crackled in the air between them, and Juliette could barely breathe.

Suddenly one hand grabbed the back of her head, roughly pulling her toward him. Harrison's mouth came down on hers and he kissed her. Again. But oh, this was not at all like the way he kissed her earlier . . . This was a hard kiss. A demanding kiss. A kiss full of frustration, passion, and even anger. She locked her arms around his neck and gave in to his assaulting kiss, matching his fervor with her own.

They kissed. And kissed. And kissed.

It was as if someone had ignited an incredible flame between them. Their fiery encounter earlier that afternoon seemed mild compared with the intensity of this one. They did not speak. Harrison did not utter a word. He just continued to kiss her until she thought she would faint from the pleasure of it, the sheer sensation of it.

Their breaths came in short gasps and she clung to him for support. She was dizzy and weak with feelings and desires she had never experienced.

His tongue possessed her mouth and intertwined with her own in a kiss so intimate, surely it had to be wrong. Sinful even. If it was, she didn't care. She didn't want to know if it was wrong or even entertain the mere possibility of it being wrong. She only wanted more of him. More of this man she barely knew.

And yet here she was, on his ship, in his bed, on her knees, kissing him. The utter excitement of the situation overwhelmed her being.

His hand move down her back, pressing her closer to him, and sending delightful shivers through her body. That same hand, firm and sure, then slid up the length of her, outlining the flare of her hip, along the curve of her waist until he cupped her breast. She gasped into his mouth and he kissed her harder, if such a thing were even possible.

Suddenly he used both hands to pull on the front of her men's shirt, ripping the buttons loose, sending them flying across the room, and tearing the remaining fabric in half. He pulled the shirt from her arms, leaving her only in her thin chemise. Juliette did not protest. She could not. Not when she wanted him. Not when she wanted to tear the clothes from her own body herself. Not when she wanted to tear his clothes off as well.

Reaching out, she tugged on his shirt front, mimicking the motion he had made, but her hands trembled so much her fingers could do nothing more than cling to the fabric.

Finally, Harrison tore his mouth from hers. Again they stared at each other, their eyes locked in a magnetic gaze, unable to break free. His stormy gray eyes mesmerized her. The handsome planes of his face. The bronzed tone of his skin. The golden streaks in his hair. The windswept scent of him. The strength and wildness of him intrigued her. She had never met anyone quite like Harrison Fleming. He did not care what she wanted or what she thought. He ordered her about and carried her bodily where he wanted her. He did not treat her with deference and admiration as other men did. She was unable to resist the feel of him and the wild sensations he created within her. Juliette tugged on the front of his shirt pulling him closer to her.

"Harrison," she whispered low. She kissed him, her lips covering his.

She had never kissed a man before. Men had always kissed her. It was odd, but she *wanted* to kiss Harrison Fleming. She wanted to taste him, to feel him. Her tongue slipped into his warm mouth moving with his tongue. She sucked in her breath, reveling in the feel of him.

Harrison growled low and wrapped his arms tight around her waist. He moved his lips along her jaw, down her throat. Juliette closed her eyes and arched her back, tilting her head back with her arms clutching his shoulders. Harrison's heated kisses moved lower, kissing her neck, kissing her collarbone, kissing her chest along the edge of her cotton chemise. When his mouth sought her nipple through the fabric of her chemise, Juliette gasped.

Her eyes flew open and they shared a heated look before he lowered his head to her chest again. With her heart pounding erratically, she let Harrison kiss her breasts. The very sensation weakened her, melted her.

Gently he eased her back on the bed, until she lay flat. Grateful for the pillows beneath her head, Juliette looked to Harrison, wishing for him to continue. Laying there in her men's trousers and her kiss-dampened chemise with her hardened nipples clearly visible she suddenly felt quite exposed and somewhat vulnerable. And undeniably excited.

Harrison loomed over the bed, staring down at her. A hard look suddenly crossed his face, and his golden brows drew together in a frown. "This is not going to happen between us."

She blinked in mute surprise.

He repeated again, his voice hoarse, "This is not going to happen."

Suddenly cold, she wished she could pull the blanket up to cover herself. But she would not do so in front of him. "Are you saying that to me or to yourself?" she finally murmured, her voice thick with emotion.

He gave her another hard look. "To both of us."

Before she could respond, Harrison stalked from the room and left the cabin, closing the door behind him.

Stunned by his abrupt departure, but not sure if she was more relieved or disappointed by it, Juliette lay in Harrison's bed mutely staring at the low-beamed ceiling. Her cheeks reddened in a burning mixture of mortification and shame. Covering her face with her hands, she groaned softly. The swaying of the ship seemed to increase, rocking her, as she clutched a pillow to her chest and curled up in ball on Harrison Fleming's bed.

What had just happened between them?

She had allowed him to take ridiculous liberties with her.

Admittedly, she had enjoyed every second of those liberties, but still, she should not have allowed it in the first place nor should she have enjoyed it so much.

An odd thought occurred to her.

Had Harrison not enjoyed it? Had *he* not enjoyed being with *her?* He had seemed as though he were taking as much pleasure in their encounter as she was. The way he touched her, looked at her, kissed her all indicated that he was enjoying himself. Had she done something wrong? Why had he left her with such abruptness? *Again?* And why did she feel so terribly that he had left her feeling . . . so . . . unfulfilled?

She should be relieved. And thankful.

But she only felt an odd sense of hurt and the ache of unfulfilled desire.

Juliette knew what happened in a man's bed. Well, not literally and certainly not from personal experience, but she had gathered enough information during her life to know what the technicalities entailed. Hadn't she and Colette spent hours secretly reading that intimidating medical text in their father's bookshop, *A Complete Study of the Human Anatomy and All Its Functions*? Didn't they spend countless more hours trying to figure out what it actually meant? When finally Colette became experienced in that area, her older sister had eventually, after much coaxing and begging and pleading, enlightened Juliette with some of the nuances of the act. Colette had assured her that it was pleasurable and nothing to be fearful of as long as it were done with the proper person under the right circumstances.

All things considered, Juliette should be relieved that Harrison hadn't pressed matters further with her. He had acted as a gentleman. Well, perhaps not *quite* a gentleman, if the truth were told. His actions were not what one would define as those of a proper gentleman. He *had* captured her as if he were a lusty pirate and she were a tavern wench for the taking, dragging her back to his cabin and dropping her on his bed, of all places. Then he had kissed her, without even asking permission. Quite passionately. *And* he had torn open her shirt and fondled and kissed her breasts as if he had every right to do so.

No, those were definitely not the acts of a gentleman.

But then again proper gentlemen had never really held her interest in the least.

She groaned anew as the image of Harrison's mouth on her nipples flashed through her mind. An unexpected thrill coursed through her body at the thought. She had reveled in his every touch and had wanted even more from him.

She had wanted him to show her everything she did not know.

No, Harrison was not a gentleman, for a true gentleman would have never allowed such an opportunity for passion to arise between them in the first place. He had simply regained his self-restraint before their situation had gotten too far out of hand.

Why did she not feel the least bit relieved? Why did she feel like she wanted to hit something? Why could she not ignore the hurt that flooded her as well?

How dare he kiss her that way and storm out as if it were her fault! And he had done so twice now! Juliette sat up. She reached for her shirt, which she found on the floor at the foot of the bed. All of the buttons were missing and the bottom half was split down the center. How dare he tear her clothes! Especially when she had a limited wardrobe as it was. Who did he think he was? She shoved her arms into the sleeves and pulled the front tight across her chest. Standing on shaking legs she made her way from the bedroom through the open doorway to the office of the cabin. She would find Captain Fleming and give him a piece of her mind.

She angrily wrenched the brass door handle and was quite surprised when it did not move. She yanked it again, harder. The door was locked from the other side. Which could only mean that Harrison had locked her in his cabin when he left!

With a shrill scream, Juliette kicked at the door. She pounded on it with her fists. After a series of outraged shouts and angry yells, to which no one on the other side responded, she came to the bitter realization that even if anyone could hear her calls, apparently they were not going to let her out. She kicked at the door once more in utter frustration.

Good heavens, he had locked her in!

He had locked her in his cabin, punishing her as if she were a small child. Could he still be upset with her climbing the mizzenmast? She knew it had been a risky stunt, but still, his reaction seemed a bit extreme.

Her little tirade at the door left her somewhat deflated, but still irate. She leaned against it with a heavy sigh, pondering her next move. When she saw Harrison, she would have no qualms about slapping his handsome face yet again.

In the meantime, practicality won out. He had to release her at some point. He couldn't very well let her starve in there.

A triumphant grin spread across her face. She obviously could not go back to scrubbing the deck. So much for his grand idea to treat her like a stowaway! If Harrison thought he was punishing her by holding her captive in his cabin, he certainly didn't know her very well. Juliette could lie in bed and do nothing for the entire voyage to New York without a single qualm.

New York!

Once she arrived in America, she could do as she pleased. She would answer to no one. The restlessness that had plagued her for as long as she could remember would finally be assuaged. While her sisters loved the family bookshop and London, Juliette had been suffocated by it. She felt trapped her whole life. Entering society last year under her uncle's supervision had only intensified her deep sensation of confinement. She had always chaffed under the strict rules and codes of behavior for women. Juliette craved independence, adventure, and excitement and knew intrinsically that prim and proper London could never provide those necessary elements in her life. The youth, vibrancy and freedom of a new city, a new country, a new life in the United States, filled her with a fervent hope and optimism she never thought possible.

Now her dream was almost within her grasp. She simply had to endure this ocean crossing with a very vexing gentleman. Then she would be free. If she had made it this far, she could manage the rest. In the meantime, she had to admit that she *was* having an adventure. Something she had always wanted to have. If sailing the Atlantic Ocean on a beautiful ship with a handsome American captain kissing her passionately didn't qualify as an adventurous experience, she didn't know what did.

Still clutching her shirt closed, she slowly made her way back to the bedchamber. She noticed a few of her

buttons on the floor. Some had landed on the carpet near
the bed, some on the polished wood planks. Gathering
them up, she searched until she had found most of them.
Holding them in the palm of her hand, she glanced
around the two adjoining staterooms. She really had not
given either space much notice before.

Harrison's rooms were quite luxurious. Far more spacious than what she would have expected on a ship, the
captain's quarters were almost as well appointed as any
room at Devon House. The walls of his office were pan-
eled with dark wood, a thick navy-blue carpet covered
most of the floor, and brass sconces and gilt-framed pic-
tures of seascapes adorned the walls. One tall shelf was
filled with books. Forest green leather upholstered chairs
surrounded the large, round table in the center of the
cabin. Tasteful and decidedly masculine mahogany furniture enhanced the decor. She found it surprising that
Harrison indulged himself in such comfort and style,
for he seemed quite a no-nonsense type of man.

The adjoining bedchamber held the enormous bed, upon
which she slept last night. The walls held brass sconces
also, as well as a wall of closets. Several small windows
framed with curtains allowed light to stream in.

Under the pretense of looking for a sewing kit to re-
fasten the buttons of her shirt, which *he* had so carelessly
torn, Juliette poked around Harrison's cabin without
compunction. Even after she found the sewing kit.

Opening every cabinet, drawer, and chest in the room,
Juliette ignored the slight pang of guilt at rummaging
through his personal items by reasoning that if Harrison
hadn't wanted her to go through his things, he should not
have locked her alone in his cabin in the first place.

Harrison was surprisingly neat and organized, unlike
Juliette who could never be bothered to take the time to

put her possessions away properly. All of his clothes were neatly folded in drawers and arranged in closets. She lifted one of his shirts from a drawer and inhaled the scent. She suddenly realized that she could now recognize the distinct scent of Harrison: a mixture of sea and salt air, soap, and an utter masculinity. She breathed deeply again, holding it close to her, then replaced it very carefully. Juliette made her way back into his office.

She rifled through the stacks of papers and maps in his desk drawers, ignoring most of it, deeming it boring and inconsequential. She wanted to learn about the man, not his ship. Frustrated by the lack of any personal memorabilia, Juliette continued her search. Inside one drawer she found a small black leather case. Opening it, she paused at the daguerreotype photographic card of a woman. A very lovely woman, who possessed fair curls and somewhat sad looking eyes.

Now this was something. Juliette lingered over this particular find, wondering who the lady was and how Harrison knew her. Was this his sweetheart? She did not recall Harrison mentioning any family during his visit to Devon House, but then she had not paid him too much attention. Harrison did not seem to be one who was overly eager to divulge personal history anyway. She was positive he was not married, for Lucien surely would have shared that information when they were first introduced, and she certainly would have remembered something like that. But perhaps he had a fiancée? Maybe this sweet, fair girl was his intended bride? It was not entirely out of the range of possibility.

Perhaps that is why Harrison stopped kissing her so abruptly. And left the cabin. Had he been riddled with guilt for kissing her when he had a fiancée?

Staring at the face on the photograph, Juliette realized

she actually knew very little about Captain Harrison
Fleming. Not that they had had much opportunity to dis-
cuss his life since she had been aboard the *Sea Minx*.
He was too busy either ordering her about or kissing her.

She mentally recounted what she could recall being
told about him.

He hailed from New York and had built his own shipping business. And she knew next to nothing about either
New York or shipping. She wished she had questioned
Jeffrey about him. Jeffrey would have told her anything
she wanted to know about him. But then he would have
wanted to know why Juliette wanted to know such
things. She had feared arousing Jeffrey's suspicion by
her interest in Captain Fleming so she had prudently kept
her mouth closed.

What did she really know about Harrison?

She surmised that he had to be a successful businessman or her brother-in-law and Jeffrey would not be involved with him in the first place. She knew he was
strong and handsome. She knew his crew respected him.
She knew he cared enough about her to make her wear a
proper hat while out in the sun. She knew he was capable of kissing her senseless.

And now she also knew Harrison kept a special photograph of a beautiful woman in his desk.

Slowly, she turned the sepia-toned photograph over.
Anderson's Photographers with an address in New York
City was printed on the back. And scrawled in pencil was
written the name Melissa and the year 1870. Who was
Melissa? Whoever she was, she must be important to
him to have this picture in his desk, for photographs were
a rarity. Only last year, Lucien had arranged for a family
photograph to be taken on his and Colette's wedding day
and that had been a very special event.

The sound of a key rattling the door set her heart to pounding. Goodness! Had Harrison returned? Juliette hastily placed the leather case with the photograph back in the drawer and scurried away from the desk. She certainly had no wish for Harrison to catch her in the act of snooping. Shaking, she sat herself in a chair and clutched the front of her shirt closed just before the door opened.

A sigh of relief escaped her when Robbie entered the cabin, carrying a cloth sack. He gave her a sheepish smile, his freckled face lined in apprehension.

"Hello, Robbie," she said, relaxing somewhat. "Have you come to let me out?"

He shuffled his feet awkwardly. "You made the captain pretty angry there, Miss Juliette."

She laughed in spite of herself. "Oh, I don't care that he's angry. I just hope I didn't get you into any trouble."

Robbie shook his head. "I wouldn't worry about me. The captain doesn't stay mad for long. He was more worried about you than anything else. You gave us all an awful scare watching you climb up that rigging."

Juliette had no regrets over her actions. "I'm sorry for worrying you all. I did have a grand time though."

"You did fine up there," he said in admiration. "I would think you'd been on a ship before."

"Thank you for being man enough to admit that to me." A feeling of pride coursed through her.

His face flushed again. "You're welcome."

She eyed him closely. "Does Captain Fleming want me back up on the deck scrubbing now? Is that why he sent you?"

"No . . ." Robbie hesitated nervously and gave a little shake of his head. "No, the captain wants you to stay in here for a while. He thinks you'll be safer this way."

So he intended to keep her locked up in his cabin for

the duration, did he? Well, she would just see about that! Just as she became irate at the prospect of her enforced captivity, she paused for a moment as an idea occurred to her. If she was to remain in Harrison's cabin, she could not scrub the decks. If being inside freed her from manual labor, she truly didn't mind. And she *was* being kept in the nicest and most luxurious cabin on the *Sea Minx*. For all that she had stowed aboard, Juliette truly could not complain about their treatment of her.

Robbie handed her the large burlap sack.

Curious, Juliette peered inside. The bag held an odd assortment of worn shirts, wrinkled trousers, socks, and what looked like men's underclothes. With her mouth open, she stared at Robbie as realization slowly dawned.

"He says you're to keep yourself occupied by mending some of the fellows' clothes and things," Robbie explained, confirming what her intuition had already told her.

"He wishes for me to become the seamstress of the *Sea Minx*, does he?"

"Well, it would keep you busy and safe inside. You'd be helping out us fellows too. And the captain thinks you'd be earning your keep at least." Robbie, who thought the situation well settled, nodded in agreement with his captain's philosophy.

Harrison thought he had found a way to put her to work after all. Juliette suppressed the laughter that bubbled within her but could not hide the grin on her face.

It truly was a shame that she had never learned how to sew properly.

~ 7 ~

A Friend, Indeed

Lord Jeffrey Eddington hugged Colette Sinclair one last time, her pretty face full of worry and her unwieldy frame making him slightly uncomfortable. Women in the family way always caused him to feel nervous, especially when he was not supposed to remark upon their state of being according to society's dictates. With ladies in such a delicate condition, he feared hurting or injuring them in some way. Seeing his closest friend's wife this way only intensified his awkwardness.

Colette whispered in his ear, "Please find her, Jeffrey."

"Of course I will find her," he reassured Colette, patting her back briefly as he released her. He wondered how it was possible for her to look any more beautiful carrying a baby than she did the first day he met her. Her skin positively glowed. Her blue eyes, although tinged with anxiety, beamed with an inner radiance. Of course, he could never say that to her, but he wished he could. The errant thought that perhaps one day a woman he loved would bear his child and look lovely doing so caused his heart to constrict.

"We appreciate you taking this journey for us," Lucien added.

Lucien's words dragged Jeffrey back to the task at hand. He had hardly needed encouragement to search for his beautiful and headstrong friend, for he had been frantic and consumed with worry since he first learned of Juliette's disappearance. After a thorough search of the London docks and numerous inquiries, he and Lucien could find no sign or trace of her. This led them to the only conclusion that they could bear to contemplate; Juliette had successfully boarded Harrison Fleming's ship in spite of numerous obstacles. Jeffrey secretly prayed that was the case, for he knew she would be safe in Harrison's care.

Any other possibility of Juliette's whereabouts was too horrifying to entertain.

Through his connections with the crown, he had immediately made arrangements to sail on the fastest steamship to New York. With Colette about to have a baby, Lucien could not in good conscience leave his wife. So Jeffrey had volunteered to make the voyage across the Atlantic Ocean to bring the wayward Juliette back to her family.

He could do nothing less.

Aside from being afraid for her safety, Jeffrey was filled with admiration for her gumption and spirit at doing something so outrageously daring. To his complete astonishment the chit had actually made good on her threat to sail to New York City one day. Only Juliette could do such a thing.

It was what had always intrigued him the most about Juliette. She had no fear and she would go after exactly what she wanted. However, he had a feeling that this time she might have gotten more than she had bargained for.

"You must make sure you stay safe, as well, Jeffrey," Lisette said to him.

"And you must come back home to us," Paulette announced with a worried frown. "We can't lose you to America too!"

Yvette piped up, "Oh, that would be dreadful!" Her wide blue eyes sparkled with tears.

Jeffrey glanced at the three younger sisters. They had all come to the dock to see him off. Lisette, another Hamilton beauty, had charmed him with her sweet and unassuming nature. With her dark blonde hair and steady eyes, she possessed an innate calmness that the others lacked. The fourth sister, Paulette, about sixteen years old now and on the verge of womanhood, would be a stunner to match her sisters. Intelligent and lively, she had a quick mind and a lovely face framed with blonde curls. Yvette, the youngest at fourteen, still had the youthful look of a child about her, but Jeffrey had a feeling she might be the most beautiful of all the sisters one day.

How he had come to be so involved in their lives, he was not quite sure, but he now loved them as if they were his own sisters. Last year when he and Juliette had wildly conspired to force a stubborn Lucien, his trusted friend since childhood and the closest thing to a brother he had ever known, into admitting his true feelings for Colette, Jeffrey had unwittingly made himself a part of the Hamilton family. Colette and Lucien's marriage had solidified his position in their family, for the Hamilton girls had welcomed him with open arms.

This little band of sisters had given him a sense of family Jeffrey had never known. Lord knew his father, the Duke of Rathmore, hadn't bothered to. Jeffrey had spent most of his childhood and adult life alone, living down the terrible shame of his illegitimacy and trying to prove his worthiness to the world. So Jeffrey would go to New York gladly and drag Juliette, most likely kicking and spitting fire the whole way, back home. He owed at least this much to the Hamiltons for all they had given him.

These women stood before him, hopeful and anxious, placing their trust in him. Jeffrey, for the first time in his life, could think of nothing witty or amusing to say to lighten their somber mood. He felt his cheeks redden under their regard. *Good God!* He was actually blushing.

"I'll do my best," he said to all of them.

He only hoped he could find Juliette, for their sakes as well as Juliette's.

∾ 8 ∾

In the Stars

For three days Harrison managed to avoid contact with Juliette. Not an easy feat on a ship, but he had deftly kept his distance from her at all costs. For three days he had only gone to his office when he was assured that Juliette was walking the deck with Robbie. For three days he had thoroughly occupied himself with the business of sailing the *Sea Minx*.

And for three very long nights had slept on a bunk in the third mate's cabin and had thought of nothing but the feel of Juliette's silky skin and the passion of her kisses, the sweet scent of her dark hair, the sensation of her breath on his cheek. For every one of those nights he had been tortured by sensual images of Juliette lying willing and eager beneath him, naked, in his bed.

He had come dangerously close to crossing a line with her that first afternoon. A line which he had no intention of crossing. He regretted that encounter with her after he carried her to his cabin, and he was a man who rarely had regrets in that area of his life. The last thing he needed now was to be entangled with a woman like Juliette Hamilton. He had a little over a week left to endure before they reached New York, where he would send her safely back to London on the *Freedom*, one of his fastest steam packets with one of his most trusted captains. Then he would be rid of her.

Then he could breathe easily once again. Only one more week to survive.

There were too many issues that needed his complete attention. Once he returned to New York, he would meet with his shipping manager and then head straight to his new farm in New Jersey and see Melissa. His worry for her had continued to grow. He could only imagine the state she would be in by now. Annie's last letter had been full of foreboding and Harrison sensed her frustration and concern in dealing with Melissa. He only wished he had answers or knew how best to help her.

Now Harrison remained on deck watching the sky and enjoying the quiet solitude of the ship. Except for those on watch, most of his crew were below deck or already in bed and Charlie had the wheel for the night. Harrison would retire soon himself, but he felt too restless to go below just yet.

He leaned over the mahogany railing and inhaled the bracing sea air as his elegant ship silently cut through the dark waves. Looking up at the sky, he noted that an eerie cloud ring had formed around the waning moon and he knew bad weather was ahead. Harrison could sense it, feel it in the very fiber of his being. He could smell the change in the air and had had it confirmed by the mahogany and brass barometer that indicated falling pressure, a sure sign of rain. Bad weather would only slow them down and cause difficult sailing conditions. If they were very lucky they would avoid the brunt of the brewing storm.

And he'd be very lucky if he could avoid the dangerous little storm in his cabin.

Who *was* this woman on his ship?

Yes, he was acquainted with her family. Well, at least he had known Lucien Sinclair and Jeffrey Eddington for years. He had spent a few weeks at the Sinclairs' beautiful home and had a few brief conversations with Juliette while in the company of others. He noted her remarkable beauty, for who could not? She was stunning, but he knew better than to become involved with a woman like that, and he had not sought her out. Nor had he sensed any overt interest on her part.

Now, he couldn't stop thinking about her. And to make matters worse he was responsible for her welfare and safety.

From the second he found her on his ship, he was haunted by thoughts of her. He could not think straight. He had misplaced his maps and misread the barometer. He had been unreasonably short-tempered and quick to anger with his crew, barking at them for the pettiest of reasons. Robbie practically hid from him. Even Charlie had remarked on his foul mood and wondered at his distractedness. Just that afternoon Harrison had made a careless error in his calculations with the sextant, almost sending them off course. Harrison had laughed off his blunder, blaming his temporary and uncomfortable sleeping arrangements for his distractibility and foul humor.

Although Harrison suspected the true reason for his bothered state rested deeper within him.

Juliette Hamilton had somehow gotten under his skin, causing him to act out of character. He never had such a problem with a woman before, yet this one made him crazy with desire. She had only to look at him with those wild blue eyes and he became aroused. After their last encounter, when he had recklessly ripped open her shirt like some callous youth, he had to lock her in his cabin and give his key to Robbie to keep himself from her. The fact that he could not dally with her, made his plight that much more painful. Juliette was not a woman he could have. In any sense of the word.

Besides, she was already in love with someone else.

What kind of man could claim a wild heart like hers? Did the man have any idea of how reckless she was? That this beautiful woman was crossing an entire ocean to be with him? What would it be like to have the love of a woman like that?

"What are you looking at?"

The feminine voice shot like fire through him. Harrison did not move an inch, nor did he turn to face her, but a muscle tensed along his jaw. Silently he wondered how Juliette had managed to escape the cabin. Robbie had been very diligent about locking the door. She must have sweet-talked him into letting her out. Damn the fool.

Harrison answered her slowly. "I'm observing the stars and clouds to predict the weather."

She paused a second before asking in an amused voice, "And just what is it you see in them?"

Harrison sensed her stepping closer to him, but he still did not turn to her. "We've had fair weather so far, but I think we are in for some rain by morning."

"A little rain would be most refreshing."

"Oh, it will likely be more than a little rain," he said, his tone ominous.

She leaned against the railing next to him. A long silence ensued.

"You've been avoiding me, Captain Fleming."

"I've more important things to do than to attend to your needs."

"You've been avoiding me," she repeated, her voice throaty and low, sending an extraordinary wave of desire crashing over him.

Harrison then made the monumental mistake of looking at her.

Staring intently at him, Juliette smiled triumphantly, her face luminous in the pale glow of the moon and stars. No longer wearing the men's clothing, she had on one of her own dresses, a pretty confection that outlined her numerous charms. He swallowed hard. Her long black hair hung loose around her shoulders, blowing in the breeze. Looking like she should be the figurehead on the bow of the *Sea Minx*, he sucked in his breath at the sight of her. He steeled himself.

"After what happened between us, it's best if I avoid you, Juliette," he managed to reply.

She nodded her head gently. The exact reason why he needed to stay away from her hung unspoken in the air. God help him, but he fought the urge to take her in his arms and kiss her sweet mouth again right then and there.

"When will we reach New York?"

He felt himself relax as she changed the subject. "If we can manage to bypass this storm, we should be there in little over a week."

She turned her face toward his. "This is a very fast ship, isn't it?"

He grinned at her. "One of the fastest clippers on the sea."

"It's a beautiful boat." She glanced out over the water and breathed deeply. "The ocean is so dark at night and something about it terrifies me. The vastness and mysteriousness of it, perhaps. But I'm sure you're not afraid of the ocean anymore."

"It is a very foolish man that does not possess a healthy fear of the ocean."

Juliette turned back to face him again. "You have been sailing since you were a young boy, haven't you?"

He nodded in agreement. "When I was thirteen, I started working on the docks on South Street. When I was old enough I became part of a crew on a tall ship."

"And now you've traveled all over the world and have had great success with your own shipping line."

"Yes, that's true," he admitted. "I've come a long way from where I began as a boy."

"You must be very proud of your accomplishments."

"Proud enough."

"Do you ever intend to stay in one place and settle down?"

Noting the highly inquisitive tone in her voice, he held back a smile and gave her a noncommittal shrug. "Perhaps."

"Do you want to have a real home on land someday?"

"I have that already."

"What about marriage?" she questioned.

"What about marriage?" he countered evenly.

"What about having a wife and children?"

"I had not given that much thought." Which, oddly enough, was the truth. He had been so consumed with succeeding with his shipping line, making money, and taking care of Melissa that the thought of a wife and children had not entered his mind in any practical terms. He supposed in a vague, far off fashion he had assumed he would settle down one day when he met a woman he could love. "What about you, Juliette? Do you wish to have a husband, a home, and children?"

"If I wanted to be married I would have remained in London!" she exclaimed with a rueful laugh. "I don't wish to marry. At least not now. Not yet. Perhaps someday." Juliette sighed heavily. Changing the subject, she asked abruptly, "Have you any family? Brothers? Sisters?"

"I have a brother and two sisters." Saving her the effort of more questions, Harrison continued in a matter of fact manner. "I am the eldest. Both of my parents are deceased. My birthday is July third. I'm twenty-nine years old. My favorite color is blue. My shipping business is quite successful. I have sailed around the world at least half a dozen times. I have a town house in Manhattan and a house and farmland in New Jersey, where I am currently building a stable for racehorses. Is there anything else you care to know?"

Juliette, looking somewhat chagrined, shook her head. "That about does it for now, although that information begs me to ask a whole host of new questions."

"Well, let me ask you a few questions for a moment or two."

"I suppose that's only fair," she conceded amiably. "Fire away."

"How old are you?"

"I'm twenty-one."

"And your birthday?"

"Was March eighteenth."

A silence lengthened between them, before Harrison spoke again. "Since we are sharing information about each other, I would like you tell me something, Juliette. What is the real reason you wish to go to New York so desperately?"

Disarming him, Juliette looked directly in his eyes. "I told you the reason already."

"I don't think going to visit a friend on another

continent is enough to lure a young lady from her home." He gave her an assessing gaze. "Who is he?"

"*He?* There is no *he*. It is difficult for me to explain why, but I simply had to leave London."

He stared at her for a long moment, noting the sincere look on her face. She sounded earnest enough, but he did not believe her. Her story did not make sense. This woman was on a mission and there was no doubt in his mind that it was a mission to capture a certain gentleman in New York. A woman in love following the man who claimed her heart made sense to him, but Harrison would be damned if he could figure out why any man would leave behind a woman like Juliette.

He played along, hoping to lull her into a false sense of security. He would get the truth out of her soon enough, and definitely by the time they docked in New York. "All right then. Who is this friend you are going to see?"

Juliette sighed easily. "Oh, I've known her for years. My father used to tutor her in our bookshop. Christina Dunbar is now married to an American gentleman and they settled in New York about two years ago. She invited me to stay with them, so I thought this would be the perfect opportunity to see a part of the world that isn't London."

Harrison could not believe this was the whole story. Surely she had dissembled or conveniently omitted certain aspects, as most women tended to do. Somewhere there was a man involved, he was certain of it. Was he a relative of this Christina person, perhaps? What Juliette did not know was that she would have no opportunity to see her friend when they arrived in New York since he would be shipping her directly back to London as soon as they docked. He humored her anyway. "Does *she* have any idea that you will be there in a week?"

"I believe so. I sent her a letter days before I left home informing her that I would be arriving before long. She will be happy to see me in any case."

"I see." He turned and leaned one elbow along the railing and faced her. "How long are you planning to stay in New York?"

"I honestly don't know yet. It's all just an adventure for me right now." Her smile lit up the night and caught Harrison off guard.

Her lips beckoned him and he was sorely tempted to kiss her. He could do it so easily too. He already knew how heavenly her lips tasted and he ached to have her again. He knew that path could only lead to trouble for him. He cleared his throat rather loudly and stood up straight. "Well, I think it's time to go below for the night." He made a move forward to take his leave.

She put her hand up, gesturing to stop him. "About that."

Harrison paused and looked at her, wishing to the good lord above that she were not so temptingly beautiful.

Juliette hesitated for a moment. "When I boarded your ship the other night, I swear to you that I had no intention of inconveniencing you in any way. I simply needed a way to get to New York. I would have stayed in that storage room the entire voyage if that was what it took. However, I do appreciate you allowing me to stay in your lovely cabin, but I never meant to put you out of your own bed, Captain Fleming."

Harrison froze at her casual reference to his bed. The image of her sleeping between his sheets, naked and warm with her long hair spilling around her, almost undid him. He stated haltingly, "You have not put me out. There simply was no other room suitable for you."

An uncomfortable silence ensued between them. At least it was uncomfortable for Harrison. He made another motion to leave.

"You're bothered by me."

He stopped and eyed her with a careful glance. Did she know that he had barely slept the last three nights for being bothered by her? "What makes you say something like that?"

"You have locked me in your cabin."

"Only to keep you from falling overboard."

She held up her chin. "I feel I am being held captive."

He titled his head toward her. "When you stow away on someone's ship, you are taking your chances, my dear. You have been exceptionally well-treated for a stowaway, so you have no reason to complain." He knew she had the best of the food on board, for Cook had seen to it that the "pretty lady" did not perish for want of sustenance. She was supposed to have been mending some of the men's clothes to earn her keep, but she had proved surprisingly inept at that task. He was aware that Robbie had even filled the small bath for her earlier that day. She had been given every luxury and treated as a princess. So in essence she had been lounging about in his cabin for three days, without a care in the world.

"Yes, that's true enough and I do thank you," she conceded easily. "Yet still, I was locked inside for days with no word from you."

Struggling with the delectable and arousing image of Juliette naked in the bath, he refocused on her recent comment. "What word could you possibly need from me?" he questioned her.

"Oh, I don't know . . . You kissed me, quite passionately I would say, and left without so much as a good day."

He needed no reminders from her of their heated exchange that afternoon. He had been tortured enough by his own traitorous mind ever since. "How the hell did you get out of my cabin this evening anyway?" he said roughly.

Juliette held up a small brass key that was not unfamiliar to him.

He nodded his head in concession while grudgingly admiring her spirit and determination. "It took you long enough to find it."

She twirled the key around her forefinger. "It was in the last place I would have suspected you to hide it."

He had stored the spare key to his cabin in a detailed china figurine of a ship that sat on the top shelf beside some books. She must have investigated his cabin quite thoroughly all right. She ought to be spanked for such behavior. He gave her a hard look, still amazed by the sheer beauty of her face. "So, I am to assume that you have gone through all of my personal possessions?"

She shrugged in a careless gesture. "You locked me in. What else did you expect me to do to alleviate my boredom but search for the key?"

She had been confined to his cabin for three days, so he supposed she had a point. Still, it rankled him to the core that she had looked through his private belongings. "Obviously your parents did not raise you as a respectable lady with proper manners."

Her melodious laughter filled the air around him. "Have you just come to that conclusion, Captain Fleming? Did you expect a respectable lady with fine manners to leave her family and stow away on a ship with a virtual stranger?"

No, he was certain he sensed that about Juliette from the moment he met her. She was not a proper lady. She was nothing but trouble. He reached out to take the key from her, but she snatched her hand away before he could get it.

Juliette laughed again and he realized the key was looped through a ribbon that was tied around her neck. In one quick movement she tucked the key down the front of the pretty gown she was wearing. The dark blue dress, although displaying her ample bosom quite nicely, sported a high enough neckline that the key was well hidden.

"Oh, it's my key now," she taunted in a low voice. "Finders keepers."

Spurred on by an impulse he could not control, Harrison grabbed her hand tightly and pulled her hard against his chest. "Make no mistake, my dear, it is my key and it belongs to me. Just like everything on this ship is mine to do with as I wish. Including you, Juliette Hamilton."

They regarded each other warily, and their eyes locked. Harrison's heart pounded wildly at the nearness of her, while he reveled in the feel of her warm body against his. She did not stiffen or pull away from him. Juliette stood her ground, and if he were not mistaken, pressed her body ever so lightly against his, which only heightened his desire. The scent of jasmine lingered around her and he breathed deeply of her. She stared up at him, her small chin against his chest.

She whispered, "If you want your key back, Captain Fleming, then you'll just have to get it yourself."

Good God! The audacity of her words left him speechless for a moment. The implications were staggering. He took a quick breath and muttered, "You, Miss Juliette Hamilton, are definitely more trouble than you are worth."

Then he crushed his mouth over hers and he was lost.
Once again he surrendered all self-control.

She kissed him as fervently as he kissed her. Her arms
wound around his neck and she pressed her body hard
against his. He felt her fingers spread out through his
hair, caressing his head. He held her tightly, devouring
her with his mouth and tongue, losing himself in the
heady sweetness of her lips and mouth. Small, yet curvy
in all the right places, she fit in his arms so perfectly it
was as if she were made for him.

Under the twinkling stars on the swaying deck of the
Sea Minx, they kissed each other with a ravenous hunger,
passionately locked in an embrace.

Unable to bear any more, Harrison swept her up in his
arms. By God, if she was going to tempt him in such a
way, then she was going to get what she asked for. Without uttering a single word, he carried her with purposeful strides to his cabin. When they reached his quarters,
he set her down, slowly sliding her body along the length
of his, while he again devoured her lips.

Breaking free, Juliette kissed him on the cheek and
little by little pulled the key from beneath her dress. With
a mischievous look, she locked the door to the cabin
from the inside. Turning back to face him, she placed the
key back down her dress.

With a wicked smile and a gleam in her blue eyes, she
whispered, "Now, you're locked in with me, Captain
Fleming."

Good sense dictated that he run, but in that moment
he knew he was doomed. With a swift movement he
grabbed her, pulling her hard against his chest.

"Do you know what you are doing?" he growled, more
aroused than he had ever been in his life. This wild,
beautiful vixen had just locked them both in his cabin

and placed the key down her dress. To get out he had to obtain the key, most assuredly a pleasurable endeavor, and in so doing he would certainly not have the strength to use the key to escape. The very idea of retrieving the key left him undone.

Juliette stared up at him with heavy-lidded eyes. "Do you truly wish to leave me?"

She was a sea siren, that was what she was. All the tall tales he'd heard all his life were true. Juliette had cast some sort of spell over him. That was the only explanation for his lack of control. His answer was a scorching kiss. It was as if a splendid fire ignited between them, glorious and hot and all consuming.

But Harrison had a dreadful suspicion he would be the one consumed by the flames when all this was done.

∞9∞

Just a Little Adventure

Juliette could not breathe and did not care. Harrison was kissing her and that was all that she wanted, or needed, quite frankly. For three days she had been trapped in Harrison's cabin, sleeping in his bed and being tormented by the memory of his kisses.

Now she kissed him back just as thoroughly as he kissed her. She gasped as his hands slid over the curves of her waist and along her back. She felt his fingers brush the buttons at the back of her dress. Slowly he unfastened them, one by one. She opened her eyes. In the dimly lit cabin she could see Harrison's face, the rugged line of his jaw, as he kissed her, nuzzled her neck.

She reached up and again splayed her fingers through the softness of his golden hair. The sensation aroused her even more. He slowly walked her back to his bedchamber; with her heart in her mouth, she allowed him to lead her, guide her to his enormous bed. She had no one to blame but herself for what was about to happen. She had willed this. She had, in fact, sought Harrison out. After being deprived of his company for days she had ached for him with a longing she had never experienced. Yes, this would be the first of her many adventures.

And she did not doubt that being in Harrison's bed would be a great adventure. And in all honesty, what did she have to lose? Her reputation would be considered lost already by everyone who knew her, so why not take her pleasure where she might? Harrison certainly promised pleasure, with his mouth, his hands, with his body.

Juliette shivered in breathless anticipation as he continued to undress her with infinite care. With slow, methodical deliberateness he inched her dress from her, and she shimmied to ease herself from the garment. His breathing heavy, she stood before him in nothing but her chemise.

"You are incredibly beautiful, Juliette," he murmured low.

A heated blush crept over her skin.

He reached for the key around her neck. With a wicked grin, he removed it from her and tossed it behind them. She smiled before she stood on tiptoe and wrapped her arms around Harrison's neck, pulling him toward her. He groaned as his lips found hers once again. As they kissed, she began to unfasten the buttons down the front of his shirt, exposing a long vee of his skin. His bare chest visible, Juliette felt her stomach tighten at the sight. With a hesitant gesture, she touched his warm and silky smooth skin as she traced the lines of his muscled chest.

In a swift movement, Harrison lifted the shirt over his head. Juliette sucked in her breath, mesmerized by the broad expanse of male chest. She leaned in close and pressed her lips to his heated skin. She had no idea a man could be so soft and hard at the same time. Her tongue licked one flat nipple, and then the other, marveling in the feel of a man's body. This close to him, she could feel his heart hammering inside the walls of his powerful chest. Drawn by the incredible warmth he exuded she kissed the taut ridges of his stomach. His body tensed under her mouth, but she continued to lean down, pressing her lips against his body. Spurred by his obvious desire for her, in a brazen move she reached lower and unfastened the front of his trousers and tugged them down. With shaking fingers, she untied the laces of his drawers and pulled them down as well. He stepped out of them with an ease and quickness that startled her. Faced with his nakedness, she suddenly lost her courage and glanced frantically up at his face. His stormy eyes were so intent on her, it felt as though he could see into the deepest recesses of her soul. Her mouth went dry.

He lifted the hem of her chemise, and without a word she raised her arms over her head as he removed the last remaining vestige of covering she had. Now completely naked next to his bare and brawny body, her legs ceased to support her. She began to sink. Harrison, sensing her sudden weakness, grasped her in his arms again; covering her mouth with his in a kiss so possessive that Juliette lost herself completely. She pressed herself against him, holding on for dear life.

Gathering her in his arms, Harrison placed her in the center of the large bed, covering her body with his. Juliette closed her eyes and kissed him, clung to him, her heart pounding erratically and about to burst from her chest. The intimacy of having a naked man atop her, his legs positioned firmly between hers, brought home the realization of her little adventure.

He pulled away and her eyes fluttered open in alarm.

Her words came out in a frantic whisper. "You're not leaving me now, are you?"

Harrison stared at her for a long moment. "Not unless you tell me to," he murmured softly in her ear. Leaning on one elbow, Harrison brushed her face with gentle fingers, slowly tracing the line of her cheek. His seductive touch melted her.

"No." She swallowed hard. "I don't want you to leave me." There was no mistaking her meaning. At least she hoped not. Unsure why she desperately wanted to be with this man, she simply gave in to her desires.

"Juliette."

Her name fell like a caress upon her and her stomach tightened. She reached her arms around his neck and stared at his ruggedly handsome face.

He looked down at her, his gaze unwavering. "If I stay, you know what will happen between us?" he asked.

Her mouth went dry. She merely nodded at him. Of course she knew what would happen between them. She was dying for it to happen. She practically locked the man in his cabin with her. If it didn't happen, if *something* didn't happen soon, she would surely die of this intense wanting. Juliette had no frame of reference for this situation with Harrison. Lying naked in a bed with a man's naked body on top of hers had to be the most delicious experience of her life. That old medical text never described this sensation, that was certain. If Harrison didn't get on with it already, she would perish from unfulfilled desire.

As if he read her mind, Harrison leaned down and began kissing her again, and Juliette melted into him. Yes, melted. There was no other word for how her body virtually became part of his. Her mouth eagerly sought his, their warm tongues entwined in a spiral dance, his kisses leaving her hungry for more.

And he gave her more. He kissed her mouth, her cheek, and made his way along the curve of her throat, the hollow of her neck, down her collarbone and up to the peak of her breast. Again, the fervent touch of his lips on her sensitive skin left her reeling. The intimacy of his touching her was like nothing she had ever experienced. An intense thrill coursed through her body and pooled low inside her, causing her to arch her hips.

"There's no rush," he said in a husky voice. "We have all night, angel."

Juliette held her breath. With a languid pace, he brushed delicate kisses upon her other breast, leaving her shaking with pleasure. His hands caressed her, while she clung to him, her fingers mindlessly stroking his neck and splaying into his hair as he moved between her breasts.

She blew heatedly into his ear, kissing and nibbling. His blond head moved lower, kissing an impassioned path along the taut lines of her stomach. She shivered and trembled in anticipation as he leisurely kissed his way around the curve of her hip and down her upper thigh. While gently massaging her leg with his free hand, he continued to kiss her ever so gently, circling the area of her greatest need. Juliette thought she would shatter into a million pieces if he didn't touch her and would just as soon shatter if he *did* touch her. His teasing assault on her senses seemed to last forever.

A wild gasp escaped her when his hand finally cupped her and her back arched in response to his touch.

Harrison grinned wickedly as he rose to meet her mouth with a kiss, while his hand continued to move magically below. He then whispered, "Ah, it seems I have finally found the way to capture your complete attention."

The exquisite sensations he created within her left

her wanting to cry. When he gently and slowly slid one finger inside of her, Juliette did cry out.

"Oh, Harrison," she gasped, her fingers digging into his shoulders. She truly could not bear any more pleasure, yet she knew there would be more. There had to be. But good lord, how would she survive it? This intimate act involved more than she could possibly have imagined. No wonder Colette could not describe it to her.

He kissed her again and Juliette let herself drown in the feelings Harrison evoked as he continued to arouse her with his skilled fingers. Wicked fingers. Heavenly fingers. Time and space lost all meaning. The cabin disappeared and her entire focus narrowed to the man next to her and how he touched her so intimately. The pleasure built within her and she held her breath, frantic and clinging to him. A sudden burst of pure bliss descended upon her.

Again she called to him. He kissed her lips and she called his name into his mouth. Juliette clung to him, her fingers digging into his broad shoulders.

In that instant, Harrison moved over her and pushed the hardness of himself inside her in one even thrust. Unprepared for the impact of Harrison inside of her, her eyes flew open. His eyes stared intensely down at her, a look of longing on his handsome face. Surprised by the force and strength of him, but welcoming him all the same, Juliette arched up to meet him, matching his thrust.

He groaned and began to move steadily within her.

"Juliette."

He uttered her name as if it were a plea. Not sure exactly what it was he wanted, Juliette willingly let him lead her, moving with him. She matched his rhythm.

Now this, *this*, was what she had been craving. Longing for. This is what she needed. She could not even think coherently. She could only feel, and touch, and kiss, and enjoy . . . Good God, her whole body throbbed with pleasure.

As their rhythmic movements coincided with the swaying of the ship, Juliette lost herself in Harrison's embrace. He surrounded her, filled her, completed her. The utter maleness of him engulfed her being. She reveled in the feel of him, while another peak began to build within her. Giving in to the increasing waves of pleasure that coursed through her body, Juliette's breath came in short, frantic gasps that matched the increasing frequency of Harrison's thrusts. She thought of nothing but him, of Harrison making love to her in his bed on his ship. This man wanted her. And she had let him have her. The power and closeness of this profound exchange overwhelmed her.

As Juliette's pleasure peaked, so did Harrison's. They both cried out each other's names as ecstasy claimed them.

Juliette frantically hoped that Harrison did not notice the stray tear that escaped her eyes as passion crested within her. Never had she felt anything so intense and astounding. She lay curled in his powerful arms, reveling in the feel of his skin against hers, attempting to regain her breath. Harrison continued to press kisses into her hair. They held each other tightly as the ship rocked beneath them. In a caring gesture, he pulled the quilt over the two of them and settled back next to her.

She snuggled into the crook of his arms, not the least bit uncomfortable or embarrassed by what they had done. She murmured to him, "Never mind climbing the mizzenmast, *that* was the most thrilling, most exhilarating thing I have ever done in my entire life."

Harrison chuckled and kissed her. "Good God, Juliette. You are something exceptional. Do you know that?"

"Of course, I do," she said sleepily. She closed her eyes, unable to keep them open another second, and snuggled even closer. Her head rested in the curve of his neck. She had never felt as at home as she did then. She sighed contentedly.

Harrison hugged her tightly to him. He whispered something to her, but she could barely make out his words. She could recall nothing else, except a deep sense of complete and utter peace and contentment.

∾10∾

There's Got to Be
a Morning After

As usual Harrison woke before dawn. What was completely unusual was the naked woman beside him. Everything came crashing back to him in a split second.

He had bedded Juliette Hamilton.

Christ! He never should have done something so irrevocably stupid. He did not dally with innocents. Despite his belief that Juliette was on her way to reunite with her lover, he was now quite sure that this man of hers had not taken any liberties with her, for Juliette had been a virgin. His heart turned over in his chest.

There she lay, sleeping sweetly in his arms, the most terrifying angel he had ever met.

He took a breath and shook his head at what he had done. He held Juliette tighter to him, enjoying her warmth. Glancing out the small window, he saw the faint lightening of the dawn sky. The rough movements of the ship told him how stormy it was and he could hear the rain. He should get up and go above deck.

But first he had to deal with the beautiful woman sleeping in his bed.

Juliette's silky, black hair spilled around them, her head resting on his chest. Her warm naked body pressed closed to his. She seemed a quiet and peaceful girl, not the impetuous and reckless beauty who had seduced him last night. Good God! She had seduced *him*. And he was not a man who was easily tempted.

Harrison would have to marry her now. The relentless thought pounded in his head. He did not want a wife particularly. As he had informed Juliette the night before, a wife and family were vague notions in his future. They were certainly nothing he was contemplating now. Yet here he was, with Juliette Hamilton in his bed. What was the old saying? Time to pay the piper? It went something like that. There was no help for it.

Harrison had taken advantage of her, and now he must take responsibility for what he had done, no matter what her plans in New York were. Juliette belonged to him now. He certainly could never allow her to marry someone else.

An odd possessiveness overcame him as he gazed down at her in the dim predawn light.

Now that was the most thrilling, most exhilarating thing I have ever done in my entire life. When Juliette declared those words to him last night, he silently agreed with her. It *had* been thrilling and exhilarating between them and he loved that she had compared the feeling to when she had climbed the mizzenmast and felt like she was flying.

He pressed a kiss on her cheek and breathed deeply of her scent. Strands of her silky black hair lay against his arm. The feel of her body next to his awakened something in him that he could not define. He would marry her. Not only because it was the decent thing to do and Lucien would more than likely shoot him if he did not, the mere thought of another man touching her caused his heart to pound ridiculously in his chest.

What was it about her that caused him to react this way? What was so damned special about Juliette Hamilton? Yes, she was beautiful. And exciting. Stubborn and fearless. But there was something else, something more, about her that he could not easily put into words.

Her eyes fluttered open and they stared at each other for a long moment. She leaned up and kissed him before flinging her head back on the pillows. "Good morning, Captain." She flashed him a sleepy smile. "It's not time to get up already is it?"

"No," he shook his head. "Not quite."

"Good." She wrapped her legs around his and snuggled deeper into his arms.

He welcomed her soft closeness by holding her tighter. He whispered in her ear. Such a small, delicate ear she had. "Are you saying you are not ready to get out of bed?"

"If it's still dark out then that is exactly what I am saying," she mumbled with her eyes closed.

Her warm body warmed his. "I take it that you are not an early riser?"

She muttered something unintelligible into the crook of his neck, which he took to be a negative response, and he grinned mischievously.

"Oh, well, it seems we must change your outlook on this matter. Don't you realize how important it is to start your day early, Juliette? To rise with the sun?"

She did not move. He heard a sort of a snore.

He gave her a little nudge. "Wake up, Juliette!"

Frowning at him with her eyes closed, she grumbled, "It's an ungodly hour, Harrison. The sun is not even up yet, so why should I be? Go back to sleep."

"I'm the captain. This is my ship."

"Then you can get up. I'm staying here."

"There is a storm brewing," he threatened.

"Even more reason to stay in bed," she said remaining firmly entrenched in place. "Who wants to be out on deck on a rainy morning, anyway?"

"That is not a good enough excuse to remain abed all morning." Although if anyone could tempt him to do just that, it would be in a bed with Juliette.

"I'm tired." She yawned unabashedly. "If you recall, we were up half the night."

"Yes, you have a valid point there," he agreed in an amiable tone, a helpless smile on his face at the memory. They had been up more than half the night. They had not been able to keep their hands off each other. It had been incredible, unlike anything he had ever experienced before.

"You can get up if you like, Harrison, but I'm staying right here." Juliette tightened her hold on him with her legs and her eyes closed in determination.

"My, my, Miss Hamilton." Harrison shook his head and made "tsk, tsk" sounds, while trying not to laugh. "You have proven yourself to be a dreadful seamstress, useless at scrubbing a deck, and now I detect a most disconcerting lazy streak in your character." He gave an exaggerated sigh. "It seems the task is up to me to find some way for you to earn your keep aboard this vessel."

He tapped his fingers along her shoulder. "Hmm . . ." He continued tapping thoughtfully on her bare, slender shoulder. Creamy smooth and delectable. Yes, it was a very tempting thought, indeed. Staying in bed with Juliette all day.

After a sudden bright flash of light, a tremendous explosion of thunder rocked the cabin, causing Juliette to sit up with a startled, high-pitched shriek.

Harrison laughed at her. "Now I know how to get you to wake up!"

She slapped his arm in exasperation and sank back into the depths of the warm blankets. "You are terribly mean. That was directly on top of us."

He continued laughing. "Come now. Get up and come on the deck with me. I want to show you something." In a swift movement he pulled the covers off, leaving her beautiful naked body revealed to him. He paused at the sight.

She stared at him, irritation evident in her blue eyes. "You are simply not going to let me sleep are you?"

"No." He grinned wickedly at her. "You can't beat me, so you might as well join me." He leaned down and kissed her.

"Are all Americans as annoying and arrogant as you?" she snapped as she tried to tug the covers back over herself.

"Not quite." He yanked the blankets away from her and gave her a nudge toward the edge of the bed. "Now get moving."

"Aye, aye, Captain," she grumbled miserably as she staggered from the bed.

Harrison chuckled at her sarcasm while suddenly feeling cold at her departure from the warm blankets. He swung his legs over the edge of the bed, enjoying the view of Juliette's bare bottom as she crossed the room and began to dress. For a long moment, he debated grabbing her and pulling her back into bed and making love to her all day, but as the ship lurched on the waves of a storm, his sense of duty swayed him in the other direction.

A half an hour later, after hot coffee, they both stood on the captain's deck behind the wheel. Juliette was bundled up in his clothes, covered in oilskins and boots with a large southwester hat pulled down low over her head, and screaming in delight as the *Sea Minx* bounded over the roaring waves. It was a rough and wild ride and Harrison loved the fact that Juliette was loving every minute of the high waves and wind. He had certainly weathered more severe storms than this one, but it was a fairly strong squall just the same. It would not last much longer. Most people would be losing their breakfast over the side of the boat, especially a first-timer like Juliette. But there she stood, gamely hanging onto the railing, her blue eyes alight with excitement and a beaming smile on her beautiful face as she stared out at the ominous sea and clouds. She amazed him.

A blinding flash of lightning streaked across the sky, followed by a tremendous crash of thunder. Juliette did not flinch.

"You're not even a little afraid, are you?" he called to her over the pounding rain.

She turned her sparkling eyes toward him. "Are we going to capsize?" she asked.

"Not a chance." Not in a storm this weak they wouldn't and certainly not on his watch. He would not risk having Juliette up on deck if he thought she was in any danger, which is why he had also insisted she wear a cork lifejacket tied over the oilskins.

"Then I'm not afraid." She grinned at him, her angelic face wet with rain.

Harrison's heart flipped over in his chest at her sheer

bravery and beauty. He had never met a woman to compare to her.

When the storm abated, Harrison and Juliette returned to his cabin to change out of their drenched clothing.

As she plucked his oversized, wet shirt from her body, she chattered in excitement. "That was absolutely thrilling! I've never seen waves that high before! Oh, my heart is still racing! That was by far the most adventurous thing I've ever experienced. Everything on this ship makes me feel as if I am truly living!"

"*Everything*?" he asked, eyeing her naked, damp body. Slowly, he held out a dry towel to her. She was more than stunning. Last night in his arms she had been more than passionate. Juliette seemed to live every opportunity to its fullest.

She took the towel, her eyes lingering on him. "Yes, everything."

The light in her eyes as she looked at him caused an odd sensation in his chest. He smiled back at her, watching at she modestly wrapped the towel around herself, covering her luscious breasts. "Why do you think that is?" he asked, unable to take his eyes off of her.

She cast him a triumphant smile. "Because for the first time in my life I am doing exactly what I want, without anyone telling me what I should or should not do. I have no mother or father scolding me about my behavior and how I should show more decorum and act more ladylike as my sisters do. I have no prim aunt or stuffy old uncle lecturing me on my deportment. I have no sisters or brother-in-law, however well meaning, warning me that I am causing a scandal. I am free."

"You are forgetting someone." With leisurely movements, he stripped off his own wet clothing.

"Am I now?" She stared back at him in blatant appreciation.

Because he knew she was watching him, he ran the dry towel over his naked body with deliberate slowness. "Most definitely."

"I'm sure I don't know to whom you are referring," she responded in a somewhat flirtatious tone, her eyes lingering on his lower body. "I don't believe I've forgotten anyone."

"What about the captain of this vessel?" He gave her a wolfish grin. "Are you already forgetting that you must obey all his orders?"

"Ah, yes." Her hands still clutching the towel closed in front of her, Juliette took a step toward him. Her blue eyes twinkled. "How could I forget? It seems I have a handsome sea-captain ordering me about."

"Handsome, eh?" He liked that, coming from her.

"Oh, yes, handsome. Very." She stepped closer, a smile playing around the corners of her mouth.

"It's the rule of the sea. You must obey all orders from a captain."

"All orders?" she questioned in mock surprise, her eyebrows arching.

"Yes," he said. "To the letter."

"I see." She nodded at him, her eyes directly upon his.

Fascinated by the interplay between them, Harrison felt his body respond heatedly to her nearness. "Come closer," he commanded.

She moved until she stood an inch or two from him. He could smell the sea spray in her hair, which hung in dark, damp tendrils around her face. God, but she was a beautiful woman. She stared up at him expectantly.

"Drop the towel."

Her amused expression vanished as her sultry eyes

darkened with desire. Without the slightest hesitation, Juliette let the white towel slip from her fingers. It fell to her feet on the floor with a quiet swish. She stood naked before him. He sucked in his breath at the sight. Her creamy white skin glowed luminous in the candlelight. He fought the impulse to touch her. For now.

"Now kiss me," he murmured how, his voice husky with hunger for her. He held his breath, waiting to see if she would follow his order.

"Aye, aye, Captain," she whispered before standing on her tiptoes to place a kiss on his lips.

Her bare breasts brushed against his chest and he suddenly could not breathe. Harrison wrapped his arms around her, easing his mouth over hers in a slow and deep kiss. A small sigh escaped her as their tongues met. He could easily drown in the sweetness of her and not care if he ever came up for air again. Her fingers splayed through his damp hair, massaging his scalp in slow, easy motions sending shafts of pleasure through his body. Their lips clung together as his hands stroked the length of her back, reaching lower to caress the curve of her smooth buttocks. Her skin warmed under his touch and she seemed to melt against him. He lifted her easily in his arms and carried her to his bed. He lay beside her, placing delicate kisses along her cheeks, her nose, her chin, and down her soft neck to the hollow of her throat, aching to feel every inch of her with his mouth.

Harrison made love to her all afternoon as the *Sea Minx* sailed into calmer waters. Afterward, they dozed in each other's arms and didn't even dress when they finally roused themselves enough to eat. Robbie had brought food to the cabin, his eyes as wide as saucers when understanding dawned that Harrison and Juliette where in the cabin together. Undoubtedly they were the talk of the ship, but there was no help for it now. His crew would take it in stride, and Juliette did not seem to mind; at least not at the moment. But he would deal with that issue later.

Draped in sheets they sat in bed and shared a loaf of warm, crusty bread and fine cheese, paired with a bottle of wine that Harrison had gotten from a vineyard in France a few years ago.

"I feel so decadent," Juliette whispered in a confidential tone.

"Because you're naked with a man in bed?" he asked.

"No"—she shook her head—"because I'm eating in bed."

He could not help but laugh at her before placing a kiss on her wine-sweetened lips.

"I'm very serious, Harrison," she explained. "I've never spent such a lazy day."

"I hardly think that last bit of exercise we engaged in could be described as lazy."

"That's not what I meant," she giggled, a slight blush suffusing her cheeks.

"Forgive me," he teased her. "I forgot you are used to toiling away the hours in a bookshop."

"That's true. I used to have to spend hours working in the shop day after day. But ever since Colette married Lucien, I am no longer required to tend the shop. Thank heaven!"

"I would have thought you would enjoy managing a store."

Juliette took another sip of wine. "Well, I didn't. To be honest with you, I detested it. Oh, Colette and Paulette, they loved working there. They lived for the bookshop and would have done anything to keep it, while I despised it."

"Why is that?" he asked, breaking off a piece of bread.

She sighed heavily. "It was deadly dull. All those books! Ugh. I felt suffocated by the heaviness and weight of it all. I suppose I take after my mother. She hated the bookshop too, which did not help her marriage to my father."

Harrison was aware that her father had passed away, but he had not met their mother while he was in London. "I seem to recall hearing that your mother is French."

"Yes," she nodded, "that's why my sisters and I all have French names."

"And you all look remarkably alike," he offered. He remembered that distinctly from his visit to Devon House. In fact he had difficulty telling the extraordinarily beautiful Hamilton sisters apart at first, especially the two younger ones, but even from the little amount of time he actually spent in their company he had found all of them to be very intelligent and charming women.

Juliette gave him a lazy smile. "Yes, we've been told that we look alike." She leaned back against the pillows, propped up by the massive headboard, and held out her glass to him.

Harrison refilled it.

"I like your accent," she said to him.

"I don't have an accent," he retorted. "*You* have an accent."

She giggled lightly. "Yes, but do you like my accent?"

"As a matter of fact I do." He kissed the tip of her pert nose and then sipped his wine.

"Who is Melissa?" Her voice dropped to a whisper.

More than a little surprised by her abrupt question, he asked, "How did you hear about Melissa?"

Without the slightest hesitation or sense of shame, she confessed, "When I was locked in your cabin and went through your things looking for the key, I found a photograph of her. She's very beautiful."

Yes, Melissa was beautiful. Delicately beautiful. Heartbreakingly so. "She's my younger sister."

"Oh . . ." Juliette breathed. "She's your sister."

If he were not mistaken, an expression of relief crossed Juliette's face. Or at least it gave him great satisfaction to think that was what is was. He nodded and drank some wine. He did not discuss Melissa with anyone, except Annie, because Annie took care of her and needed no explanations from him.

"Where does she live?" Juliette asked. "Is she married?"

"She lives with me. And no, she is not married." Unfortunately. He doubted Melissa would ever get married.

"I see." Juliette murmured, but clearly she did not see.

"Melissa is not well. I have a nurse looking after her."

Juliette thought for a moment before asking, "Didn't you tell me you had two sisters? And a brother as well?"

"Yes."

She would not let up. "Where are they?"

"My brother Stuart is aboard a ship on his way to China. He is employed by my company. My sister Isabella is married to a clothing manufacturer and lives in Boston."

"How old were you when your parents died?"

He paused. His family was not a topic he discussed readily. "I was fifteen when my mother died." The day his mother passed away filled him with regret. He was sailing off Cape May and had not been able to return in time to say good-bye to her.

"And your father?"

"I never knew my father."

Juliette's puzzled expression forced him to explain.

"You see, Juliette, my sisters, brother and I all had different fathers."

Her voice rose an octave in surprise. "Your mother was married four times?"

He smiled ruefully at her naïveté. The familiar shame he felt about his childhood welled uneasily within his chest. "Unfortunately, my mother was never married. She was a prostitute."

"Oh, Harrison." She stared at him, her blue eyes wide in astonishment yet filled with compassion. "I don't know what to say."

Harrison looked away from her. "There is nothing to say. Unfortunately, it's not an unusual or new story. My mother was an uneducated but pretty young woman struggling to survive under terrible circumstances and she did the best she could." He shrugged lightly, surprised that he had divulged as much as he had to Juliette.

Yet for some reason, he felt compelled to continue, to explain. "Apparently she loved the man who was my father. He simply did not love her. She was the daughter of a small farmer near Carlisle, Pennsylvania, and he was a farmhand who worked there one summer. When he learned she was going to have a baby, he disappeared. So at sixteen her father banished her from her home and she ended up traveling to New York with another gentleman, George Fleming, who eventually became Melissa's father. My mother gave me his name when I was born. He was a salesman of sorts, of housewares. She stayed with him for some time, but they never married, because he already had a wife back in Philadelphia. They rented a small tenement apartment in New York City and that's where I was born and spent the majority of my childhood."

"Then what happened?"

"Eventually Melissa was born, and we were a happy enough family for a time. George taught me to read and write. He even tried to teach my mother to read but she was hopeless. He had odd spells of melancholy when he would not leave the house for long periods of time. My mother would cry and try to coax him out of his dark moods. Then suddenly, he would be fine and things would go back to normal. During one of his particularly dark moods when Melissa was six years old and I was eight, George Fleming shot himself in our kitchen. Melissa and I found him first, covered in blood and lifeless on the floor."

Although her blue eyes widened, Juliette said nothing, but reached out and took his hand in hers. In spite of the look of horror on Juliette's face, he continued. He could not seem to stop himself from telling her things he had never told anyone before.

"My mother had a very difficult time after that. Practically illiterate and possessing no skills, she did the only thing she could. She found another man to take up with. This one only lasted long enough to father my brother, Stuart. I barely even remember him. Then she met an Irish dockworker named Dan O'Malley, and he was a big bear of a man. He took a liking to me and showed me around the ships that he helped to load and unload. I adored him and would have followed him anywhere. He was very good to us and more importantly good to my mother. The only time I remember my mother really laughing was when Dan lived with us."

Harrison paused and drank more wine. "But Dan ended up in jail, accused of stealing from one of the ships. I don't know if he was truly guilty or not, but we never saw him again. After she lost Dan, I think that's when my mother truly turned to prostitution. She never knew who Isabella's father was. But she loved us and kept us safe for as long as she could. And when she died, as the oldest I took over the job of looking out for my younger brother and sisters. I never wanted the girls to have to go through what my mother did."

"Oh, Harrison," she murmured, full of anguish.

The compassion in her voice forced him to continue. "I wanted to have some semblance of a family. So I did what I had to do to protect them. I worked hard and I learned everything anybody taught me and I saved every penny I could. When my mother died we moved in with an older woman who lived in the same building. She was like a grandmother to us. Her name was Margaret. She watched over my sisters and Stuart and taught them to read and write, while I worked on the ship. Whenever I made any money I sent some of it to Margaret to help with my sisters and brother, and I saved the rest."

"And you bought your first ship?"

"No." He cast her a reluctant grin. "No, I won my first ship in a card game. I was nineteen."

"That's quite impressive."

"Partly." Harrison shrugged. "And partly very good luck that my opponent was extremely wealthy and too drunk to play well."

Juliette stared at him, her expression one of awe and respect. He felt an odd tingling sensation in his chest at the thought of her admiring him.

"You are a very remarkable man."

Surprised, he shook his head. "No. I just did what I had to do."

Which he did, while making the decision that he never wanted to be without money. He wanted enough money so that he did not have to worry about where their next meal was coming from. Or that they would be evicted from their home and thrown out on the street because they couldn't afford the rent and could live in a safe place. He wanted enough money so that his little sisters would never have to face the life their mother had in order to survive. He wanted to protect them.

He sold that first ship he had won in the card game, took the money, and invested it in a small shipping company, which did extremely well. Over the years, he kept buying and selling ships at a profit, always going with his gut instincts and always investing wisely, which it seemed he had a natural gift for. Harrison had sailed the world, founded his successful shipping enterprise H.G. Fleming & Company, as well as other businesses, and owned a number of homes. But most importantly he had managed to keep his siblings safe, because he was an extremely wealthy man.

"Harrison?"

He pulled himself from thoughts that he had not dwelled on in many years and looked to Juliette. She lay back on the pillows, looking quite relaxed and stunningly sexy. Naked with a sheet loosely draped around her breasts, her shapely legs lay exposed on the bed. Her silky dark hair was tousled seductively about her face. She had not the faintest idea how desirable she appeared.

"Yes?" he asked.

"Do you know that you've led an extraordinary life?"

He winked. "I'm not finished living yet." Harrison took their glasses and plates and placed them on the bedside table.

Juliette's expression remained serious, almost contrite. "I feel ridiculous for complaining about working in a bookshop."

He gathered her into his arms and sank back into the pillows with her, enjoying the feel of her next to him.

Placing a kiss on her soft lips, he beamed at her. "You are the most amazing woman I have ever met. You don't need to feel ridiculous about anything."

"Don't I though?" she asked.

"Not at this moment."

He then gave her a kiss that definitely did not make her feel ridiculous.

∾11∾

One of the Boys

"Just so you don't end up killing yourself by doing something foolish, I will show you how to get around on the *Sea Minx*," Harrison declared with determination.

After the day they spent in bed together, Harrison put Juliette to work in a different way, learning about the workings of a clipper ship. No longer confined to his cabin, Harrison now allowed Juliette full rein of his ship.

The better she knew Harrison, the more she admired him and the more she found that she could not resist him. Since that first night in his bed, their relationship sped into vastly uncharted waters. Now that she was finally let in on a widely kept secret of the great mystery between men and women, Juliette felt a glowing sense of triumph in her glorious discovery. There was so much more involved than she would have guessed!

Harrison's kisses filled her with passion and evoked sensations within her that she had never imagined. She slept with him each night, lying in his arms, watching him sleep, listening to the sound of his breathing. Having Harrison's muscular, naked body next to hers gave her a sense of contentment. For the first time in her life, she did not think of the future or the past. She simply lived in the moment. Every delicious and thrilling moment.

Being on the *Sea Minx* gave her the freedom to do things that she never would have done at home in London. It was as if she and Harrison were suspended in a special cocoon, separated from reality. Nothing and no one else seemed to matter but the two of them.

Sometimes Juliette and Harrison dined alone in his cabin, where they talked and made love for hours. Sometimes they joined the crew in the main galley. Harrison had introduced her to every man on board, from the cook to his first mate, Charlie. Although Juliette assumed they knew what was going on between her and Harrison, the men were incredibly respectful to her and never let on. They regarded her as the captain's lady and she couldn't refute that claim.

She spent nights in Harrison's arms and days at his side, learning about the things he loved.

Harrison showed Juliette every part of the ship, from the cargo hold, which was stowed tight with barrels and crates to the officers' mess and the galley. He explained to Juliette in detail how the many sails captured the wind to increase the ship's speed. He defined nautical terms, described how the rigging was laid and how the sails were lowered and raised. He taught her how to read the compass which was housed in the binnacle box, how to use a sextant to find their latitude, how to use a chronometer for determining their longitude and how to chart a course on a map. He even admitted that he was amazed by her aptitude. He showed her how to make entries in the logbook about the weather and had her ring the bell to signal the change of the watch. He let her climb the rigging again, but only once, when the sea was extremely calm. When he discovered that she had never learned to swim, he demanded that she wear the cork lifejacket, in case she fell overboard.

At first the crew treated her as a special and most welcome guest, and then as they got to know her better, they considered her as one of the boys. They called her "Miss Juliette" and assisted with her nautical education, insisting she learn the ropes of a clipper ship. They enlightened her on everything from the correct usage of the basic terms of stern, bow, fore and aft to teaching her how to tie strong knots in the ropes to the names of the many sails on the masts. Juliette could easily tell the difference between the tiny skysails, the royals, the topgallants, and the wide topsails and mainsails, but did not think she would ever be able to distinguish which rigging lines were main-topmast backstays and main-topsail buntlines. However, she now knew that eight bells meant noon and could tell which bells signaled when a watch began and ended.

Robbie Deane, delighted with her progress and apparent elevated status on the ship, took over her sailing lessons when Harrison needed to devote his attention to the actual sailing of the *Sea Minx*.

"It's good to see you and the captain getting along so well," Robbie said shyly to her.

Slightly uncomfortable with his veiled reference to her intimate relationship with Harrison, Juliette merely said, "Thank you."

"The captain ain't never had a woman on the ship before."

"You look up to Captain Fleming, don't you, Robbie?"

"Of course I do! We all do. He's a good captain. The

best. You always know where you stand with him and he's fair. And there's not one of us on this ship that he hasn't helped out in some way or another."

"How does he help?" she asked curiously.

"Oh, he pays us well, first off. And he has helped with our families and problems like that," Robbie explained, as he slowly coiled up some rope. "Last year the captain gave money to my mother for a house, when my father died and left her with nothing.

"He just helps that way. Quiet-like and without a fuss," Robbie continued easily. "You won't find a crew more loyal to their captain than us."

Juliette could not argue that point. Even she had picked up on the fact that Harrison's crew admired and respected him.

"That's why it was so unusual to see him angry with you. He hardly ever gets angry."

"Yes, he was quite angry with me for climbing the mast that first day," Juliette admitted, recalling how he had dragged her to his cabin.

"That was something!" Robbie laughed. "Afterwards I told the captain straight off that I thought you were a natural born sailor," Robbie stated with a bit of awe in his voice. "You took to those rigging lines like I've never seen anybody do. Me and the other fellows couldn't get over it."

Juliette too had wondered at her easy adaptation to life at sea. "It is funny, isn't it, considering I have never been on a ship before in my life?"

"My point exactly," Robbie agreed. "And that you are a lady to boot!"

Yes, she was a lady. But she was also a woman. That was something that Harrison never let her forget once she was in his arms. And she did not mind it one bit.

Nor did she mind the company of the other sailors.

The men sang bawdy songs, including one about a sailor named Barnacle Bill, which they promised they toned down just for her, but she laughed with them just the same. One night they held an impromptu concert and took turns dancing with her. Dancing with Harrison had been the highlight of the night for her, for he surprised her by lifting her off her feet and spinning her around until they both collapsed with laughter.

The crew let her join in on some of their card games as well. The men confided in her about their families, their wives, and their sweethearts and asked her advice, which she readily gave. Having spent her entire life in a household dominated by women and feminine ideals, Juliette delighted in this sudden exposure to male company. She had never laughed so heartily or so often before.

Harrison had changed in his approach to her as well. He allowed her to be herself on the ship. He didn't censure her or demand that she behave like a lady. He let her do as she pleased. If that meant wearing trousers all day or playing cards with Robbie and Charlie and others, he did not mind. Harrison was almost amused by her.

He seemed to be oddly fascinated by her interest in his ship and he took pride in showing her how to do whatever it was she wanted to do. With his guidance and by placing his hands over hers, he let her steer the wheel of the ship one afternoon.

"You have the sea in your blood, Juliette," Harrison declared with a sense of wonder. "I should take you on as one of my crew!"

Feeling happier than she could ever remember being, she gave him a sly glance and whispered pointedly, "I think you have already taken me on."

He grinned lustily, drew her into his embrace and kissed her, heedless of the crew watching them.

Nights in his cabin were no different than her days aboard the *Sea Minx*. She gave herself over entirely to the captain's expert tutelage. In Harrison's bed, Juliette became completely uninhibited as she learned how to give and receive pleasure, as they spent hour after hour endlessly making love.

~12~

Land, Ho!

Land. As the sun set Juliette could see the pale blue outline of the shore in the distance and her heart nearly burst with happiness. Although she loved her time aboard the *Sea Minx*, she had never been so glad to see anything in her life. She looked forward with great relief to the time she could once again place her feet on solid ground.

She stood on the deck near the forecastle and gripped the railing tightly. The billowy white canvas sails of the foremast, mainmast, and mizzenmast floated like clouds above her as the *Sea Minx* flew across the waves. This was it. She had finally arrived in the United States. A little thrill raced through her at the thought. She had never been a studious girl and had shunned most of the academic books her father had pressed her to read in the bookshop, but she had picked up enough information to know that she had more in common with this young, innovative, and daring new country than she ever had with England.

Suddenly not sure what to expect when she arrived, she experienced a brief moment of panic. What if America did not meet her expectations and proved just as disappointing as London? What if all she had done was for nothing? She shook her head and took a hearty gulp of sea air. No, she would not think negatively. She could not, would not, fail now. Not after everything that had happened to her.

Harrison's arms wrapped around her waist and he kissed the top of her head. Juliette sank back against him, breathing in his now familiar scent. He stood behind her, his head resting over her shoulder. A strong breeze blew around them, ruffling the skirt of her gown and causing her hair to whip around them.

"We'll be docking by morning," he whispered low in her ear. He pointed out toward the land. "We'll be coming up near Sandy Hook where a pilot schooner will meet us and guide us in through the Narrows to the East River and to a berth at South Street in New York. Your little journey has come to an end, Juliette."

"It's so thrilling!" She squeezed his hands, which rested comfortably on her waist. "I cannot believe that I am finally here in America."

"Well, you are not quite there yet," he teased.

"I know that!" She playfully swatted his hands. "But now that I can actually see land, I know that I am close and at last it all seems more real."

Harrison held her tighter. The strength in his arms sent a jolt of desire through her.

He said, "I had originally intended to send you back to London on the next ship."

"And now?" She asked, her heart suddenly pounding

an erratic rhythm. He couldn't still mean to do that to her, could he? She could not go back to London. Not now, not yet, anyway. Oh, of course someday she would go back home, after she had lived a little and had had a taste of life on her own.

Stowing away on the *Sea Minx* had been a grand adventure so far. While being with Captain Harrison Fleming had proven to be a most wonderful adventure as well, one that Juliette had not anticipated when she had first climbed aboard. Their intimate relationship had been an eye-opening experience for her. She felt more sophisticated and like a mature woman of the world. She had dallied with a man, with no thought of marriage or the future. She had behaved scandalously and it was very freeing. Admittedly she had grown fond of Harrison. Her heart constricted a little at the thought of leaving him, but the idea of having to return to London immediately made her nauseous.

"Your family must be overcome with worry about you. We should inform them at once that you are well. I will send them a cable to let them know you arrived safely and are under my protection."

"And then?" She held her breath.

"Then what?"

She could barely utter the words. "Are you going to send me back home on another ship?"

As if weighing his options, Harrison did not immediately reply. "I should."

"But you won't, will you?" She hated that her voice squeaked when she asked that question.

He thought for a moment before giving his response, increasing her tension. "If I had any sanity left, I still should send you home. Your behavior has been dangerous and reckless."

"I cannot go back yet, Harrison," she said decisively, pulling away from him. "I simply cannot."

"Then tell me, who is he?"

"Who is *who*?"

"Juliette." He sighed heavily and drew her into his arms again, forcing her to look at him. "Things between us have changed."

She blinked. "I am not sure what you mean." But in her heart she knew exactly what he meant.

"Don't act the fool," he snapped. "It doesn't become you."

She attempted to break from his hold, but he held fast. She stilled and stared up at him. "Nothing has changed, Harrison. When we dock, I will be on my way and you need never worry about me again."

He grimaced ruefully. "If only it were that easy."

"But it is."

"You've spent practically the entire last week in my bed, Juliette. We have to make it right. You know as well as I do what that means."

"It means naught, if we don't share that information with anyone."

"My crew is not stupid. They all know exactly what has been going on between us."

She gave a slight shrug. "I don't believe that they care, do you?"

"I care." His steely eyes pinned her in place.

"Don't play the white knight to my virtue now, Harrison," she said heatedly. "It's too late for that."

"What if you are carrying my child?"

What if she were carrying Harrison's baby? That thought had worried her, but she had pushed it to the back of her mind. She did not wish to consider the consequences. Juliette turned away.

He called after her. "Juliette!"

She came to a stop but did not face him. Her back went stiff.

Harrison came up behind her, placed his hands on her shoulders and spun her around. His mouth came down hard upon hers and he kissed her with a possessiveness that sounded alarm bells in her head.

He released her suddenly. Her head spun but she managed to focus her eyes upon his. He stated in a very low voice, "You have no choice in this, Juliette. I am not asking, I am telling you. I am marrying you as soon as we get to New York."

Before she could utter a response, he kissed her again, weakening her resolve. Her traitorous body melted under his touch and she found herself responding to his kisses passionately. In one powerful movement he swept her into his arms and carried her to his cabin.

Juliette smiled to herself at Harrison's typical behavior. He simply thought he could tell her what to do and that she would do it. He believed that he could pick her up and have his way with her. He certainly had a lesson or two coming his way. No, sir. Harrison may be used to being a captain and giving orders and being obeyed, but she was not going to allow him to order her about for the rest of her life.

Well, maybe he could this time. This one last time. For she simply could not resist his incredibly sensuous mouth and the feel of his mouth on hers. And his wickedly skilled hands . . . Juliette melted against him.

For just this one last time.

∼13∼

All Ashore That's Going Ashore

It felt good to be home again, back in the city he loved There at the dock at South Street on the East River, Harrison was back where he belonged. Even after he had traveled around the world, nothing compared to being in New York City.

As usual, Harrison rose before dawn that morning to oversee the massive responsibility of the docking of the *Sea Minx* and unloading his precious cargo of glassware, fine china, and cutlery, as well as French wine. He left Juliette sleeping soundly in his bed, positive that she would sleep until at least midmorning, since they had been up most of the night. Just before they fell asleep, they had made plans for Juliette's first day in New York. Reluctant to leave her but not wishing to wake her, he had kissed her cheek softly before going up on deck.

Once he had taken care of the business of unloading

the ship, he would take her into the city. There was so much he wanted to show her while she was here. He wanted to bring her to a theater in Union Square to see a play and to hear one of the concerts at Central Park. It would even be fun to take her to see a New York Mutuals baseball game at Union Grounds. He wanted to show her his office building. He found that he looked forward to showing her the sights. And of course, they would get married.

Harrison became so absorbed with his work that he hadn't given Juliette another thought until it was close to noon.

"Have you seen Miss Hamilton at all this morning?" he asked one of his sailors.

The man shook his head. "No, Captain. Should I have?"

Harrison went down to his cabin, thinking he would have to resort to dragging Juliette's pretty bottom out of bed to get her to wake up. Instead he stared at the rumpled bed. He glanced around the empty room. Juliette was not there. And neither was her little satchel of belongings.

Harrison could barely suppress his panic. He raced to the deck and called to his crew, "I want the ship searched for Miss Hamilton."

Even as he said the words, Harrison knew they would not find her. He sensed without a doubt that she had already left the ship. Sickened, he turned to look at the city. In the dazzling sunlight, he squinted at the buildings along South Street and beyond to Wall Street, now bustling with people, horses, carts, and carriages. He could see his own building, where the offices of H.G. Fleming and Company were located.

He could not believe that Juliette had left him.

She had left him and ventured into an unknown city

on her own. Harrison was momentarily stunned, his mounting anger tempered by an overwhelming concern for her immediate safety. Did the stubborn wench even know where she was going? Or how dangerous it was for her to be alone in a strange city? Was what they had shared together on the *Sea Minx* meaningless to her?

Of course, he knew where she went.

Fortunately for him, Juliette had left her things strewn about his cabin so he had seen the letters from her friend Christina Dunbar and noted Fifth Avenue as the address. Now Harrison knew he had to go after Juliette, if only to wring her neck for taking such a terrible risk and to assure himself that she was well.

Then . . . then the little baggage could be on her own, if that was what she wanted so desperately. He would wash his hands of her. Not only had she scorned his offer of marriage, she had fled from him. No woman had ever done that to him before! Torn between irritation and wounded pride, Harrison stormed across the deck of his ship.

"Captain!" Robbie Deane ran up to him, out of breath and his expression anxious. "I'm sorry, Captain. I thought it was okay, because Miss Juliette said that you knew, but now I see—"

"What is it, Robbie?" Harrison asked, his heart pounding.

The young man spoke hurriedly, his freckled face full of contrition. "I'm sorry. I guess while you were in the shipping office, Miss Juliette asked me to get a hired carriage for her. I just figured she was going to your house, so I helped her. That was a couple of hours ago. Now you have everyone on the ship and the dock looking for her, as if she were missing. So I thought I should tell you that it is all my fault that she's disappeared. I'm sorry, Captain."

Harrison shook his head in disbelief. "Don't worry, Robbie, I have a pretty good idea of where she went. I appreciate that you helped her." Harrison's heart turned cold at the confirmation of Juliette's disappearance.

Robbie shook his head. "You mean she just left us?" The wounded expression on the young boy's face must have mirrored the one on Harrison's own.

Hearing the harsh truth said aloud almost brought him to his knees. He gave Robbie a sympathetic look. "It seems that way."

With a sickening feeling in his gut, Harrison gave some brief instructions to Charlie and left the *Sea Minx* in his first mate's care while he went ashore.

He found the house of Christina Dunbar easily enough, since he was quite familiar with that particular neighborhood. It was a grand five-story brownstone on a very fashionable section of Fifth Avenue near Thirty-fourth Street, almost as impressive as his own house. He stared up at the front door, feeling something of a fool. He had followed a woman who did not want to be followed. A woman who obviously did not want him, after he asked her to marry him. What could he say to her now? Nothing. He just prayed that she had arrived without mishap.

Harrison took a deep breath and climbed the stone steps. Lifting the brass knocker, he rapped on the door.

A weary looking butler answered his knock. The distinct frown on the man's face signaled his displeasure at being disturbed so early. "May I help you?"

Harrison stood quietly, wondering how to word his question without sounding as if he were a crazed lunatic. "I apologize for intruding. This is the Dunbar residence, is it not?"

The man nodded his head. "Yes."

"My name is Captain Harrison Fleming, of the clipper ship the *Sea Minx*, and I . . . I was wondering if a young lady had arrived here this morning."

The butler eyed him skeptically.

"Miss Juliette Hamilton traveled from London on my ship. We docked this morning and she left, without waiting for an escort. I just wished to be certain she arrived at Mrs. Dunbar's safely."

The man relaxed at Harrison's explanation. "Why yes, sir, a Miss Hamilton did arrive just a short time ago. She is upstairs with Mrs. Dunbar now. Shall I inform her that you are here, Captain Fleming?"

Harrison shook his head. "Thank you, but no. Now that I know she is here and safe, I shall be on my way. Good day."

With a heavy heart he returned to his ship, which seemed strangely empty without Juliette on board. His crew eyed him carefully as they finished the final unloading and he gave them leave. Later that afternoon, he had a telegram sent to Lucien Sinclair, informing him that his sister-in-law was safe at the home of her friend. He did not wish for her family to continue to worry about Juliette.

Then Harrison threw himself into his work, attempting to block Juliette Hamilton from his mind. For two days he worked nonstop in his office at the H.G. Fleming & Company building near South Street, where he could see the beginning efforts of the construction of the caissons for a new suspension bridge being built from New York across the East River to Brooklyn. He rescheduled meetings he had missed, brokered deals for his shipping line, checked on the status of his steamships, met with investors and merchants, and took care of correspondence, including a long letter to his sister Isabella in Boston.

On his third day in New York, he made plans to travel to his estate in New Jersey. He had put off seeing Melissa for too long now and he needed to get home to her. He also had to oversee some of the new construction on his estate.

While he sat at his desk, a knock on his office door caught his attention. "Come in," he called, expecting his assistant to enter. Harrison did not look up from the letter he was writing to a gentleman who wished him to invest in a device that could transmit speech electrically. The idea intrigued him.

"Well, if it isn't my old friend Harrison Fleming."

Startled, Harrison glanced up to see Lord Jeffrey Eddington standing in front of his desk, and he dropped his ink pen in surprise.

"So they sent you after her, did they?" Harrison asked, assuming that Lucien Sinclair was searching for his sister-in-law.

"No one 'sent' me after Juliette," Jeffrey said easily, but his expression remained anxious. "I offered to find her. And here I am."

Harrison grinned lazily. "Well, it's nice of you to visit me for a change."

Jeffrey gave him a tense look. "Sorry to disappoint you, but I'm not here to visit. Where is she?"

"She's perfectly fine and in remarkably good health. I've already sent a cable to Lucien informing him that his foolhardy sister-in-law arrived in New York three days ago. So sit and have a drink with me." Jeffrey, visibly relaxed at his words, sank into a leather chair beside the desk, mumbling his thanks to God in a faint whisper.

Harrison poured them each a shot of bourbon. He handed a glass to his relieved friend and sat in the chair behind his desk, pushing the papers he had been working on to the side.

Jeffrey took a drink, and so did Harrison. The reddish liquid burned his throat in a familiar way and it surprised him how much he needed it. He glanced back at Jeffrey.

"I cannot even imagine how worried Juliette's family has been."

Jeffrey shook his head. "No, you cannot." He took another sip and stared at Harrison intently. "Did you know she planned to run away with you?"

"No!" Harrison laughed at that possibility. If he had known Juliette Hamilton was aboard his ship that night he set sail, he never would have left London. "Does anyone know what wild schemes Juliette is planning in that crazy, clever head of hers?"

A wry smile crossed Jeffrey's face. "I see you have gotten a chance to know our darling Juliette quite well during the voyage."

That is a vast understatement, Harrison thought to himself, as images of all he had done with Juliette flashed through his head, but even when he thought he knew the woman who had enchanted him, he had not known her at all. More was the pity for him.

"We discovered her onboard that first night, after we had already set sail," Harrison explained. "She had hidden in a storage room. When she was brought to my cabin, I was half tempted to turn the ship around and bring her home right then."

"Why didn't you?" Jeffrey questioned, his eyes narrowing.

"Because I was angry. I was already behind schedule as it was and I have some pressing family issues to take care of. I could not afford to be inconvenienced and delayed because some reckless, stubborn girl decided to have an adventure. In the first place, she was not invited nor welcome aboard my ship, and in the second place, she was not my responsibility."

"Point taken," Jeffrey acknowledged reluctantly. "But still, as a gentleman, you might have—"

"As a gentleman, nothing. I figured she was hell-bent on getting to America one way or another and was just crazy enough to stow away on someone else's ship. At least if she stayed with me, I could keep her safe until—"

Harrison stopped speaking in midsentence, as his words hit home. Had he kept Juliette safe? Had he not taken advantage of her innocence? No, he had not quite kept her safe for he had not been a gentleman with her. Even when they docked in New York, he had tried to do right by her, but then she had fled from him, without even a good-bye. His heart began to thump loudly in his chest. He ignored it.

"Keep her safe until . . . ?" With one eyebrow raised in question Jeffrey prompted him to finish his sentence.

"Until other arrangements could be made for her." Harrison declared, finishing the rest of his bourbon and setting the glass back on his desk with a louder thud than he had intended.

"And now that you are here, I leave all future arrangements to you. Juliette Hamilton is your responsibility. I officially wash my hands of her."

"Where is she now?"

"She is staying with that friend of hers who lives on Fifth Avenue."

Jeffrey nodded his head. "Ah, yes, Christina Dunbar. In the letter Juliette left her sisters, she mentioned that she would be going to see her friend. That was to be my next stop after I checked in with you."

After a thoughtful silence, Harrison asked, "Who is he?"

"Who is who?" Jeffrey's puzzled expression gave Harrison pause.

"The man she came to New York to be with. Do you know who he is?"

"Juliette came here to be with a man?" Jeffrey moved to the edge of his seat and appeared utterly incredulous.

"I'm asking *you* that question." Harrison kept his irritation in check.

"Did she tell you that?"

Harrison recalled all the denials Juliette had given when asked the same question. He had refused to believe her. Uncomfortable now, Harrison stammered. "Well, not exactly, no. But what other reason would a beautiful woman have to run away from a loving family and a wonderful home to travel to another country to . . . ?" His voice trailed off at the sound of Jeffrey's laughter.

Jeffrey's loud guffaws echoed through the office, "Maybe you didn't get to know Juliette that well after all!"

"What do you mean?"

"I have grown quite close to Juliette over the last year. If you haven't noticed, she's not like other women. I'm probably her closest friend and I would wager that I know her better than even her sisters do. I can tell you this with the utmost certainty: Juliette Hamilton never does anything to please anyone other than herself. And she would never do anything to try to win over any man."

Harrison felt a strange pang of uneasiness in his chest at Jeffrey's words, yet he said nothing.

"Juliette has threatened to leave London for as long as I've known her. Her friend gave her an open invitation to visit so I suppose that proved to be too much of a temptation for her to resist. To add to that, her mother had expressly forbidden her to go, which was probably just the same as sparking a match to a powder keg. Your ship simply provided her with an opportunity she waited a long time for. Juliette lives in the moment and takes chances. She has a mind more like a man's, despite having the face of an angel."

Harrison recalled images of Juliette climbing the mizzenmast, Juliette wearing the key to his cabin around her neck, and Juliette sewing closed the tops of all the socks she was supposed to be mending. In spite of himself, he grinned. "Yes, I've noticed that about her."

"Believe me, if Juliette had come to New York to be with a man, I would know about it."

Harrison was still not totally convinced. "But you didn't know she had stowed away on my ship, or that she was leaving London at all."

"That's true enough," Jeffrey admitted reluctantly. "I'm impressed that she could keep a secret of that magnitude from me. But I would know if Juliette were in love. She would have confided in me. I'm sure of it."

Harrison gave Jeffrey a long look. "What are your interests in Juliette?"

"What are yours?" Jeffrey countered.

After a tense silence, Harrison finally said, "Listen Jeffrey. I did not ask for the responsibility of Juliette's welfare, but I did get her to New York unharmed. As soon as I arrived, I sent a cable to Lucien to let him know that his sister-in-law was safe. She is now happily ensconced at the home of her childhood friend. What more do I need to do?"

Jeffrey held up his hand in concession. "Nothing. Nothing at all."

Harrison stood.

"Good, because I need to visit my sister in New Jersey. As I mentioned, she has not been well."

"I'm sorry to hear that," Jeffrey commented. "Is there anything I can do?"

"Thank you, but no." He could not help himself from asking, "So what are you going to do about Juliette? Are you taking her directly back to London?"

Jeffrey hesitated before smiling. "First I thought I would wring her pretty neck for putting herself in such danger and scaring her sisters and me half to death. My main concern was to ascertain that she had been on your ship and that she had arrived safely. But I suppose I shall have to bring her home. Colette and the rest of them would have my head if I returned without her."

"She won't go."

"Why do you say that?"

"Because I wanted to send her on my next ship back to London, but she left for her friend's home before I could stop her."

Jeffrey's broad grin spread across his face. "That's my Juliette."

Harrison bristled at the possessiveness in Jeffrey's words. Quickly changing the subject, he asked, "How was your voyage?"

"Sea travel is not my favorite, but it was fine."

"Where are you staying?"

"No where at the moment, since I just arrived this afternoon. Can you recommend a nice hotel?"

Harrison shook his head. "You are more than welcome to stay at my house. I'll be leaving for the New Jersey shore on a steamboat tomorrow, but my staff will take good care of you for as long as you stay. Come with me now, and we'll get you settled. Then you can pay a visit to Juliette quite easily. I live only a few houses away from the Dunbars."

Jeffrey could hardly refuse.

∞ 14 ∞

What Goes Around, Comes Around

"Oh, Juliette, that looks lovely on you!" Christina clapped her hands with glee as she admired the elegant gown of blue silk that Juliette wore. "Doesn't it look lovely on her, darling?"

Maxwell Dunbar nodded in agreement with his wife, but barely glanced in her direction. A large, barrel-chested man, Maxwell Dunbar kept his dark, intense eyes fixed squarely on Juliette. Uncomfortable with her friend's husband's stare, Juliette continued walking with them into their elaborately decorated dining room.

"Thank you very much for lending the gown to me," Juliette said as she took her place at the lavishly set table.

"You are most welcome. Now we shall have to host a party to introduce you to all our friends."

"Oh, Christina, that really is not necessary—" Juliette began.

"Of course it is," Christina insisted. "My dearest friend has come all the way from London to visit me. And you are the sister-in-law of an earl! I simply must show you off to all my new friends."

"While I'm wearing your clothes!" Juliette laughed at the absurdity of it.

Christina patted her softly rounded belly and smiled. "Well, I certainly cannot wear my gowns now, so you might as well enjoy them."

"You mustn't even consider having a party for me in your condition," Juliette protested. "I won't hear of it."

Maxwell chimed in with a too-bright, too-eager smile. "Miss Hamilton is quite right. You should be resting, Christina."

"I suppose you are both correct. Besides, anyone who is anyone is out of town," Christina admitted cheerfully. Her light brown hair curled in ringlets around her face and her brown eyes sparkled. "But since your trunks were misplaced while they unloaded the ship, I'm happy to have you wear my gowns for as long as you need them."

When she arrived at the Dunbar residence three days ago, Juliette had confessed to Christina just how she had come to be in New York and how she had slipped away from the *Sea Minx* in a hired carriage. Leaving the ship that morning had been quite a difficult decision. Juliette regretted leaving Robbie and the other crewmembers in such an abrupt manner, but she knew she had to break free or she would end up as Mrs. Harrison Fleming. She did not dwell on Harrison's reaction to her departure. She had had to put that to the back of her mind.

Her friend, however, realized that Juliette simply could not tell everyone that she had left London without the consent of her family or that she had stowed away on a clipper ship with dozens of sailors without a proper chaperone. Christina had stressed the importance of not revealing those details to anyone, especially her husband. Even as reckless as Juliette was, she understood the necessity to hide her scandalous behavior. So they led Maxwell Dunbar to believe that she had been under the protection of the captain of the ship, with the blessings and good wishes of her family. And was it not a terrible shame that her trunks full of clothes had inadvertently been lost on the dock? Juliette's story seemed more acceptable that way.

While Christina had been astonished by Juliette's outrageous and unorthodox mode of travel, Juliette had been equally shocked to learn that Christina was expecting a baby. Had Christina mentioned that little fact in her last letter, Juliette would have thought twice about descending upon her friend in such an unexpected fashion. And Juliette had been surprised by more than just Christina's pregnancy. She had known that Christina's parents had quickly married her off to a wealthy American, but Juliette had had no idea just how wealthy. Their lavish and ornate Fifth Avenue mansion displayed their vast prosperity in a staggering manner.

Nor had Juliette been prepared for Christina's husband. With his gray hair, avaricious eyes, and gaunt features, Maxwell Dunbar was older than his young wife by at least twenty years. His overt attention to Juliette made her skin crawl.

Although Christina had never uttered a negative word about her new life and seemed quite satisfied with her situation, Juliette's heart grew heavy at the thought of her friend married to such a man and now having his baby. She merely said, "Well, again, I thank you for being so generous with me and for having me in your home."

Maxwell Dunbar said, "We are happy to have you

here. Especially now. It's wonderful for Christina to have some company."

Christina beamed her wide grin at Juliette. "It's true. The timing of your visit couldn't have been more perfectly arranged. Everyone has gone to the shore in Newport or Long Island or New Jersey for the summer months but I don't feel comfortable traveling at this point, and I wished to be near my doctor. And now you are here to keep me company!"

Juliette nodded with a bright smile, but inside her stomach tightened with a familiar dread. She loved Christina to be sure, and her friend had been nothing but kind and welcoming since her surprise arrival, but Juliette did not just journey across an ocean to be the companion of an expectant woman. If she had wanted to do that she would have stayed at home with her sister Colette, for heaven's sake!

She had come to America to have adventures and explore the country and see all there was to see. She had not planned on spending all her time at Christina's home, beautiful as it was. It was only meant to be a stepping-stone to further adventures, just what those adventures would entail she hadn't quite thought through yet.

It seemed as if she were constantly escaping those who would confine her.

"So, tell us more about life on the clipper ship," Maxwell encouraged her, his flinty eyes glittering. "How was the crossing?"

"It was an exciting adventure," Juliette managed to say.

A sudden and intense longing to be with Harrison overcame her as she recalled the *Sea Minx*. For a moment she could barely breathe while thinking of the feel of his strong arms around her, holding her to his chest. Thoughts of Harrison had frequently come upon her like this, in startling and unexpected moments since she had left him, leaving her unsettled and full of yearning. However, on her second day at the Dunbars, she had been most relieved to discover that she was *not* going to have a baby. Now there was nothing to tie her to Harrison Fleming, except her private memories of the two incredible weeks on his ship. Again, an odd sensation of yearning coursed through her and it was with a great effort that she forced herself to continue her description. "Sailing on a clipper ship is quite beautiful, like flying on a cloud, if you can imagine such a thing."

As they finished a rich supper of roasted quail, the Dunbars' butler, Ferris, entered the dining room. He cleared his throat before stating, "Mr. Dunbar, there is a gentleman at the door. He claims to be a friend of Miss Hamilton."

Juliette could not miss the pointed look Ferris gave her. Surprised by the butler's insinuating manner, she almost blushed. He made it seem as if she possessed an inordinate amount of male friends visiting her. But then her blood tingled.

Good Heavens! Harrison had found her! He must be here to take her home. She said a silent prayer that he would not cause a scene before dragging her back to the ship. Noting that both Christina and Maxwell were looking to her for guidance, she instinctively nodded her head.

"The only person I know in New York would be Captain Fleming," she explained hesitantly.

Ferris looked down his long nose at her. "It is not Captain Fleming. This is an English gentleman who claims he is a Lord Eddington, from London."

"Jeffrey!" Juliette exclaimed loudly, while jumping to her feet.

Christina giggled at Juliette's reaction. She turned her attention to her butler. "By all means, Ferris, please show Lord Eddington into the front parlor, since Miss Hamilton is obviously acquainted with him. We shall join him there momentarily."

Ferris nodded in assent. Juliette pressed her hands together nervously. As happy as she was to see Jeffrey, she needed no explanations as to why he had come to New York, and that fact induced a twinge of fear within her. He had come to take her back to London. He would also inevitably describe to her how hurt and worried her sisters were about her. Juliette's heart sank. She did not possess the strength to bear the recriminations and disapproval that were sure to come from Jeffrey.

"Who is this lord, Juliette?" Christina asked in a singsong tone, as if she suspected a romance. "Is he someone you met on your sea voyage?"

"No. I've known him for quite some time. Lord Eddington is a close family friend."

"Did you know he was visiting New York?" Christina asked.

"No, I had no idea he intended to come to New York." Juliette shook her head helplessly, her stomach in knots. "I suspect he is here with news of my family."

"Well, then," Maxwell said anxiously. "Shall we join Lord Eddington now?"

Sensing that Maxwell was overly impressed with the prospect of meeting a member of the London aristocracy, she smiled. Jeffrey was the illegitimate son of a powerful duke who, out of guilt, had a courtesy title bestowed upon Jeffrey when he turned twenty-one. She did not think now would be the best time to explain this to Maxwell Dunbar.

As he escorted the two women to the elegantly

furnished parlor, Juliette felt Maxwell Dunbar's hand on the small of her back. Her spine went rigid at his touch. Just as they reached the entrance, Maxwell's hand squeezed her. She turned and flashed him a disdainful glance. He gave her a sly smile, while Juliette fought the urge to slap him. She knew she could not remain in this house much longer, if he were going to behave that way.

Jeffrey stood up as they entered the room, looking for all the world as if he were a guest who stopped by the Dunbars' everyday. As handsome as ever, he exuded charm and good humor. The familiarity of his presence and the understanding gleam in his eyes almost brought tears to Juliette's own. She relaxed. Jeffrey did not intend to reproach her. At least not at the moment. She hurried to him, throwing her arms around his neck.

"Jeffrey! This is such a wonderful surprise to see you here!" His hug invoked a wave of homesickness and she blinked back tears.

"I am simply relieved to find you safe and well," he whispered before releasing her.

Juliette turned to Christina and Maxwell, feeling her cheeks redden slightly under their regard. With a surprising amount of poise, she introduced them to Jeffrey. They greeted each other warmly and the Dunbars invited him to stay for dessert, as Ferris wheeled in a silver teacart laden with pastries and cakes.

"What brings you to New York, Lord Eddington?" Christina asked politely after they had all taken their seats.

Jeffrey glanced briefly at Juliette before stating, "I had some very important business that needed my immediate and personal attention."

Eyeing them carefully, Maxwell asked, "How did you know that Juliette was staying with us, when we barely knew she was arriving?"

Once again, Jeffrey's eyes met hers. "Shortly after Juliette's ship left, I received word that my presence was required in New York to oversee an urgent matter. Juliette's sisters provided me with your address, Mrs. Dunbar, and asked me to call upon you both to express their good wishes and to ascertain that Juliette had settled safely in New York."

Releasing the breath she had unwittingly held, Juliette took a bite of lemon cake.

"Well, it's lovely to have both you and Juliette here." Oblivious to the silent exchange between Juliette and Jeffrey, Christina continued to chatter away. "I have not had any visitors from my home since my marriage. My mother refuses to make the journey, not that I blame her at her age, but my sister could certainly find the where-withal to come stay with me. Although I love it here too, I do miss England at times."

"Of course you do," Jeffrey smiled winningly at Christina.

"How is my sister Colette? Has the baby arrived yet?" Juliette asked.

"Being that I left immediately after you did, I have no way of knowing either. But I'm sure the baby will not make its arrival for a few more weeks."

"How long are you planning to stay in New York, Lord Eddington?" Maxwell questioned.

"That depends upon a number of things," Jeffrey answered with another meaningful glance at Juliette.

Christina asked brightly, "Where are you staying? With friends or at a hotel?"

"I happen to be staying with a good friend of mine. He lives down the block from here actually."

"Oh, how convenient!" Christina exclaimed in surprise. "Shall we be seeing more of you then?"

"Most assuredly . . ." Jeffrey paused before turning his attention to Christina. "Mr. and Mrs. Dunbar, could I impose upon you both to allow me a moment of privacy with Miss Hamilton? I'm afraid there is a personal matter regarding her sisters that I must discuss with her."

"Oh, why yes, of course." Christina rose slowly from her chair. "Maxwell and I will leave you both, won't we, Maxwell?"

Her husband stood. "Certainly." He gave Juliette a suspicious glance before he followed his wife from the parlor.

When the door closed behind them, Juliette and Jeffrey simply stared at each other in silence for a few moments.

"Please don't say anything," Juliette finally murmured.

"Don't say anything?" he echoed incredulously. "After following you halfway across the globe, I'm not supposed to say anything to you?"

Juliette whispered softly, "No."

Jeffrey shook his head in disbelief. "Do you have the slightest inkling of how much you have wounded and worried the people who love you the most in the world?"

"Please don't do this to me, Jeffrey," she pleaded with him, unable to bear the hurt expression on his face. Or the thought of her sisters and how they must feel.

"Only you, Juliette, could turn this around to be about your feelings," Jeffrey chided her. "Have you even thought about Colette? In her delicate condition? Or your poor mother?"

Juliette could say nothing in response. Since the night she left Devon House, she had blocked those thoughts from her mind. If she considered how hurt Colette would be at her leaving, she never would have had the courage to leave. Yes, she loved her sisters, and in spite of everything she loved her mother too, but did that mean she had to stay bound to them for the rest of her life at the expense of her own welfare and sanity?

If she had stayed in London and had done what society expected of her, she would have perished from unhappiness. If she had dutifully married one of those staid, proper gentlemen her uncle Randall had forced upon her and had settled down in some dull country estate in the middle of nowhere to have babies, she surely would have died of suffocation. Or she would have gone stark, raving mad.

Was it really that dreadful of her to have wanted something different, something exciting? Was she appallingly selfish and greedy to want to go after it? Was she that odd, that freakish or that unusual in her desire to live life on her own terms, that no one could possibly fathom her need for a different life?

If a man had done this, he would have been applauded for his resourcefulness and initiative, while she was chastised for hurting the feelings of her sisters and being reckless. Juliette did not understand this vast discrepancy in judgment and it angered her.

She glanced up from her seat to find Jeffrey staring at her with a sharp intensity. They looked at each other for a quiet moment. He finally moved to sit beside her. He took her hand in his.

"I apologize, Juliette. I'm an idiot to think that you did not consider the feelings of your sisters and your mother before you left. I know how much you love them."

She still could not speak.

Jeffrey continued. "My real concern, and theirs, was for your safety. What you did was incredibly dangerous, Juliette. Anything might have happened to you."

"But it didn't," she could not help but point out.

"Don't fool yourself. You were extremely fortunate."

"Yes," she nodded slowly. "I realize that now."

"You could have been killed." He paused, before adding ominously. "Or worse."

"There is no need to go on in that vein," she protested. "As you can see, I am perfectly fine."

"Why would you take such a risk with your life?"

Juliette sighed with a weariness she had not felt since she was in London. "Because, my darling Jeffrey, that is what makes life worth living. I thought you above everyone else would understand that. Understand why I had to get away from all that." She waved her hand to indicate to her life back in London. "And if I had asked permission, I would have been categorically denied and you know it."

He became thoughtful at her explanation. "I do see your point, but I hate to have such a beautiful woman I care about put herself in unnecessary danger. It would be a pity to lose you."

The sparkle in his eyes lightened the mood and Juliette gave him a halfhearted smile. If Jeffrey was flirting with her again, he could not still be upset or angry with her.

"Why didn't you tell me what you were planning to do?" he questioned softly.

She could sense the hurt in his voice. "Because you would have tried to talk me out of it. Or worse you would have told Lucien or Colette and I would have been watched like a hawk and would not have been allowed to leave the house alone. You would have seen to it that my plan was put to an end. I never would have gotten away."

He could not refute her claims. So he grinned at her, in a way that only Jeffrey could. "That's not entirely true. I know you've wanted to come to New York since I've met you. I might have tried to assist you. I could have at least made sure that you were welcome on Harrison's ship before you tried to sneak on board."

Juliette laughed aloud at his outrageous claim. "That is completely untrue! You would not have lifted a finger to help me. You are only saying that now because it's too late to help me and I have no need of you."

He ignored her accurate assessment and changed tactics. "Would it really have been so terrible if you had stayed?"

A sudden lump in Juliette's throat made it hard for her to speak. If she had stayed she would have been pressured into another dreary London Season, while a parade of dull and straitlaced men who possessed nothing in common with her vied for her attention. She had dutifully experienced the social season the year before in order to secure a wealthy marriage to assist her family out of their dire financial situation. Fortunately Collette had successfully managed that feat, while Juliette had only earned herself a reputation for being outrageous and unmanageable. However, Juliette could not and would not fake her way through the niceties of a season again. She could not stomach the hypocrisy of pretending she wanted to marry, when she knew she could never live the life of a proper wife of an English gentleman without doing something scandalous or losing her mind from boredom.

"More than you can imagine," she said. "And you, Jeffrey should know that better than anyone else."

"Well, I cannot say that I understand it entirely, although I must admit I admire your courage. There is not a single woman of my acquaintance who would have done what you did. But Juliette, we can't have you taking risks like this anymore."

"Oh, no?"

"No."

She considered him evenly. Dark-haired with intense blue eyes and a classically handsome face, his easy smile and charming manner only added to his winning personality. Everyone loved Jeffrey, including the countless women who vied for his attention and his bed. Aware that he kept a string of lovely mistresses, Juliette had never held that against him. They had become fast friends last year from the moment they met at Lady Hayvenhurst's ball. It had been Juliette's first foray into the London Season and she had danced with him. Jeffrey sported a scandalous reputation and Juliette had taken an instant liking to him. The two had spent the entire evening laughing and teasing each other while surreptitiously poking fun at most of the guests. She adored Jeffrey and knew he only had her best interests at heart. Didn't he just cross an ocean to make sure she was safe and sound?

She squeezed his hand. "You are a wonderful man, Jeffrey."

"Let's get married, Juliette," he said in a voice that almost trembled, his eyes on hers. "I can look after you properly and give you the freedom you desire."

Her first instinct was to laugh at the absurdity of his offer, but she would never dare wound him in that manner. Jeffrey meant what he said. As flippant and carefree as he could be, deep down he was a true gentleman. Amazed by her second marriage proposal within mere days, she smiled at him, and again squeezed his hand. "That is a very tempting offer and I am honored that you would ask me to be your wife. But you know as well as I do that it would never work between us. I would make you miserable."

"Why wouldn't it work? We are good friends. I find you attractive and I know you must find me quite handsome in a rakish way." He gave her a quick wink.

She did laugh then. "Oh, Jeffrey."

"Is it because I am the bastard son of a duke?"

"Of course not! Don't be ridiculous."

"Then let's get married." He stood beside her, but still held her hand. He gave her his most charming smile. "We would have a grand time together. Your family already loves me and my illustrious father would be thrilled with you. We could travel the world and host outrageous parties. We'd never have to settle into a boring routine. What fun we could have together, Juliette!"

"Yes, we would have a grand time. But I don't love you and you don't love me."

He let go of her hand and remained oddly silent at her words.

"That is, I love you as a dear friend, but I don't love you the right way. As a wife should love her husband . . ." Juliette's words faltered. "Besides, I don't wish to get married."

He turned his back on her, moving to face the tall windows, which overlooked Fifth Avenue. "It was just an idea. A suggestion. Your escapade may make it difficult for you to return home."

Good heavens! He was trying to save her reputation! Juliette rose from her seat and went to him. She placed a gentle hand on his shoulder. "Thank you, Jeffrey. But you truly don't wish to marry me. When you marry, and you will, it shall be to a woman who loves you more than life itself. Besides we are too much alike and would get into all sorts of mischief and scandalize our poor families."

"I daresay you are right." Jeffrey turned around to face her. "But what type of man will you marry now?"

"I already told you, I don't wish to get married. Do you think I'd ever let a man have control over me?"

He laughed, the smile reaching to the corners of his

blue eyes. "Oh, but you will. I predict that one day you'll fall in love, Juliette, and I will laugh harder than anyone when I watch you obey the man you love . . . and see you bending to his will in order to please him. Now that will be something to see!"

She shook her head in protest. "You'll not see me wed."

He gave her a pointed look. "You're still looking for your highwayman, aren't you?"

Her brows drew together in puzzlement. "What are you talking about?"

"I remember one time at the bookshop you told me you wanted to marry a man who was adventurous and dangerous. Someone like a pirate or a highwayman."

"I never said such a thing," she paused. "Did I?"

"You did. In fact you said you would know him when you saw him."

An unbidden image of Harrison Fleming standing at the wheel of the *Sea Minx*, his blond hair glinting in the sun and his powerful arms moving the massive wheel, flashed in her mind. Was a sea captain like a pirate? Suddenly annoyed by Jeffrey's teasing, she changed the subject. "What a funny thing for you to remember. Enough about marriage now."

He sighed in resignation. "Honestly, Juliette, what are you planning to do? Will you stay in New York?"

"I am not entirely sure."

"Your sisters want me to bring you home as soon as possible."

"I know they do," she nodded reluctantly. "But I just arrived. I can't leave yet. I need more time to think."

"Well, I do need to return at some point in the near future. I do have other obligations in my life. I will give you a week to figure out your next move. I would like to escort you back home safely. In the meantime, I'll be at Harrison Fleming's house. It's just down the block—"

"You are staying with Harrison?" She could not control the high-pitched sound her voice suddenly made.

"Yes."

"Harrison lives a few houses from here? From Christina's?"

Jeffrey immediately gave her a suspicious glance. "Yes."

Her heart hammered erratically. She attempted to ignore it. "Is he there now?"

Jeffrey's eyes narrowed at her. "Yes, he's there until tomorrow. Then he is going to New Jersey. Wherever the hell that is."

"Oh." Juliette turned away from him. Harrison lived just down the street and had not yet come to see her. She felt guilty about leaving him. And she had been somewhat surprised that he had not come looking for her. She had half-expected him to, but was also relieved that he had not. He must be very angry with her. She did not understand why that bothered her, but there was much about her feelings for Harrison that she did not understand.

"Juliette?"

The tone in Jeffrey's voice caused alarm to rush through her. Afraid to turn around where he could see her expression, she remained still. "Yes?"

"What happened between you and Harrison on the ship?"

She said nothing.

"Juliette . . ."

She was incapable of describing what had happened between her and Harrison on the *Sea Minx* because she was not entirely sure what *had* happened. She could not speak. Jeffrey would never understand and would most likely be upset with his friend for taking advantage of her, but she knew Harrison had in no way taken advantage of her. If anything she had been the one who seduced him, if the truth were told, but Jeffrey would not see it that way.

After an uncomfortably long silence, Jeffrey finally said, "Your avoidance of the question leaves little doubt in my mind what might have transpired between the two of you."

Still Juliette remained quiet, her cheeks heated.

"And your continued silence only confirms my worst suspicions, Juliette."

Slowly she turned around, but she said nothing.

"Well, you Hamilton sisters certainly have a way of sweeping men off their feet and causing them to lose their heads, do you not?" He gave her a wry look.

She knew he referred to Colette's tempestuous courtship with Lucien. She and Jeffrey had been instrumental in bringing the love-struck pair together. And Jeffrey had been privy to some information of a highly personal nature. His teasing remark told her he had a pretty good guess as to how far her relationship with Harrison had progressed.

Jeffrey continued, "Well, now I don't feel so insulted at your refusal of my proposal, but he has to do right by you. If he doesn't, by God, I will see to it that—"

"I turned him down."

The shock was plain on his face. He looked completely baffled. "Why?"

Juliette remained silent.

"Do you love him?"

Jeffrey's question caused a knot of conflict in her stomach and she felt flustered. "It is not a question of love."

"Why not? He's a good man."

"Yes, I agree with you. Harrison is a wonderful man, but I don't wish to get married," she said for what felt like the hundredth time that evening.

"He hurt you."

"No," she protested. The last thing she needed was for Jeffrey to become righteously outraged at Harrison for something he did not do to her. "He did nothing in the least to hurt me. He was exceptionally caring and kind to me—"

Juliette stopped as the door to the parlor opened and Maxwell Dunbar entered, signaling the end of their private moment. Maxwell's glittering eyes took in the intimate scene between her and Jeffrey. "Would you care to join me for a cigar, Lord Eddington?"

Jeffrey responded with a breezy calm. "Thank you for the offer, Mr. Dunbar, but I am afraid I must decline. I need to be on my way." He turned to Juliette, his expression one of sympathy. "I shall call upon you tomorrow. We still have much left to discuss. Perhaps we can tour some of the city."

"That would be lovely," she said. "I shall look forward to it."

Jeffrey bid them all farewell, and Juliette retired for the evening, too emotionally drained to make pleasant conversation with the Dunbars.

She had a feeling she would not sleep well that night.

∾15∾

An Englishman in New York

As promised, the next morning Jeffrey called on Juliette, and the two of them set about to spend the day exploring New York City together. If he was not mistaken, Juliette seemed inordinately excited for the opportunity to escape the Dunbars' house.

"Is it not as nice to see your friend as you had hoped?" he asked her as they rode along Fifth Avenue, admiring the lovely houses. The carriage driver Jeffrey hired for the day was taking them to Central Park. The warm June sun sparkled in a cloudless sky, creating a perfect summer day.

"Oh, yes, of course it is. I'm thrilled to see Christina."

Jeffrey laughed at her. "You are lying to me. Out with it, Juliette."

She stuck her tongue out at him.

"You know I love when you do that," he teased her pleasantly. She had done that the first night he met her.

She blithely ignored him. "I've been cooped up with

them since I arrived and have not had an opportunity to do anything fun at all."

"Poor Juliette." Jeffrey shook his head. "She crossed an ocean to find more of the ordinariness of the life she led at home."

She gave him a sharp look. "How did you know that is what I was thinking?"

"Because I know *you*."

"Well, it's true," she continued. "The only real fun I've had so far was while I was on the *Sea Minx*, and that was utterly thrilling."

"I imagine it was, at that." Jeffrey had thought a good deal about what he had learned had happened between Juliette and Harrison on that ship. And it worried him greatly. For all of Juliette's bravado, he was concerned about her being hurt.

The night before Jeffrey had waited for Harrison to return home for an hour before he learned that Harrison had already departed for his other home on the Jersey shore to tend to his sister who was ill. Jeffrey had been disappointed for he had wanted to speak with his friend to discover the truth of what his feelings for Juliette were.

He glanced at Juliette, sitting beside him in the carriage, looking as lovely as a rose in a pale pink muslin gown and holding a frilly parasol to shade her from the sun. No one would guess that she had run away from home. With her angelic face and feminine attire, she appeared the epitome of a well-bred English lady.

"Did you pack that gown with you?" he asked with a wink.

"No, I was traveling considerably lighter than this when I left London," she pointed out, knowing full well he was aware of that. "I was planning to have new clothes made when I arrived, but Christina gave me her entire wardrobe since her clothes no longer fit her properly and they will be out of style by the time she can wear them again. I am merely putting them to good use until I can have my own made."

"Very good use," he added, looking her up and down. "The Dunbars seem like nice people."

"They were very impressed to meet you, *Lord Eddington*."

He took her meaning and laughed. "Little do they know that my title is empty!" Jeffrey loved the irony that the people who fawned over him would normally scorn him if they knew the circumstances of his birth.

Juliette smiled at him, her blue eyes alight with excitement. "Imagine, Jeffrey! We are in New York City. Isn't it exciting? Who ever would have thought that we would be here together?"

"I can't think of anyone."

And that was the truth. He had imagined doing quite a lot of things with Juliette, and some of them did not bear repeating, but seeing the sights of New York was not one of them. He wondered what had prompted him to propose they get married last night. It was not as if he had a sudden wish to be married or planned on acquiring a wife any time in the near future. Marrying Juliette would have been a mistake in the long run. She was quite right about that.

Now he worried over her feelings for Harrison. The more Jeffrey thought about it, the more he realized that Juliette and Harrison were perfect for each other. Harrison was the only man he knew who had the fortitude to put some restraints on Juliette's reckless behavior, yet he would be able to provide her with the excitement that she craved. He also sensed that Juliette cared for Harrison more than she led him to believe. She was usually quick to provide a litany of faults of men she found lacking. She did no such thing when he questioned her about Harrison last evening. Juliette had remained uncharacteristically silent. Which told Jeffrey more than she realized.

Harrison was a bit tougher to read. Although now that he considered it more carefully, Harrison had questioned him about a mystery man in Juliette's life and was under the misconception that Juliette had fled to New York to be with a man. And Harrison had questioned *him* about his own motives regarding Juliette. Harrison had acted as a jealous suitor might, which told Jeffrey that Harrison definitely had feelings for Juliette, even if Harrison was unaware of it himself.

"Oh, look!" Juliette exclaimed. "That must be Central Park over there."

An indeed it was. Their driver explained that over twenty thousand workers and engineers had reworked the land in the center of the island of Manhattan to create a countrified and well-landscaped park, which first opened over a decade earlier. With rolling green fields, wide meadows, and hundreds of leafy trees, it provided a much-needed pastoral respite for the citizens of New York and instantly became a popular place to see and be seen while ice skating on the lakes in winter or attending outdoor concerts in the summer. Many walking paths, carriage drives, and equestrian trails lined the park, which also boasted a meadow filled with sheep and a brand new zoo.

As their open-air carriage winded its way through the shade-covered lanes of Central Park, Juliette fell into a thoughtful silence. Jeffrey could hardly resist.

"What are you thinking about?" he questioned.

"Nothing."

"You looked very far away."

"Did I?"

"Yes, you did." He paused. "Are you thinking about Harrison?"

She shook her head, twirling her parasol.

"I believe you were and just so you realize what a sporting chap I am, I'm going to tell you something." He smiled knowingly at her.

Juliette's eyes narrowed in suspicion. "What is it?"

"Harrison is no longer in New York."

Surprised by the news, Juliette's voice rose higher. "He's not?"

"Ah, I see that got your attention." He smiled wickedly at her. "No, he is not."

"Where is he?"

"He has gone to see his sister."

Her elegant eyebrows shot up. "Melissa?"

"Is there another?" Jeffrey asked.

"Harrison has two sisters, Melissa and Isabella, and a brother, Stuart."

"He's gone to visit the one who is ill."

"That would be Melissa," she announced with a certainty that surprised him.

"Yes, I believe that's the one." He found it very telling that he had known Harrison for some years and knew next to nothing about his family, yet Juliette knew the names of his brother and sisters.

"How long will he be gone?"

Ah, another telltale question for Juliette to ask. Jeffrey maintained a neutral expression and shrugged casually. "I'm not sure. He seemed to leave rather abruptly."

She fell into a long silence, staring off into the trees.

"Were you hoping to see him again?" he asked.

She turned sharply to him. "You are very manipulative, Jeffrey, and I don't care for it one bit."

"You might as well confirm my worst suspicions and simply tell me the truth."

"There is nothing to tell."

"Isn't there?" he said in a low voice.

She sighed. "I hate that you know me so well." Her eyes were downcast.

"That's part of my charm." He grinned at her. "You know that I would never judge you. Lord knows I'm not one to put anyone up on a pedestal, least of all myself."

She smiled at that. "You would love to be on a pedestal."

"Maybe." He thought for a moment. "If the right person placed me there. The view could be rather nice."

Juliette's bubbly laughter floated around them.

As their carriage left Central Park, Jeffrey instructed the driver to take them to Fifth Avenue and Fourteenth Street to Delmonico's for lunch. Juliette had never been to a restaurant before and happily added the experience to her list of adventures. In a private room, they dined on "eggs á lá Benedick" and Delmonico steak and champagne.

"Juliette, you have to think about what you will do next. You can't possibly stay with the Dunbars forever."

"Nor would I want to," she responded tartly. "Maxwell Dunbar is a lecherous bore and I cannot imagine how Christina can bear to be married to him."

"Lecherous?" he questioned.

"He never stops staring at me."

"Not that I blame him for doing so but if that is the way the wind blows there, you must leave. That's a disastrous situation for you to be a part of."

"I am quite aware of that, but I have not decided where to go yet."

"Well, what are you looking for that you haven't found?"

She looked into his eyes, her frustration evident. "I don't know, Jeffrey. I can't describe it to myself, let alone to you, but I will know it, I will feel it, when I find it."

"No." He shook his head. "No, I think you've already seen it and it has scared you to pieces. And you ran away."

"Whatever are you talking about?"

"Captain Harrison Fleming."

At her startled look, he pressed further. "I think he scares you because you cannot control him like you can control everyone else."

Juliette waited until their waiter brought them baked Alaska for dessert and left, before she let loose a diatribe. "I have never had control over anything in my life. I'm a woman if you hadn't noticed. Women control nothing. If you are confusing the fact that I may from time to time use what little charms I possess to get my way on occasion with control or power, then you are an idiot. Women have no options, no say in anything that happens to them. Even in a country as equality based and founded on freedoms and rights as America, women have no vote, no voice, in anything that happens here either. Don't you dare speak to me of control, Jeffrey! A man can do whatever he wishes and no one blinks an eye. But if a woman—"

"Why did you stop?" he asked, when she abruptly came to a halt. She had been talking a mile a minute, her fury mounting.

"Because I might as well be talking to a wall." Juliette folded her arms across her chest. "And you are smirking at me."

"I am not smirking," he protested, attempting to keep the smile from his face. "I happen to agree with you."

She bit into her dessert and ignored him.

"Let's put politics aside, shall we? And concentrate on the larger picture."

She glared at him while stabbing her cake with her fork. She remained silent.

"You are in a new city, staying with friends you are uncomfortable with and which could quickly become an untenable situation. You have no plans to go anywhere else. You have become involved with a man whom you claim to have no interest in, yet I think you protest too much, as the old saying goes. You executed a grand plan to get here, but did not have a plan for what to do once you arrived. You cannot continue traipsing about by yourself. You have only the companionship of a very handsome and dear male friend with unlimited means and resources for guidance." He looked directly into her eyes. "Do I overstate the picture?"

She grudgingly shook her head in acknowledgement.

Jeffrey continued. "So I suggest you follow my advice." He put up his hand to stop her from speaking. "And I furthermore suggest you listen to what I am proposing first, before you put up any resistance."

She gave him an arch look and said sarcastically, "Pray, go on, dear Jeffrey. I am on pins and needles waiting to hear what you have to say."

He grinned at her. "I will ignore your sarcasm because I know how much you love me."

She rolled her eyes heavenward.

"Do you wish to hear my plan or not?"

She managed to place a neutral expression on her face. "Yes, please."

"That's better." He patted her hand. "I think we should continue your adventure." He paused, waiting for her reaction.

"You're not insisting I return home?" Her expression turned to one of suspicion.

He shook his head. "No. I think you are quite correct. There is more adventure to be had here for you in the Untied States and I say we should take advantage of this opportunity. As the closest thing you have to a male relative on this continent, I shall be your escort, chaperone, protector, whatever."

"Wonderful. You can be my protector," she said with increasing impatience. "Just where do you propose that we go?"

He gave her a pointed look. "I've done a bit of investigating and I have heard that the New Jersey shore is quite lovely in the summer."

∽16∽

Down the Shore

Harrison had not slept all night. When he arrived home yesterday, he had not expected to find Melissa in such a state. She had not had one of her violent episodes in some time and the toll this most recent one had taken on her shocked him. She had not even recognized him.

He feared that Melissa would take her own life the way her father had done. Harrison had noted over the years that she and George Fleming had similar behaviors and habits. He remembered the man who had been the father figure in his life to have had great mood swings. He would be almost frantic and overflowing with ideas on how to make more sales of the houseware products he sold. Full of energy and bursting with activity he would be up all night, planning and thinking. Then would follow the time when he would sink into a black mood. Irritable and withdrawn, he would retreat into his bed and not come out for days. His mother would explain that George needed rest and quiet and to not make a sound or that they needed to not disturb him because he was busy working. The patterns continued until the day George Fleming shot himself.

Over the years, Harrison discovered that Melissa experienced those diverse periods of great elation and deep despair and it broke his heart. As she aged the episodes became more frequent and more terrifyingly violent. Once he had found Melissa threatening Isabella with a knife. The doctors he had taken her to see could offer no cause or explanation or cure, except for Harrison to try to keep her as calm as possible.

As Harrison's wealth increased he was able to provide better care for her, ignoring the advice of many doctors who bluntly recommended that Harrison place her in an asylum for the insane. Instead he hired a woman to watch over her and care for her. Annie Morgan had proven herself invaluable. Last year he had moved Melissa and Annie from his home in New York City to his newly constructed home in a small village on the Jersey shore called Rumson. Near the beach but within a beautiful country setting, the change in location had improved Melissa's constitution and her episodes had almost ceased. She had ridden horses, walked along the river, and spent more time outdoors in general, which did her good. Living at Fleming Farm had proven to be a wise decision.

However, now it seemed her troubles had returned with a vengeance, her violence escalating in the last months. Annie's letters to him had not been exaggerations.

His first sight of Melissa sickened him. His sister had always been beautiful, possessing fair and delicate features with pale blonde hair, but now she appeared nothing but skin and bones. Wan and gaunt, she stared at him from lifeless, glassy eyes.

"How long has she been like this?" he asked, incredulous at the change in his sister's appearance. He barely recognized her, and even more frightening was the fact that she did not seem to be aware of him at all.

"About a week now, after her last violent outburst. She's been refusing to eat," Annie explained. "I'm lucky if I can get her to sip some water and have a bit of toast. The doctor in town gave her some laudanum and that calmed her down, but look at her now. She's not even living. She just sits there."

Harrison had liked Annie Morgan immediately when he first interviewed her for the position. In her forties, she had been a private family nurse for two decades. Annie's demeanor exuded calm and efficiency and he trusted her judgment completely.

"Then don't give her anymore," he suggested.

"I haven't. We used the laudanum when she was threatening to jump out of her bedroom window," Annie said. "That's why I have her down here in the sun room on the ground floor. She can't jump from here and I think the light is good for her."

"Do you think we should take her back to Doctor Reynolds in New York?"

Annie answered with sage practicality, "I don't think she could survive the trip. Would you want to risk her jumping off the train?"

"No, I suppose not." Harrison reached out to stroke Melissa's hair, which hung limp and pale around her face. "Melissa," he whispered. "It's me. Harrison. I'm back from London."

She did not move or in any way indicate she heard him. Her eyes stared past him as if she could see something that he could not. He placed a light kiss on her cheek.

"Melissa!" Annie called to her in a firm voice. "Speak to your brother."

Harrison shook his head at Annie. "Don't."

He felt sick, and the last thing he needed was for Melissa to be goaded into greeting him. Not when her pretty jade green eyes used to light up and she would run and throw her arms around him when he came home.

But then for the briefest instant Melissa's eyes seemed to fix on him. In that flash of recognition he saw his sister trapped inside. Then just as quickly she disappeared again.

He turned away, unable to stomach the emptiness.

Annie followed him from the sunroom, leaving her assistant nurse to keep an eye on Melissa.

"What happened?" he asked.

"I don't know. She just seemed to become more and more despondent. Nothing I did or said could coax her out of that mood. Usually a ride to the river perks her up, but she was having none of that. None of her usual activities would tempt her. She would not even engage in her painting."

The painting had been a wonderful outlet for Melissa. He had designed a studio for her at Fleming Farm and she spent many days creating pastoral scenes. He wondered what had happened to cause such a decline in her mental state.

Harrison had gone to bed that night, but he had not slept, thinking that somehow he had failed to protect his sister. All his money, all the doctors, all the special care, and still she seemed destined down the same tragic path as her father. He did not know what to do to prevent it.

He had had more success with Isabella and Stuart. Stuart was a sea captain also, and a damn fine one. Harrison had put him in charge of his South China Sea trade. His younger brother would be fine. And Isabella was safely and happily married in Boston with a healthy son and another baby on the way. Her husband, James Whitman, was a decent fellow and would take good care of her.

Melissa was another story. He had failed her and it weighed heavily upon his conscience. Failure of any sort did not sit well with him.

A matter of another kind weighed heavily upon his conscience as well.

Juliette Hamilton.

He had left New York unwillingly. He knew he had to return to check on Melissa and a trip to Jersey was unavoidable, but he had not wanted to leave the city. He feared that by the time he got back there, Juliette might be long gone. He had warred with the conflicting desires to never see the little vixen again and to go to her, hat in hand, and convince her to marry him.

He reminded himself for the thousandth time that *she* had turned *him* down, as ridiculous as that sounded. She had been an innocent, despite her passionate nature, and he knew he had to do right by her. For the first time in his entire life he had made a proposal of marriage to a woman, and what did the fool woman do? With not so much as a by-your-leave, she had run away from him. It rankled him that she had spurned him in such a blatant manner.

He hoped that staying at Fleming Farm would provide him with some solace. But so far, it had not. Seeing Melissa broke his heart. Thinking of Juliette tortured his heart. And so he lay awake all night, deeply troubled, in his beautiful home.

The next morning, exhausted but still unable to sleep, he went about inventorying the grounds and meeting with his estate manager, Tim O'Neil. Together they discussed the plans for the new stables, which were now complete and the arrival of the new racehorses he had purchased and planned to race at Monmouth Park. He spent the remainder of the day riding the extensive length of his property and visiting the village of Oceanic. A few years back he had visited Long Branch and had stopped by the Rumson area with a friend. The quiet country beauty and lush greenery of the locale, surrounded on three sides by the Shrewsbury River and the Navesink River, called to something in him and he immediately bought property and began to build a grand three-story home with the very latest and most modern conveniences.

Before returning to Fleming Farm, Harrison rode along River Road overlooking the Navesink River and bought some fresh flounder and crabs from a fisherman. By the time he got home, he had checked in with Annie and Melissa, and there being no change in her condition, he retired to his room for a nap. Just as he was finally dozing off, a knock on his bedroom door roused him.

Mrs. O'Neil, his housekeeper and the wife of his estate manager, called to him through the door. "Captain Fleming? Captain Fleming? You have visitors."

Harrison struggled to rouse himself and staggered to the door. His housekeeper's eyes widened at the sight of his bare chest. He ignored her. "What is it, Mrs. O'Neil?"

"Excuse me sir, I didn't mean to wake you," she whispered, while attempting to avert her eyes from his chest. "It's just that you have visitors. A fine gentleman and an elegant lady. They said they just arrived on the *Sea Bird* and hired a ride here. I already sent one of the boys back to the dock to fetch their trunks."

His sleepy brain tried to make sense of what his housekeeper said. The *Sea Bird* was the steamboat ferry from New York City. His heart began to pound. "Who did you say was here?"

"A Lord Eddington and a Miss Hamilton, from England. I have them in the formal living room, Captain Fleming. You didn't tell me that you were expecting company and I was a bit surprised by their arrival. I told Lucy to ready two guestrooms for them. Would you like me to serve those crabs for supper then?"

"Yes, yes, Mrs. O'Neil. That's fine. Please tell them that I'll be down directly."

After he shut his bedroom door he stood immobile, reeling from the unexpected turn of events. Juliette Hamilton was in his house. Downstairs. At that very moment. What was she doing here? Jeffrey obviously brought her here, but why? Was she going to return to London? Was she here to say good-bye? But why would she bother saying good-bye to him at this point?

Suddenly Mrs. O'Neil's words sunk in with a dreadful certainty as it occurred to him that she had mentioned guestrooms. Of course, Jeffrey and Juliette would at least have to stay the night because the next ferry didn't leave for New York until tomorrow. He would have Juliette under his roof. In a bed a few doors down from him. *Good lord.* If he thought he had difficulty sleeping last night, he knew for certain that he would not sleep at all during the night to come.

Walking to his adjoining bathroom, the newest innovation in his house, Harrison splashed his face with cold water, ran a comb through his blond hair, and donned a clean white shirt.

When he entered the formal living room, he could barely catch his breath his heart was beating so rapidly. He immediately saw Juliette sitting on the green and gold striped sofa, looking calm and serene. She wore a pretty muslin gown of pale blue, which accentuated the color of her eyes. He had not seen her so fashionably attired since they were in London, and he suddenly longed to see her once again wearing nothing but one of his shirts, the sleeves rolled up on her arms and her shapely legs visible. But either way she was dressed, she was beautiful. Her mere presence aroused him and the familiar scent of the jasmine perfume she wore affected him more than he cared to admit. He fought the desire to go to her and pull her in his arms.

Jeffrey stood quietly before one of the tall windows, gazing out at the sprawling, green front lawn and the curving gravel carriage drive that led up to the front of the house.

Juliette must have sensed his arrival for she suddenly glanced up. Their eyes locked and they stared wordlessly at each other. Harrison's gut wrenched at the contact. Her eyes were unreadable. They held no clue to her feelings for him, although he desperately searched for one. He had no idea how long they stared that way, neither one breaking their silent hold on the other.

Jeffrey happened to turn around. "Oh, Harrison, good afternoon!" he said in that easy manner that only Jeffrey possessed. He greeted him as if his stopping by Harrison's New Jersey home, which entailed a four-hour ferry ride from Manhattan, was a common occurrence.

Harrison pulled his gaze from Juliette. "Welcome to Fleming Farm," he uttered quietly. "To what do I owe this unexpected pleasure?"

Jeffrey explained with breezy charm. "Juliette and I thought an excursion to the seashore was in order while were in the area. And who better to visit than our dear friend, Harrison?"

"I see," Harrison responded. He turned his attention back to Juliette. "Bored with New York already?"

She shook her head, but said nothing. That was quite unusual for Juliette.

"I wouldn't say bored exactly," Jeffrey continued, ignoring the obvious awkwardness between Harrison and Juliette. "I think restlessness describes it more accurately. We've heard the Jersey shore was lovely so we decided to see for ourselves. Your butler was kind enough to provide me with the directions we needed to get here. And judging from our ferry ride, the accounts we have heard were not overstated. The area is quite lovely and your home very gracious, Harrison."

"Thank you," Harrison mumbled. "I'm glad that you like it." It was not often that he entertained, because he never knew how Melissa would react. He hosted a business client from time to time in Manhattan, but Juliette and Jeffrey were his first visitors to Fleming Farm. He nervously wondered if Melissa would even notice that they had houseguests at this point, and if she did, would they upset her? He would have to have a word with Annie to see if she could keep Melissa away from their guests.

Mrs. O'Neil entered the living room and asked if Lord Eddington and Miss Hamilton would like to freshen up after their long journey, she would take them upstairs to their rooms. Their trunks would be along shortly. As Jeffrey followed Mrs. O'Neil from the living room, Juliette lingered behind.

"Harrison?" she asked.

"Yes?" He looked at her expectantly.

"It was not my idea to come here. It was Jeffrey's. He insisted."

"But you came anyway."

She hesitated as if searching for the right words,

her brow furrowed. "If it is uncomfortable . . . or awkward . . . for you to have me here I will return to New York tomorrow."

"It's fine, Juliette. Your being here does not bother me in the least. It's a very large house. Stay as long as you like." His words were uttered casually, but Harrison wondered if she knew that he was lying and that her presence in his house shook him to the core. All he could think of was that he wanted her. He wanted to reach out and touch her. He wanted to take her in his arms and thoroughly kiss her, even though he was still angry with her for running away from him that morning they docked.

She glanced at him and nodded her head. "Thank you." She left the room on silent feet and Harrison was alone.

He sank onto a velvet loveseat with a heavy sigh and held his head in his hands. If ever there was a time he wished he were out sailing the *Sea Minx*, without a care in the world, it was now. He had never *not* had a care in the world and idly wondered what the freedom of that would feel like.

But all he could think about was Juliette.

He had known Juliette Hamilton would be trouble from the instant he met her. She had boarded his ship un-invited and caused him nothing but trouble since. Now here she was at his house, uninvited yet again. This time she claimed that she only came to Fleming Farm at Jef-frey's insistence, did she?

Well, he would just have to have a little chat with his friend Jeffrey.

∽17∽

A Quiet Life in the Country

Juliette stood motionless in the pretty guestroom at Fleming Farm. Decorated in shades of blue toile, the light and airy room overlooked the green fields where horses grazed. Cool and lovely with a slightly sea-scented breeze wafting through the large open windows, the room had a large canopy bed and elegant yet simple furnishings.

Still she could not move, filled with a mounting sense of dread. It had been a mistake to come here. Jeffrey's impulsive plan to visit Harrison and have a seashore adventure seemed like a good idea while she was still in New York. She had to admit that she had a secret longing to see Harrison again and Jeffrey was providing her with the perfect opportunity, because she never would have ventured to see him on her own. But now she was filled with regrets.

Harrison was not in the least bit happy to see her and

had acted cold and distant with her. How odd to see him and not have him hug her or kiss her.

She should not have come, for she was obviously not welcome.

Now she found herself not quite at the seashore as she expected, but in a house in the country with fields, woods, gardens, and horses grazing all around. The area was so lush with greenery it wasn't to be believed. The scenic boat ride there was a refreshing change from the noise and dirt of the city. She was more of a city girl than she had imagined, having spent her whole life in London and this country surprised her. As did Harrison's house. It was enormous and quite beautiful and very modern. It seemed odd that he lived here alone, except for his sister Melissa.

Juliette wondered how ill the girl was and if they would have a chance to meet her.

She slowly wandered around the elegant bedroom.

Seeing Harrison had been more difficult than she had imagined. She had wanted to run to him. She wanted to fling her arms around him and kiss him as she had done so freely aboard the *Sea Minx*. She wanted him to hold her close to his chest. She wanted him to show some happiness to see her. Instead, he looked almost sad. And very tired. And he had seemed most displeased to have her in his living room.

She flung herself atop the large canopied bed, feeling the soft down mattress beneath her. Pressing her hands to her temples she closed her eyes tightly in an attempt to block out that long look they shared when he first saw her. His eyes had seemed so shuttered and cold. She could not detect an ounce of warmth in them or a glimpse of the man whose bed she had shared only a week ago.

When she was on his ship, she had felt very sophisticated and modern about her involvement with Harrison. She had not a care for the future. She was sharing a man's bed with no thought of marriage and she enjoyed each moment as it came. She had felt so safe and loved in Harrison's arms and nothing else seemed to matter. They seemed suspended in time in the middle of the ocean where society's mores and dictates and judgments of women did not matter. She had been free and independent.

Now she did not feel sophisticated, or modern, or like one of those liberated women who took lovers at all. Now she just felt an aching loneliness in her heart and a burning sense of shame. Perhaps society knew best after all. Perhaps all those rules were there for a reason, that reason being to protect women. Was that why intimate relations with a man without marriage were so frowned upon, because female hearts were too easily wounded?

Juliette suddenly sat up on the bed.

Was her heart wounded?

Had she allowed Harrison into her heart enough to be hurt?

If that were true, could that mean that she was in love with Harrison? She was not entirely sure. She did not want to be in love with him. She wished desperately and not for the first time, that she could confide in Colette. Her sister would know what to do.

Juliette had received one letter from Colette since she arrived in New York, which was mailed to Christina Dunbar's address as soon as she left Devon House. Seeing her sister's neat and elegant handwriting had brought tears to Juliette's eyes. Colette had not scolded her, only writing to enquire if she had arrived safely and to please let them know as soon as possible that she was safe. Juliette had written back immediately. She wanted her sisters to know that she had enjoyed her journey immensely, describing her adventures at sea in great detail, but omitting the intimate nature of her relationship with Harrison. She told them news of Christina and her husband and waxed poetic about New York City. She assured Colette that she was quite safe.

But was she really safe?

Here she was, in a strange house a world away from all that she had ever known with a man who—a man who—what? Hurt her? No, Juliette, could not in all honesty say that Harrison had hurt her in anyway. Yet she felt hurt. Terribly hurt. And the worst part was she did not know why.

Harrison had acted the gentleman and had offered to marry her. She had turned him down.

Because she did not want to marry him.

Juliette did not wish to marry anyone. Not yet anyway. But she supposed if she *had* to choose a husband, she just might choose someone like Harrison Fleming. He possessed many qualities she found attractive in a man. He was strong and handsome, and he did not judge her or seem to care for the rules of society any more than she did. In fact, Harrison seemed to make his own rules. He had worked his way up from nothing to become successful and quite wealthy, judging from his home on Fifth Avenue and his estate here. He provided for his family. He was a good man, who took care of his younger siblings, including his ill sister. Yet he was adventurous and exciting. She never felt bored or suffocated when she was with him. They could argue heatedly yet still end up kissing passionately. And there was that other part of their relationship. When Harrison kissed her she came alive.

She found herself wondering which bedroom belonged to Harrison.

A light knock on her door reminded her that she was supposed to be getting ready for dinner. A young maid entered at Juliette's instruction, and a male servant carried in her trunk full of clothes, and again she blessed Christina for giving her a ready made wardrobe and a trunk to pack it all in! Mrs. O'Neil had been true to her word and had sent someone back to the dock to pick up their trunks. The maid, who introduced herself as Lucy, began to unpack Juliette's borrowed clothing.

Juliette chose a simple yet lovely gown of sapphire silk and, with Lucy's help, piled her hair upon her head. Taking a deep breath, she left the safety of her room.

Juliette made her way along the hallway and down the main staircase, a wide, two tiered landing with an immense glass window. Moving along a corridor, she had the feeling that she had gone in the wrong direction. She was about to turn around when she heard the murmur of voices. She took a step or two closer to the sounds coming from behind a closed door.

Someone was singing. A man. It sounded like a lullaby of sorts but she was unable to make out the words. Suddenly it occurred to her that she was acting as if she were her sister Paulette, who was notorious for listening behind closed doors to other people's private conversations. Juliette hated eavesdropping. Just as she turned, the door opened and out stepped Harrison. He almost tripped over her.

He seemed just as startled to see her as she was to see him.

He snapped angrily, "What are you doing here?"

Had Harrison been the one singing? If so, whom had he been singing to?

Juliette stammered, feeling terrible for being caught eavesdropping. "I went the wrong way . . . I was going to the dining room, but . . . then I heard singing . . . I wasn't listening I just . . ." Her voice trailed off to nothingness and she simply looked up at him.

She had quite forgotten how tall he was. And how nice he smelled. He was dressed for dinner in an elegant black jacket. His golden blonde hair was neatly combed back from his face. He looked impossibly handsome, even with a scowl on his face.

"The dining room is in the opposite direction."

"Thank you."

They both stood in the dim light of the hallway. Neither moved. Neither said another word. They gazed at each other. Juliette could barely breathe. He stood so close, she could reach out her hand and caress his cheek. She wanted to kiss him, but wished he would kiss her. She waited in silence, pleading with her eyes for him to pull her into his arms and kiss her.

"Let's go," he mumbled as he took her by the arm. "The dining room is this way."

Startled by his roughness she held on tightly as she walked quickly to keep up with him, blinking rapidly the whole time. Inside she felt like crying. Harrison did not smile or seem happy to see her. He did not kiss her when he had the opportunity to do so. He no longer desired her. She followed him across the house until they entered the elegant dining room.

"I was wondering where the two of you were." Jeffrey gave them a curious glance as he entered from the adjoining sitting room. "I thought I would end up dining by myself."

"I got lost," Juliette explained. Not wanting Harrison to think that she was hurt she added breezily, "We would never leave you to eat alone, Jeffrey dear." The lightness in her voice surprised her.

"I apologize for keeping you waiting," Harrison said as they took their seats.

A chandelier glittering with crystals hung over the center of the table, which was set with fine white china, edged in gold. The walls were painted a rich crimson giving the room an intimate feel. The glass doors that led to a slate patio outside were open wide to let in the cool evening air and the sweet scent of honeysuckle wafted into the room. Fireflies lit up the growing darkness; their tiny bursts of golden light pinpointing the night sky.

Juliette sat on Harrison's right and Jeffrey sat across from her. Quite surprised by the formality of Harrison's house, she tried to remain calm with him so near to her. She took a deep breath to steady her nerves. Still confused by their strange encounter in the hallway, she wondered again what had been going on in that room?

The three of them dined on deliciously prepared local seafood, while Jeffrey recounted their recent outing in New York.

"I have always enjoyed visiting this city," Jeffrey said. "There is a vitality to it that I have never encountered anywhere else before."

"It's quite different from London," Juliette agreed.

"It's nice that you were able to do a little touring," Harrison said, his voice clipped.

Juliette added, "We had lunch at Delmonico's too."

"That's one of my favorites." Harrison smiled, seeming to relax a little. "How was the trip on the *Sea Bird*?"

"It was lovely," Juliette answered. "It's so pretty here."

They were barely through with the second course when a shrill, feminine scream ripped through the house, followed immediately by a series of sharp, anguished cries and the unmistakable sound of breaking glass.

Harrison dropped his fork on his plate with a clatter

and pushed back his chair with such force that it tipped over backwards and crashed to the floor. Without a word he raced from the dining room. The sounds of more shattering glass, followed by tormented screams and shrieks echoed through the house. Hurried footsteps and frantic shouts could be heard as well. Juliette and Jeffrey stared at each other, not sure what to do.

"Good lord, what is going on?" Jeffrey asked, a worried expression on his face. "Should we go and offer help?"

Juliette nodded, unable to say a word. She had a feeling she knew where the terrible noises were coming from. With her heart pounding, she exited the dining room with Jeffrey and headed down the hallway she had been lost in earlier, moving toward the growing din. Outside the door she had been caught eavesdropping behind less than an hour before, Mrs. O'Neil and few other servants huddled together. She peered over their shoulders.

The horrific scene within frightened her.

Harrison stood before a blood-splattered woman, her long blond hair tinged with red. This had to be Melissa. Juliette recognized the hysterical woman as Harrison's sister, even though she looked vastly different from her image in the photograph she had seen aboard the *Sea Minx*. The white nightgown she wore was streaked with blood, as were her hands, which she wrung together anxiously. Her eyes were wild and she sobbed desperately. Shards of splintered glass lay scattered on the wooden floor around her bare feet. A number of the tall floor to ceiling windows had jagged holes. An older woman, her hair in a neat bun, spoke in calm voice, encouraging Melissa to drink some water that she held out to her in a china cup.

The tension in the room, which seemed to be some sort of solarium, was palpable.

"It's all right, Melissa," Harrison said in a soothing manner. He took the cup from the other woman and held it out to his sister. "Just have a sip."

She seemed not to hear him, but Melissa held out a shaky, bloody hand and reached for the cup, which was filled with a brownish liquid that was definitely not water.

"Good girl," Harrison whispered in a low tone, giving her a warm smile. "That's it. Drink it. You'll feel better, I promise."

Melissa stared blankly at her brother. "Harrison?" Her thin voice was tremulous with fear.

"Yes, it's me. I'm here. I'm home."

"Harrison?" She asked again. Her thin body shook, as if she were cold.

The obvious pain in the woman's voice chilled Juliette to the bone. What could be so terribly wrong? What had happened to upset her so?

"Drink the medicine, Melissa," Harrison coaxed her. "Please. For me."

Trembling, Melissa slowly brought the cup to her lips, closed her eyes and took a sip. Then she let the cup fall to the floor. It shattered next to the broken glass, sending shards of china flying everywhere and splashing the remainder of the brown liquid around the hem of her gown. In an instant Harrison stepped toward her and picked her up in his arms, carrying her toward the bed at the opposite end of the large room. The other woman followed closely behind them.

Mrs. O'Neil whispered frantic orders to one of the maids to sweep up the broken glass on the floor. She then noticed that their houseguests were standing there as well.

"Oh, my! Please, please, you must come with me and return to the dining room at once," she said, obviously dismayed that they had witnessed such a private and unnerving scene.

With no other option available to them, Juliette and Jeffrey followed her back to the dining room. They sat in their seats at the table once again, yet neither of them could possibly eat. Wordlessly Jeffrey poured them each another glass of wine from the decanter. He handed a glass to her. Juliette found that she was shaking, but she drank the wine anyway hoping it would calm her. From the stricken expression on Jeffrey's face, he was hoping the same thing.

They sat in silence, lost in their own thoughts.

Finally, Jeffrey muttered. "Good God, that was harrowing."

Juliette whispered, "When he told me that his sister was ill, I never imagined that she was mentally ill."

He shook his head in disbelief. "I am sure Harrison wishes we had not seen that."

"But we did." Juliette did not know how she would sleep that night.

The image of Melissa covered with blood, obviously in an attempt to injure herself or worse, would haunt her forever. It had been terrifying. Yet her heart ached for the pain in that woman's heart. And her heart broke for Harrison, who obviously had been caring for his sister his entire life and was doing his best to help her.

"Are you all right?" Jeffrey gave her a concerned look.

She nodded weakly. "I suppose so. I just feel so terribly sad."

"I do too," he said somberly.

Again silence reigned in the room. Juliette sipped her wine, wishing she could be useful in some way. She had never witnessed anything so disturbing in her life, nor had she ever felt so powerless.

She finally murmured to Jeffrey as he refilled their glasses, "I have no idea what I could possibly to say to comfort Harrison after that."

"There is no need to say anything to me."

Juliette and Jeffrey both startled as Harrison stood before them. He looked haggard and weary and there were streaks of dried blood across the front of his white shirt. His jacket was gone and his hair was tousled as if he had run his hand through it many times in frustration Juliette resisted the impulse to jump up and throw her arms around him.

"I apologize," he said quietly. "I regret you had to see my sister that way."

Jeffrey stood and poured a glass of wine for Harrison and handed it to him. "Or would you prefer something stronger?"

Harrison gave him rueful grin. "No. This will do fine." He accepted the glass and drank.

Hesitantly Juliette ventured, "Is there anything we can do to help?"

"I doubt that." He glanced out the glass doors to the patio. "Do you mind if I have a cigar?"

"Not at all." Jeffrey agreed readily. "In fact, I'll join you."

Juliette watched as the two men took their wine and cigars and headed out to the slate patio, leaving her apparently forgotten and alone at the table. She sat there, more than a little stunned by their abrupt departure. Gentlemen usually had their cigars without the presence of women, but at that moment Juliette decided that was a ridiculous custom. With bold determination, she picked up her crystal wine glass and joined the men outside.

Bathed in the flickering light of the outdoor gas lamps that lined the patio, they sat on the steps which led down to the rolling expanse of manicured lawn. The lit tips of their cigars glowed in the dark and crickets chirped their song. Juliette hitched up the skirt of her deep sapphire gown and sat down between them, almost daring them to say something to her. Jeffrey merely gave her an indulgent smile and lifted his glass. Harrison said nothing. But he did not ask her to leave either.

"Does she behave that way often?" Juliette's words broke the silence among them.

Harrison exhaled deeply. "She hadn't for some time. Lately, however, she seems to be getting worse. More hysterical and more violent and more difficult to calm down afterwards."

Jeffrey questioned. "I assume you have taken her to see a doctor?"

"Many doctors." Harrison nodded. "The best money can buy. I even met with a few while I was in London. They all tell me the same thing."

"And what is that?" Juliette asked.

Harrison sighed heavily before speaking. "They all recommend that I place her in a state asylum for the insane."

No one spoke for some time after that. Juliette did not doubt, after witnessing that devastating display of instability, that Harrison's sister could indeed be insane.

Finally Jeffrey asked, "If all the doctors recommend it as best for her, why don't you do it then?" He added, "It would be easier for you."

"Have you ever been to one of those places?" Just the sound of Harrison's voice chilled Juliette.

"No." Juliette and Jeffrey echoed the same response.

"Well, I have visited quite a few of them over the years to see if one was suitable enough. They are dreadful places, some not fit for animals let alone human beings. I can't even describe how awful they are and I can't bear to think of Melissa in a place like that. I can take much better care of her here myself."

"That makes sense," Juliette concurred. "Even with her problems, she is much better off with her family around her than with strangers."

Harrison flashed her a grateful look, which sent an odd thrill through her. She sipped her wine, thinking it was much more relaxing and comfortable sitting out here with Harrison and Jeffrey than it was when they were in the formal dining room earlier.

Jeffrey stated, "It's very admirable of you, Harrison, the way you care for her. Not many brothers would be so caring."

Harrison did not respond, but smoked his cigar.

"Is she all right now?" Juliette asked. "Was she seriously hurt?"

"What little laudanum we were able to get her to take was at least enough to put her to sleep. Annie, that's her nurse, got her cleaned up and bandaged her cuts. Melissa is fortunate in that she has no serious wounds from this episode, but it wasn't from lack of trying on her part. She broke nearly every window in the solarium by crashing her fists through the glass. Hopefully she will be calmer tomorrow, but we never know how she will act or what will set her off." Harrison blew a ring of smoke from his cigar. "This is the worst I have ever seen her."

"But she does have calm moments, doesn't she?" Juliette wondered aloud, thinking how difficult it must be to deal with someone so unpredictable.

"She wavers between periods of despair, as you just witnessed, and phases of elation," Harrison explained in a matter of fact manner, "and we have no clue how long each stage will last or what causes her to shift from mood to mood."

Juliette said softly, "I can't imagine what that must be like for her."

Not for the first time, it occurred to her that in spite of what she had initially believed about her childhood with her absent-minded and disinterested father and bed-ridden, sickly mother, that she had led a very sheltered and privileged life with healthy sisters who loved her. She had no cause to complain. She could not comprehend having to have dealt with all that Harrison had experienced in his life. Her respect and admiration for him and all that he had accomplished increased tenfold.

Switching her wine glass to her left hand, Juliette slowly reached out her right hand to Harrison's, which was resting on the top of the step. She placed her hand over his. Without looking at her, Harrison turned his palm around and grasped her firmly, interlocking his fingers with hers. She squeezed him in silent support. He squeezed her hand back and did not release his hold on her. Instead he moved them closer to the fold of her gown, concealing their clasped hands beneath the fabric, and rested there. Jeffrey could not see that they were holding hands. Juliette suddenly felt like crying.

"Again, I'm sorry you had to see Melissa that way tonight," Harrison said.

"There is no reason to apologize," Juliette began. "We are the ones who arrived here unexpectedly. Had we any idea how things were with Melissa, we never would have intruded. Jeffrey and I will return to New York tomorrow, won't we, Jeffrey?"

"Yes, of course," Jeffrey readily agreed.

Harrison protested. "No. Please stay. At least for a few more days. It's nicer having company here than I would have imagined."

As he spoke, Harrison squeezed Juliette's hand tighter. Her heart flipped over in her chest at his tender gesture and she could not speak.

"Are you certain, Harrison?" Jeffrey questioned. "It's no trouble for us to go. There is no need to stand on ceremony with us."

"I'd like you both to stay," Harrison declared firmly, giving Juliette's hand another squeeze. "We could go to Long Branch and see the pier or go to the racetrack at Monmouth Park."

His thumb lightly caressed the top of her hand, tracing a path down to her inner wrist and sending shivers of delight up her spine. She closed her eyes. Having Harrison secretly holding her hand in the dark seemed incredibly intimate and filled Juliette with the overwhelming desire to kiss him.

"Well, then. We shall stay then, shan't we, Juliette?" Jeffrey asked, putting out his cigar on the slate stones.

Her eyes fluttered open at the mention of her name. "Of course," she murmured in a breathless whisper when she found her voice again. She squeezed Harrison's hand back as she spoke, but still they did not look at each other. "I would love to stay."

"It's settled then."

"I'm out of wine," Jeffrey said with a light laugh. "That must mean it is time to retire."

"That's probably a good idea," Harrison concluded. He extinguished his cigar also. "I must admit that I am exhausted."

Juliette, loath to let go of Harrison's hand, said nothing.

She could sit there on that hard, stone step all night, as long as she felt this close to Harrison.

Jeffrey stood and made his way toward the house. Neither Harrison nor Juliette moved an inch. Juliette wondered if Jeffrey intentionally left them alone. It would not surprise her if he had.

A honeysuckle laden breeze wafted over them as they sat in silence.

"We should go inside," he said.

She nodded, her throat tight, unable to speak.

Still they did not move to get up. She finally turned her head to look at him only to find that he was staring at her. He did not turn away when her eyes met his. In the dim light she could see the heat in his gaze and almost gasped aloud at the intensity.

"Juliette?"

The sound of her name on his lips shook her. It seemed as if he were going to say something to her of great importance. She leaned in closer to him, her face mere inches from his, willing him with every fiber of her being to kiss her.

He leaned toward her. "Juliette, I—"

"Are you two coming inside, or should I come out there and get you?" Jeffrey called loudly from the doorway, instantly shattering the intimate mood between them.

Harrison released her hand abruptly and straightened up. "We're coming." He rose to his feet.

Filled with bitter disappointment, Juliette glanced up at him, her heart thrumming wildly. She had been positive that he was going to kiss her. Blast Jeffrey for interrupting them! Harrison nodded to her and held out his hand to help her to her feet. Taking his hand once again, Juliette stood on shaky legs and followed him into the house. The three of them bade each other good night and retired to their separate quarters.

Alone in her room, Juliette collapsed in emotional exhaustion upon her bed, the sting of unshed tears burning her eyes. Funny, she hardly ever cried. Yet lately it seemed she was on the verge of tears constantly.

∼18∼

Some Like It Hot

Juliette awoke the next morning and did not recognize the room she found herself in. After a fitful night sleep full of strange dreams, it took a moment to recall that she was in Harrison's house. She blinked at the bright sunlight pouring into the blue toile bedroom. The clock on the mantel read eleven thirty. Goodness gracious, she slept later than usual, even for her! She stretched and yawned before making her way to the open window. Looking out at the verdant lawns and woods beyond, she could not help but admire the beauty of the landscape. The humming buzz of insects and the twittering of birds greeted her. The thick haze in the sky portended a very hot day. Indeed, Juliette could already feel the heat in the steamy stillness of the air.

She washed in the adjoining white tiled bathroom, once again marveling at the amazing modernity of Harrison's new house. He had every latest convenience and luxury installed. Once she was dressed in a simple muslin gown of pale peach and had arranged her thick hair into some semblance of order on top of her head to keep her as cool as possible, she descended the main staircase. The house was quiet. Seeing no one about, she made her way to the kitchen in answer to her rumbling stomach. She had not eaten much at dinner the night before so it was no surprise she was hungry.

Mrs. O'Neil gave her a warm smile as she entered the sunny kitchen. "Good morning, Miss Hamilton. Captain Fleming gave us orders that we were to let you sleep as long as you liked. You must have been tired from your journey to sleep this late. It's noon already! Why don't you have a seat in the breakfast room and I'll bring you some scrambled eggs and toast and coffee."

"Thank you, Mrs. O'Neil. That sounds lovely." She followed the woman into a comfortable and decidedly less formal room than the dining room, and sat at a small table near the tree-shaded windows.

"I hope you found your room to be comfortable and that you had a good night's sleep." Mrs. O'Neil bustled about, pouring her a cup of coffee, as she chattered amiably, and sat down at the table across from her. "Oh, it's going to be a hot one today, mark my words. You'd be well-advised to stay indoors this afternoon, Miss Hamilton."

"Where are Lord Eddington and Captain Fleming?"

"I believe Lord Eddington took one of the carriages and was riding into Red Bank or Shrewsbury. He mentioned something about visiting a friend."

Curious, Juliette wondered just whom Jeffrey was meeting in town and felt slightly put out that he had not seen fit to ask her to join him. "And Captain Fleming? Is he out for the day as well?"

One of the maids placed a plate of fluffy scrambled

eggs and thick sausage in front of her. Juliette's mouth watered.

"Captain Fleming is out and about somewhere on the estate with my husband. Mr. O'Neil manages the estate for him and takes care of everything on the farm when Captain Fleming is away." Her pride in her husband was evident.

Juliette smiled at the woman as she ate.

"We don't get many visitors here at Fleming House. It's nice to have guests, especially such grand ones as yourself and Lord Eddington."

"Thank you," Juliette murmured. "It's lovely to be here. Thank you for making me feel so at home."

A maid stuck her head in the doorway. "Mrs. O'Neil? Did you want me to starch those lacey napkins too?"

"I'll be right in, Fanny," she called to the girl. She rose from the table and said to Juliette, "When you are finished with breakfast, the library is down the main hallway. It's cool and quiet in there. Captain Fleming thought you might like to visit there."

"Thank you," Juliette called as the plump housekeeper hurried from the breakfast room.

Feeling much better after she ate, Juliette found the library, a dark, wood-paneled room lined with shelves of books but wondered why Harrison would suggest that she visit the library. Juliette had had more than her fill of books to last her whole life and was not the least bit interested in reading. Thinking that he must have been teasing her and sent her there as a joke, she smiled to herself. The quiet room was cooler, but not by much.

She fanned herself with a thin book of poetry that she found resting on a table. In the corner stood a rocking chair. Juliette, feeling somewhat restless, sat down and rocked back and forth, enjoying the slight breeze the movement created. She wished that Jeffrey or Harrison would return soon.

"Hello."

Startled by the voice, Juliette froze when she saw Melissa standing alone in the doorway.

Harrison's sister appeared completely normal. She would be pretty if she weren't so thin and fragile looking. She was very fair with wide green eyes and wore a simple pink cotton dress. Her long blonde hair was neatly pulled back behind her head with a pink ribbon. Aside from heavy dark circles around her eyes and thick bandages wrapped around her wrists, she displayed no outward signs of the traumatic events of the previous night. Unnerved by her presence and wondering why Melissa was unattended, Juliette swallowed.

"Hello," she murmured in response, clutching the arms of the chair tightly.

Melissa stepped into the library and Juliette noted that she had bare feet. She came closer. "Who are you?" Melissa asked.

"I'm Juliette Hamilton."

"That's a pretty name," she said softly, her voice like that of a child's, although she had to be a few years older than Juliette.

"Thank you." Juliette felt the need to explain to her. "I'm a friend of Harrison's."

"We never have visitors." Melissa sat upon a large leather chair facing Juliette. "I'm Melissa Fleming, Harrison's sister." She pulled her feet up beneath her in a very casual position. Juliette caught a glimpse of the scratches on her bare ankles, obviously from the broken glass.

"It's very nice to meet you," Juliette said, thinking the woman seemed more lucid than she had expected her to be. Again she wondered where her nurse was. Surely

Melissa was not permitted to roam about at will. Not after that scene last night. The nurse must certainly come for her shortly.

"Will you be staying with us long?" Melissa brought her fingers to her mouth and began biting her nails, which were already bitten to the quick.

The nervous gesture increased Juliette's apprehension. She did not feel comfortable being alone with Harrison's unbalanced sister, yet she did not know how to extricate herself from the situation without upsetting the woman who had apparently made herself comfortable and settled in for a sociable chat.

"I'm not sure how long I shall stay at the moment," Juliette answered. "A few days, perhaps?"

"That would be lovely. Has Mrs. O'Neil given you the blue guestroom?"

"Yes. It's quite charming." Oh, when would that nurse come for Melissa? Juliette had never had to converse with an unstable person before, even though she seemed quite rational at the moment. The very ordinariness of the conversation seemed ridiculous. Juliette could not help but fear that Melissa would suddenly do something crazy or try to injure herself.

"You have a lovely accent." Melissa stopped biting her nails and smiled at her. "Where are you from?"

"I'm from London."

"I've always wanted to go to London!" Melissa sighed dreamily. "I've only read about it in books."

Juliette smiled at her and continued rocking slowly in the chair. Imagine someone dreaming of going to England, all the while she was wishing to go to America! "I've always wanted to come to the United States."

Melissa let out a girlish giggle. "That's very funny. We

should switch places. You stay here and I'll go to London and stay with your family."

"That would be funny," Juliette conceded awkwardly. She wondered what her sisters would think of Melissa.

A shadow of sadness crossed her face and she bit her nails again. "I never get to go anywhere though. No one ever lets me do anything I want to do. Especially my brother. He makes all the rules for me. He and Annie. They make all the decisions and they never ask me what I think."

"What do you wish to do?" Juliette heard herself ask.

"Oh, lots of things!" Her eyes alight with excitement and yearning, she took her fingers from her mouth and continued. "I would like to go to different places and meet different people. I just wish to do *something*."

Although she nodded in agreement, Juliette said nothing. Melissa's words sounded painfully familiar.

Changing the subject, Melissa asked, "What is your family like?"

"I have four sisters."

"Four sisters?" Melissa clapped her hands like a schoolgirl. "That's wonderful! Are you the oldest?"

"No, my sister Colette is the eldest. I'm next. Then there is Lisette, Paulette, and Yvette. Colette is the only one who is married so far. She's about to have a baby."

"My sister, Isabella, is about to have a baby too!" She grinned happily. "I'm already an aunt though. Isabella has a little boy who is two years old, named Sam. I haven't met him yet. They may come visit us from Boston at the end of the summer. I have another brother too. Stuart is off at sea somewhere. Asia, I think. Harrison is a wonderful brother to me. He's the oldest. How do you know him?"

"He is a business associate of my brother-in-law.

Harrison stayed with us while he was in London. I came to New York with him when he sailed back." There. Juliette thought that covered that subject as concisely as she could without outright lying.

"Oh, were you on Harrison's ship?" she stared at Juliette in wonder. "I would be too afraid to sail on the *Sea Minx*. They couldn't even get me to ride the ferry to come here to Rumson. I insisted we take the train! Harrison was most displeased with me." Melissa smiled impishly.

Juliette could not deny the normalcy of their conversation. If she had not witnessed Melissa screaming and sobbing last night with her own eyes, she never would have believed her capable of such behavior. Nothing she said indicated that she was unbalanced. She appeared completely sane. She seemed like any average young woman. She loved her family, she wished to travel, yet had normal fears, and she was completely aware of who and where she was.

"Are you going to marry my brother?"

Shocked by the question, Juliette stopped the rocking chair with her feet. "Excuse me?"

Melissa seemed embarrassed, and resumed biting her nails again. "Forgive me, I didn't mean to pry. It's just that Harrison has never brought a lady home to visit before. And with you being so beautiful and accomplished, I just naturally assumed that he intended to marry you."

Juliette had no answer except the truth. "No. I'm not going to marry Harrison. We are simply good friends."

"I see," Melissa said, chewing on her thumbnail. "You're dress is very pretty."

"Thank you."

"Could I borrow it sometime?"

Feeling the awkwardness suddenly creep back into their conversation, Juliette murmured, "I suppose so."

"Melissa!" A sharp voice called. "I've been looking for you."

"Oh, hello, Annie." Melissa waved casually to the woman whom Juliette recognized from the night before as her nurse. "Have you met Harrison's good friend from London? This is Miss Juliette Hamilton. Juliette, this is Annie Morgan, my nurse."

Surprised by Melissa's ease of introductions, Juliette watched her in fascination.

Annie, still wearing a bun tightly pulled back from her face, gave Juliette a questioning look before saying, "It's a pleasure to meet you, Miss Hamilton."

Juliette smiled at the woman to let her know that everything was fine. "It's a pleasure to meet you as well. Melissa and I were just having a little chat and getting acquainted."

"That's nice." Annie seemed to relax, seeing that the situation was calm and that nothing out of the ordinary had happened while Melissa was not under her supervision. "Unfortunately it's time for Melissa to have her nap."

"Yes," Melissa nodded gratefully. "I am rather sleepy now." She uncurled her long legs and stood up. "It's been lovely talking to you, Juliette. Would you join me later for a game of backgammon?"

Melissa looked at her with such longing that Juliette could hardly refuse her. "Yes, of course."

"That's wonderful." She smiled broadly, looking like a little girl. "Shall I meet you in the drawing room at six o'clock?"

"That sounds fine." Being that Juliette had no other plans that day, what else could she say?

"Good afternoon!" Melissa gave a little wave and followed Annie out of the library.

Alone again, Juliette released a long sigh of relief. She suddenly realized how nervous she had been throughout the entire exchange. Sweat had trickled down her back and between her breasts, leaving her feeling sticky and hot. Trembling slightly, she rose from the rocking chair and thought she would retire to her room and take a cool bath. The house was still and quiet in the heat of the afternoon. All the blinds had been drawn to block out the sun and the rooms were dark as she made her way along the corridor and up the main staircase.

She walked along the dim upstairs hallway, the thick carpet muffling the sound of her footsteps. Before she reached her door, another bedroom door opened and Harrison stepped out, looking as if he were in a hurry. Juliette stopped in her tracks and so did he when he saw her. A lazy smile spread across his handsome face, and her knees went weak.

"Well, well," he said in a teasing tone. "Look who finally decided to get out of bed."

"Actually I have been up for quite some time," she retorted. His shirt was open to the waist, revealing his tanned, bare chest, and his sleeves were rolled up to his elbows. It seemed people were a good less formal about dress here in the country. She took a deep breath.

"And what trouble have you been getting yourself into?" He stepped closer to her.

"No trouble," Juliette murmured, lowering her eyes. She could not think clearly when he stood so near to her. Her dress clung to her and the loose tendrils of her hair were damp around her temples. She had a sudden impulse to tear her clothes from her body and slip into a cool bath with Harrison naked beside her. The image caused her head to spin. "It's just so . . . hot . . . I . . . I thought I'd have a bath."

Slowly she lifted her eyes to meet his.

His silver-gray eyes pinned her in place. As if he could read her mind, he reached out and pulled her to him. He covered her mouth with his in a scorching kiss. Enfolded in his arms, she melted into him. The scratchy stubble on his face felt good against her skin. Harrison was kissing her and that was all that mattered. His lips were hot and salty and their tongues entwined with a ravenous eagerness. She clung to him, devouring him. She could not get enough of him. His hands splayed through her damp hair, tugging until the tresses came loose from the pins that had held it off her neck. He continued to kiss her, while caressing her face with his fingers. She placed her hands on his cheeks, losing herself in his kisses, melting from the sheer pleasure of being kissed by Harrison once again.

There, in the stifling and silent upstairs hallway, they kissed each other as if they would never get another chance.

"Harrison." Juliette whispered his name frantically, as a plea. She needed more than this. She needed him.

In response, he backed her up against the wall, ravaging her with his kisses. He pressed himself against her and she could feel that he wanted her as much as she wanted him. A thrill raced through her as she met his kisses with her own. She ran her hands inside his already open shirtfront, her fingers feeling the heat of his bare skin. One of his hands ran down the length of her, stroking the curve of her hip and back up to cup her breast. They were both breathing heavily, and he reached his hand down the front of her pale peach gown. If he had torn the gown off her she would have screamed in delight, so desperate was she to feel him naked against her bare skin. Overheated and overexcited, she could barely breathe, but she continued to kiss him.

He began to walk her back up the hallway toward the door of his bedroom, which was just where she wanted to go. Her heart hammering, her blood tingling, she let him lead her. Filled with elation, she sighed. He was taking her to his bed! God, but she had missed being with him! Missed the feel of him. Missed the strength of him. She had not realized how much until she saw him again. And now . . . Now she could not get enough.

"Oh, Captain Fleming!"

Mrs. O'Neil's voice coming up the stairs immobilized them both. Juliette's eyes flew open to see a mixed expression of lust and frustration on Harrison's face. He immediately released her. She turned and fled down the hallway until she reached the safety of her room. She raced inside and closed the door before Mrs. O'Neil could see her. Panting and out of breath, Juliette leaned her back against the door and listened. She heard the muffled voices of Harrison and Mrs. O'Neil and their footsteps as they made their way downstairs.

Slowly Juliette sank to the floor. Shaking uncontrollably, it was some time before she could find the strength to move again.

∾19∾

Games Women Play

After spending the rest of that sweltering afternoon overseeing the arrival of six Thoroughbred racehorses from Maryland, Harrison finally returned to his bedroom to wash up before dinner. He soaked in the cool tub, still tortured by his encounter with Juliette earlier that day.

God, but he had wanted her. She had been willing and eager to have him too, he had no doubt. Kissing her in the hallway had been a terrible mistake, as was kissing her in the first place. He needed to stay away from her. He would be the world's biggest fool to be tempted by her again. And she certainly had tempted him that afternoon. And last night on the patio . . . when she had offered comfort and held his hand so sweetly.

Last night had been a disaster.

Melissa's hysterical and suicidal episode had terrified him. Annie had not been exaggerating her deteriorating mental state. Before dinner last night, Melissa had finally awakened from the stupor she had been in and recognized Harrison for the first time since he arrived home. Happy to see him, she seemed placid and calm. He even sang her a silly little tune he had made up for her years ago about sailing on the waves and drifting off to sleep.

He was utterly unprepared for her complete breakdown less than an hour later. Seeing her covered in her own blood and sobbing desperately wrenched his heart. Then learning that Juliette and Jeffrey had witnessed his sister's suffering first-hand filled him with regret. He had gone to great lengths over the years to protect Melissa and to keep her infirmity private. Somehow he felt he had let her down by allowing outsiders to see her at her most vulnerable.

Still, it had been somewhat of a relief to finally talk about Melissa's condition with Juliette and Jeffrey. They had both been very kind and offered their support. They had been shocked by what happened, of course, for who wouldn't be? But they did not seem to think any less of him because of it.

Harrison dunked his head under the water, staying under for some time, listening to the muffled stillness that could only surround him when totally submerged. When he was a little boy he had done that often, to block out the unpleasant sounds that worried him. He would count the seconds to see how long he could hold his breath, trying to stay under longer each time. Coming up for air now, he gasped and filled his lungs with deep breaths. He wiped the water from his eyes and rose from the tub, rivulets of water running down his body and dripping on the tile floor.

Wrapping himself in a thick towel, he stared at himself in the mirror. With a heavy sigh he shook himself from his reverie. He got dressed and made his way downstairs to dine with Juliette and Jeffrey, where they would make plans for their little excursion to Long Branch tomorrow.

But first he would check in on Melissa. He had seen her earlier that morning and she was quite placid, acting as if nothing out of the ordinary had happened the night before. It really was disconcerting how her moods shifted so mercurially. If she were becoming more and more of a danger to herself, and perhaps others, maybe it would be best to place her in an asylum. He hated to think of her in one of those places though.

When he looked into the sunroom, he found it empty. Puzzled, he glanced around the room, taking note that the broken windows had been boarded up until the glazier he sent for could come and replace the glass. He left, wondering where Melissa and Annie could be.

As he walked the corridor he heard peals of laughter coming from the drawing room. He paused and looked in, surprised by the sight of Melissa and Juliette seated at the card table engaged in a lively game of backgammon while Annie sat on a nearby sofa, sewing. Shocked speechless, he stood watching the scene for a few moments before the women noticed him.

Melissa looked happier and more alive than he had seen her in some time. She looked pretty too. Her hair had been washed and styled, arranged in curls around her face. Her cheeks had some color in them, which were accentuated by the cheerful pink gown she wore. Aside from the bandages around her slender wrists, the sight of which made him wince, there was no evidence of her hysteria of last night. Her light laughter filled his heart with hope.

And Juliette, well, Juliette looked breathtaking. With her dark hair and sparkling eyes, she was in direct contrast with his sister's pale beauty. She appeared cool and serene in a low-necked gown of ice blue, which revealed far more of her seductive cleavage than he could comfortably bear to see.

The sight of the two women together brought up an odd feeling in him. How the hell did they wind up playing a game together?

Finally Melissa glanced in his direction and cast him a brilliant smile. "Oh, Harrison! Thank you so much for bringing Juliette to visit me. We are having such a lovely time together."

"You're welcome." What else was there to say? He certainly had not brought Juliette to visit her. He glanced toward Annie for answers to this strange little scenario. Annie only gave him a helpless shrug and continued with her sewing.

"Hello, Harrison."

He turned his attention back to Juliette. Vivid images of their torrid kiss earlier that afternoon in the hallway flashed in his mind. He wished he could apologize to her. He wished they had not been interrupted. He wished he had made love to her in that sweltering heat and then shared a cooling bath with her. His mouth went dry. He managed to utter, "Good evening, Juliette. I see you've met my sister."

She nodded. "Yes, Melissa and I met earlier today and became acquainted. She invited me to play backgammon with her before dinner."

From the odd expression on her face, Harrison could not tell if Juliette were a willing participant in this game or had awkwardly been pressed by Melissa.

"We are just about finished," Melissa said happily. "I'm going to win."

"I'm afraid she is right," Juliette conceded. "I'm not very

good at these types of games. My sisters always played more than I did."

Melissa made her last move and squealed with delight. "I win!" She clapped her hands together and jumped up from her chair.

Juliette grinned indulgently and gave her congratulations.

Melissa's childlike happiness was somewhat unnerving, and again, Harrison did not know what to expect from her. "Annie, isn't it time for Melissa to retire?"

Annie immediately set down her sewing and rose from the sofa. "Yes, it's time she had supper. It seems her appetite has returned. Aren't you hungry, Melissa?"

For a heart-stopping moment, Harrison feared that Melissa was going to put up a protest. An angry scowl appeared on her face, and then just as suddenly, it disappeared. "I'll go now, if Juliette will visit with me tomorrow." She stared at Juliette. Apparently his sister had taken an exceptional liking to Juliette.

Juliette nodded in agreement, although her smiled was decidedly nervous. "Yes, of course. I need another chance to try to win."

"Good night then." Melissa obediently followed Annie from the drawing room.

With his eyes still on Juliette, Harrison noticed her hand trembled as she put the backgammon pieces away. During the entire voyage on the *Sea Minx*, he had never seen Juliette afraid. Yet now she appeared not just nervous, but almost afraid.

"I'm sorry." He apologized for that unfinished and frustrating encounter in the hallway. He apologized for taking advantage of her. He apologized for his sister. He hoped she understood that he was sorry for everything.

Juliette stammered anxiously. "No . . . I'm sorry. I just

don't . . . I've never had to . . . I'm not sure . . . what to do . . . how to act with her. I'm so afraid I'm going to do or say something to cause her to . . . to cause her to . . ."

Harrison went to her side and took her hand in his. "You don't need to explain. I understand how you feel and I thank you for being kind to her."

"It's just that she seems to like me so much and I'm afraid to disappoint her."

"Please don't worry so much, Juliette. Her calm moods usually last for a few weeks at least." He took her hand and brought it to his lips, pressing a kiss upon it.

She glanced up at him, and the look on her face almost brought him to his knees. Gone was the worry and fear. Her expression was filled with unmasked desire. She rose to her feet. He slowly lowered his hand, still clasping hers, and drew her toward him. God help him, but if he kissed her now he would end up taking her right there on the game table. Her lips trembled and he leaned in closer to her.

"Oh, there you are!" Mrs. O'Neil popped into the drawing room. "Supper is ready, Captain Fleming."

"Thank you, Mrs. O'Neil," Harrison said, as he quickly broke apart from Juliette. "We'll be right there."

He did not miss the censorious look his housekeeper gave him before she left. He turned back to Juliette, who was smiling regretfully.

"Her timing is impeccable," she whispered.

He shrugged and held out his arm to her. "Shall we go to dinner?"

She took a deep breath before taking his arm and followed him from the room. "Where is Jeffrey?" she asked when they were seated at the dining room table.

"Apparently he has not returned yet," Harrison explained

to her with a wink. "I imagine he found something to keep him occupied this evening."

"Knowing Jeffrey, I can safely guess what that would entail," Juliette said with a roll of her blue eyes.

Harrison had to admit that he was a little jealous of her unconventional relationship with Jeffrey. The man was far too familiar with her, sharing things with her that were entirely inappropriate for him to share with a lady. He was secretly relieved that Jeffrey had chosen to spend some time in town. "So, it is just the two of us this evening."

She cast him a warm smile. "I don't mind."

"Neither do I."

"You are quite charming this evening, Captain Fleming."

Pleased that she was flirting with him, he grinned back at her. "And you look quite beautiful this evening, Miss Hamilton."

It turned out to be a very romantic dinner, so different from their casual and informal meals in bed in his cabin or in the galley with the crew. They drank champagne and dined on a delicious seafood platter. It was the first time they were alone together for any length of time since they were on the *Sea Minx*. Before long, they had fallen into their usual banter and comfortableness with each other, their lively conversation punctuated with easy laughter.

Toward the end of a rich chocolate cake for dessert, Harrison finally brought up the subject they had both been avoiding.

"Why did you run away from the ship that morning? Why didn't you wait for me?"

Juliette grimaced, clearly ill at ease with the topic. "Let's not ruin this evening, Harrison."

"After knowing the danger you put yourself in leaving

London the way you did, have you learned nothing? You venture off alone in a strange city. You could have been——"

"Please spare me the list of what could have happened to me," she interrupted heatedly, her eyes flashing. "Obviously I am just fine."

"Why did you run away without me?"

"You know why."

"Answer me," he insisted.

"Don't make me say it, Harrison."

"Then I'll say it," he threatened. "You left because——"

She interrupted him in a very low voice. "I left because you felt compelled to marry me to assuage your misplaced sense of honor. You truly didn't want to get married any more than I did. That is why I left."

The ferocity of her words momentarily stunned him. "What?"

"I would never want you to marry me simply because I shared your bed, Harrison."

"Don't be ridiculous," he scoffed at her stubborn pride. "I offered to marry you because it was the right thing to do."

Juliette rolled her eyes. "That is exactly what I am saying. Had I stayed, you would have pressed the issue."

"Of course, I would have. It's my responsibility. We should get married."

"Simply because I shared your bed?"

"That and I don't like to think of you in anyone else's bed." He knew the words were a mistake as soon as they came out of his mouth. He stared at her.

Truly angry now, Juliette stood up from the table and stalked to the doorway. She turned back and faced him. Her words fell like ice. "You understand nothing."

Harrison was left alone in the dining room, stunned by Juliette's reaction. He almost went after her, but then thought better of it. Feeling hurt and angry when he had only been trying to do the right and honorable thing, he grabbed a bottle of champagne and walked out to the patio.

The night had cooled off very little. He removed his jacket and tossed it over the wrought iron railing that outlined the patio. He made his way to the steps where he sat with Jeffrey and Juliette the night before and made a mental note that it would be rather convenient to have some furniture out here.

She was right.

He would never understand women. Least of all a woman like Juliette. What a stubborn, pig-headed, beautiful temptress she was. He swigged from the champagne bottle and wiped his mouth with his sleeve. The whole situation made no sense.

"Looks like I'm too late for dinner."

Harrison turned around to see Jeffrey Eddington standing in the doorway. He waved to him. "Come join me."

Jeffrey staggered onto the patio and sat on the steps. He held a bottle of something in his hand. "Bourbon."

Harrison held up his bottle. "Champagne."

They both chuckled and took swigs from their bottles.

"Where the hell have you been?" Harrison asked, taking in Jeffrey's inebriated state.

"I ran into an old friend. And I made some new ones," he said cryptically, with a rakish smile.

"Business or pleasure?"

"A little of both actually. It was a productive day. Until a few hours ago, that is. Somehow I ended up at a party at a house on the river . . ." Jeffrey grinned.

"Glad you had a good time."

"I did, but I never kiss and tell." He gave Harrison an

arch look. "But I must say your name is quite familiar to certain parties."

Smiling, Harrison shrugged helplessly.

Lighting a cigar, Jeffrey asked, "Where's Juliette?" He offered another cigar to Harrison.

Taking it, Harrison lit the tip and inhaled deeply. He exhaled in a slow, even breath before responding, "She's in her room, I would imagine."

Jeffrey gave him a questioning look. "How is that going, by the way?"

"How is what going?" Harrison asked, ignoring the obvious. Cigar smoke curled around them.

"How is it going between you and Juliette?"

If he had any idea of where he stood with Juliette that might be an easier question to answer, but as it was, Harrison hadn't a clue. "What makes you think there is anything between me and Juliette?"

"I'm not blind," Jeffrey said sarcastically. "You can't take your eyes off of her."

"You're the one traveling about New York City with her, taking her to restaurants and for carriage rides in the park." Harrison had wanted to be the one to show Juliette around the city, and it had stung a little to learn that she had done so with Jeffrey. The thought of Jeffrey squiring her around made him uneasy. "What's going on between *you* and Juliette? Answer me that."

"Me and Juliette?" Jeffrey laughed aloud, his grin wide. "We're just good friends. Very good friends, actually."

Harrison's eyes narrowed at the cryptic answer. "What is that supposed to mean exactly?"

"It means, Harrison, that she and I are dear friends and nothing more." Jeffrey held up his hands in mock innocence.

Harrison pressed on anyway. He had to know the

answer, because it had been gnawing at him for some time now. "Have you kissed her?"

"Not in the way you mean. No."

"But you are in love with her, aren't you?" Their unusual friendship begged this question so Harrison could not help himself from asking. He had to know the truth, even if he did not like it.

Jeffrey gave a weary sigh. "No, I'm not. Thank God for that small favor. I don't think I could survive being in love with the likes of Juliette. There may have been a time when I briefly entertained the notion of Juliette and me together. But that is long past. Yes, I love her dearly. I love her family. But as far as the two of us together? It would never work. I tend to see myself in the role of her older brother, since she has none. Or at the very least I could be a devoted cousin. *Someone* has to watch out for her."

Harrison relaxed somewhat at Jeffrey's words. If Jeffrey had serious intentions toward her it would only complicate an already complicated situation.

Jeffrey drank from his bottle before stating, "Now that we've cleared up *my* relationship with Juliette, it is only fair turn around that you explain to me what is going on between *you* and Juliette."

Harrison felt his gut clench. "Explain to you about what?"

"I have already heard one side of the story. As her closest male protector, I demand to hear your side."

Harrison remained mute and took a long swig from his bottle of champagne.

"Ah, ha!" Jeffrey cried triumphantly. "That was the exact answer I got from Juliette. The lack of an answer on both your parts confirms my very worst suspicions."

Again Harrison remained silent. What happened

between Juliette and him while they were on the *Sea Minx* was their private business. He would not share that information with anyone. And really, what right did Jeffrey Eddington have to be asking such intimate questions and making insinuations? It sullied the beauty of what he and Juliette had shared.

"You have to do right by her, Harrison." Jeffrey said in an authoritative voice. "You have to marry her."

"You think I don't know that? I did ask her to marry me." He paused before adding, "She turned me down."

Jeffrey whistled low. "She told me that, but I didn't want to believe her."

"She told you?" Harrison's humiliation was complete. "Yes."

Harrison contemplated that for a moment. "Did she tell you why she said no?"

Jeffrey shrugged. "She simply said she didn't want to get married."

"Do you believe that?"

Jeffrey took another mouthful from his bottle of bourbon. "Well, the thing with Juliette is that you have to believe what she says. I've never known her to lie."

"I don't understand that woman." Harrison's frustration edged into his tone. "As any honorable gentleman would do, I offered to marry her. But she says no! What more can I do? What more does she want?"

"She doesn't want to get married because she doesn't want to be controlled. That's why she left London."

Harrison's brows drew together in puzzlement. "What do you mean?"

"I mean that she didn't come here to meet a lover, as you thought. She just wanted to break away, spread her wings so to speak. She wanted to see something of the world and to live her life a little without society reining her in."

That sounded vaguely familiar to Harrison. What was it she had said? His champagne soaked brain tried to recall the things Juliette had told him on the ship. Something about being free and having adventures. The entire time he suspected that was a cover up and that she really was on her way to be with another man.

"She said that too, but I didn't believe her," Harrison admitted reluctantly.

"Why not?"

"Because it didn't make any sense at all!" Harrison cried in frustration.

"This is Juliette Hamilton we're talking about. Of course it makes sense."

"No." Harrison shook his head in impatience. "No, it doesn't. I've seen her home in London, and the pretty life she has there. She was safe and secure, with a family who loves her. She wanted to give all that up for adventure? For freedom? And risk her life in the process? It makes no sense, I tell you."

In Harrison's mind, Juliette had all that anyone could ever want in life. He spent his entire childhood worried what each day would bring and worked his whole life to find that sense of security and stability.

Harrison added, "She could have married any wealthy nobleman of her choice and never had to worry about anything again."

"Yes, she could have," Jeffrey agreed solemnly. "But do you see what you just did? You just mapped out her life for her. So did everyone else, myself included. But that's not what *she* wanted."

"What does she want then?" Harrison echoed through the weary fog in his head.

"She wants to live life on her own terms, I guess. And

God bless her, somehow she's doing it." The admiration Jeffrey had for her was evident in his voice.

"What are you going to do, Jeffrey?" Harrison asked in weariness. "Are you taking her back to London?"

He rubbed his hand along his temple. "I know I should bring her home, yet I can't do that to her. On the other hand, I can't just leave her here on her own. But I need to get back to London very soon."

They sat quietly for some time, smoking their cigars. The rich, pungent smoke wafted through the still night air.

Finally, Jeffrey said, "You know you have to get her to marry you. It's the only way."

"Yes, blast it, I know that! She ran away from me as soon as we docked in New York. So where does that leave me?" Harrison's fear for her that morning still made his heart race. If she had been hurt he never would have forgiven himself. Yet he was still angry with her for it as well.

Jeffrey chuckled low. "I didn't know that bit of the story, but it doesn't surprise me."

Harrison said, "I know I should marry her. It's the only way. But what am I supposed to do? Trick her into marrying me?"

"We might just have to at that." With a gleam in his eyes, Jeffrey raised his bottle to Harrison's. "I think I have an idea."

∾ 20 ∾

Across the Pond

"Can I please hold him now?" Lisette Hamilton asked.

Colette Sinclair held her infant son in her arms, overwhelmed with the emotions flooding her at the sight of his tiny and perfect features. He had Lucien's eyes and smile. Even a week after his birth she could not stop staring at his precious little face. He had arrived a few weeks earlier than expected but was healthy and strong.

Beaming with pride, Colette passed the baby to her sister, who stood anxiously by her side. "Be careful of his head."

"I know. I know," Lisette murmured, taking the sleeping bundle in her arms and crooning to him. "Oh, he's just the sweetest little boy in the world."

"Isn't he, though?" Colette couldn't help but gush over him. Her happiness had overflowed the past week, tempered only by Juliette's absence.

"You will be married with a baby of your own soon enough, Lisette," Yvette foretold in a teasing manner.

"Don't be silly," Paulette countered disdainfully. "Lisette is not ready to marry Henry just yet!"

Irritated, Lisette took her eyes from the baby she held in her arms and cast a disapproving glance to her younger sisters. "Both of you, that's enough! Let's not discuss my future at the moment."

Colette was about to agree with Lisette's sentiment, when the door to the nursery flew open.

"*Oh, laissez-moi voir mon adorable petit-fils!*" Genevieve La Brecque Hamilton entered the room with her usual dramatic breathlessness, arriving at Devon House from Brighton to see her first grandchild. "Oh, let me see my beautiful grandson!"

"Mother! You're here!" Colette cried with excitement, surprised that she was actually happy to see her mother for the first time in a long while.

Colette had not seen her mother since Christmas and was eager for her to meet her new son. Leaving London and living near the sea had invigorated Genevieve Hamilton. Although she still used her gilt-handled cane when she walked, it was more for show than anything else. She looked younger than she had in years. The color had returned to her face and her eyes sparkled with life. Her gray hair was arranged fashionably around her face and she wore a stylish gown of deep violet. Colette almost did not recognize her.

"*Bonjour mes chéries. C'est formidable de vous voir.* Colette, my darling, I am sorry I was not here sooner." She hugged Colette tightly and after handing her cane to Yvette, she turned to Lisette. "*Lisette, donnes moi le bébé.* Give him to me."

Obediently but reluctantly, Lisette passed the sleeping infant to her mother.

"*Eh bien, bonjour mon petit. Je suis ta grand-mère.*

Il est parfait, simplement parfait. Je suis ta grand-mère. I am your grandmother." Genevieve crooned over him, smiling and nodding her head. She turned to her daughter. "*Il est tellement adorable.* He is perfect, just perfect. Finally we have a baby boy in the family! He favors his father, does he not? But I see you in him also, Colette. What did you name him?"

Paulette shook her blonde head in disgust. "They haven't decided yet!"

"Why not?" Genevieve cried in surprise. "The child must have a name!"

"Of course he is going to have a name!" Colette responded heatedly, then she hesitated. "Lucien and I just can't agree on what it is." The two of them had spent hours going over names together and finally narrowed it down to two, but they could not come to an agreement.

Her mother chuckled. "I would not have expected you to be so indecisive, Colette."

"Oh, it's not me," she protested. "It's Lucien who cannot make up his mind."

Genevieve, still holding the baby, moved to sit in a chair. "I would not have expected that of Lucien either."

"I think he looks like a Charles," Paulette offered from across the room.

"Nonsense!" Genevieve declared. "*On sait de qui il tient.* He looks exactly like a Phillip."

"Mother!" Colette cried in surprise. "That is just what I wanted to call him!" Only Lucien had a different name in mind. Godfrey. Colette detested that name.

"Then it is settled. He is Phillip Sinclair, the future Earl of Waverly and Marques of Stancliff," Genevieve announced as if the decision was hers to make.

"May I hold him now?" Yvette asked her mother.

Genevieve nodded indulgently and gave to the baby to Yvette. "He is too precious."

"How was your trip here, *Maman*?" Colette asked. Lucien had sent a carriage for her as soon as the baby was born.

"*Le voyage a été terrible. Je déteste voyager, c'est tellement ennuyeux.*" Genevieve waved her hand in the air. "It was terrible. I hate traveling. The roads are dreadful and too crowded, but then the trains are filthy. Either way traveling is terrible." She smiled as she settled back into the chair, glancing around at each one of them. "I am happy to see my girls again."

"We're happy to see you too, Mother," Lisette said sweetly.

Colette wondered what her mother had thought when not one of her daughters chose to move with her to Brighton. When Colette married Lucien, he generously offered his home to all of her sisters so they could remain in London and continue to oversee the family bookshop together. Naturally he had extended the offer to Genevieve as well, but having had her fill of city life she chose to move to a small cottage by the sea. Without her daughters. Which oddly enough, seemed to suit them all. Visits were made, of course. Genevieve would stay at Devon House for weeks at a time and they would visit her, although Lisette made the trip to Brighton more than any of them. Colette and Juliette had gone the least often.

Genevieve paused, her eyes searching the room. "Where is Juliette?"

Since that fateful night, Colette had avoided informing their mother of Juliette's disappearance for fear of upsetting her. But there was no avoiding it now. "Well, *Maman*," she began hesitantly, "Juliette is away on a trip."

Still holding the baby in her arms, Yvette blurted out,

"She ran away to New York without telling any of us that she was leaving!"

"*Mon dieu, mais que fait-elle donc à New York? Tu plaisantes j'espère.*" Genevieve cried, placing her hand over her heart. "You are jesting with me!"

Colette frowned at her youngest sister, while Paulette gave her a nudge with her elbow.

"Well, it's true!" Yvette pouted, wondering what she did that was so wrong.

"Yes, *Maman*. We would have preferred to tell you in a much gentler way." Colette shot Yvette another disapproving look. She had hoped not to tell her mother that Juliette had fled in the middle of the night and not while they were in her son's nursery, but Yvette ruined that plan. "But yes, it is the truth. Juliette hid on a ship sailing for New York."

"You were going to keep this a secret from me? How could you think I would not know?" Genevieve became more agitated. "*Vous alliez me cacher ce secret? Comment avez vous pu pensé que je ne l'apprendrais pas?*"

"We were not trying to keep it a secret from you, Mother," Colette began. "We simply did not wish to worry you."

"My God! Juliette always said she would go there, but I never thought . . . I never expected her to do this . . ." Genevieve began to breathe rapidly, her hand still over her heart. "*Comment a-t-elle pu me faire ça à moi? Je lui avais dit de ne pas y aller.*"

Without needing to be told, Lisette went to her mother's reticule and removed the small vial of smelling salts she always carried with her. She handed it to her mother.

"*Merci beaucoup, ma petite chérie.*" Genevieve smiled

wcakly at her daughter. "*J'ai très mal à la tête.* Now it is my head."

Colette sighed at her mother's usual dramatics. "Juliette is perfectly fine though. The captain of the ship is a friend of ours and he made sure she was out of harm's way. She arrived safely in New York and is staying with Christina Dunbar."

"When is she returning?" Genevieve asked, obviously having a difficult time absorbing the information about her second daughter.

"We are not sure," Paulette said quietly.

Yvette offered, "Lord Eddington sailed to New York after her. He's going to bring her back home."

Genevieve murmured in French. "Juliette has always been the headstrong one. She has a fire inside her. *Ma fille est égoiste, insouciante, c'est une tête brûlée. Juliette a toujours eu la tête dure.* But she is too foolish, too reckless and thinks only of herself. *Comment ai-je pu élever une fille aussi égoïste?* How did I raise such a selfish daughter? I forbade her to go there, did I not?"

"Yes, Mother, you did," Colette conceded.

Genevieve and Juliette had argued about it on many occasions. Perhaps if her mother had not forbidden her to go, Juliette would not have had to run off on her own, instead of arranging a proper trip for her with an appropriate chaperone.

"But she did not listen to me! Her mother. *Non, ne me parles pas d'elle. Comment a-t-elle pu briser ainsi le coeur de sa pauvre mère? Cette fille, je m'en lave les mains.* I wash my hands of her."

"Mother, please," Colette began. "You know how Juliette is—"

"No." Genevieve's anger began to increase. "No, do not speak of her to me. I will not discuss it. *Je n'en parlerais pas. Elle est l'instigatrice d'un terrible scandale. J'ai toujours su qu'elle en serait à l'origine.* She has brought shame upon our family by her thoughtless and selfish behavior."

Yvette's eyes grew larger as her mother's tirade continued.

∾21∾

Pretty Is as Pretty Does

Juliette had to make a decision. Soon.

As the carriage pulled up in front of Fleming Farm, the sun hung low in the sky. Jeffrey helped Juliette to the ground.

"I am serious, Juliette," Jeffrey said to her. "I must leave by Friday."

Harrison had remained unusually quiet and avoided her eyes.

"Yes, I understand," she murmured.

Juliette entered the house with the two of them following behind her. She made her way upstairs without saying a word to either of them. For the first time in her life, she did not know what to say to either man.

Once in her room, Lucy helped Juliette out of her traveling gown, while she retired to the cool, white tiled bathroom. After two days at the shore, she felt covered in sand and salt and she longed for a bath. She sank gratefully into the warm water.

Harrison and Jeffrey had taken her to the beach in Sea
Bright and down to see the pier in Long Branch, which
was the most fashionable city on the Jersey shore and
even President Grant had come up from Washington,
D.C., to vacation there. They had a lovely time together,
enjoying the bustling beach town and watching the horse
races at Monmouth Park.

Yet in the carriage on the way home from Long
Branch that afternoon, Jeffrey announced that he had
been away long enough and had important business to
attend to back home. He told her he was returning to
New York by the end of the week and then sailing back
to England as soon as he could. Which left Juliette in
something of a quandary. She couldn't very well stay on
at Fleming Farm without Jeffrey. Unusual as his chaperone status was, he provided a bit of respectability for
her. At the very least she would have to return to New
York with him. As much as she did not wish to return
to the Dunbars, where else could she go? The idea of returning to London filled her with even more apprehension. The thought of leaving Harrison filled her with
feelings and emotions she could not name. And did not
wish to face.

Juliette was enjoying her stay at Fleming Farm more
than she would have expected, in spite of the issues between her and Harrison. She loved the graceful and
modern house and the lush greenery surrounding it.
After spending her entire life on a city street above a
bookshop, she never thought she had any interest in
quaint country villages. But looking out a window and
seeing nothing but green grass and leafy trees was more
than a novelty to her. The pastoral scenery filled her with
a strange sense of peace.

While they were at the shore, she and Harrison had not

resumed their conversation about marriage and acted as if they had never argued that night at dinner. They were civil and polite, and with Jeffrey acting as chaperone they were never alone. Juliette could not help but sense an odd change in both him and Jeffrey but could not quite put her finger on what it was. They seemed to be in collusion about something. That did not bode well for her. She had a feeling they were finding a way to force her to return to London.

She needed to make a decision, but not tonight. Tonight Harrison was taking Jeffrey and her to party at a house by the river. As she stepped from her bath, Juliette wrapped herself in a thick towel, lost in her thoughts and pondering her options.

"Hello, Juliette."

Surprised, Juliette spun around to see Melissa sitting in the center of her canopy bed.

"Oh, Melissa!" Juliette cried. "You startled me."

"I knocked, but you didn't answer," she whispered. Her wide eyes stared at Juliette.

"That's because I was in the bath and didn't hear you," Juliette said.

"Oh." Melissa sat there, biting her nails.

"Where is Lucy?" Juliette glanced around for the maid who had laid out her gown for dinner.

Melissa shrugged. "She wasn't here when I came in."

"Well, was there something you wanted?" Juliette asked, wondering what Melissa was doing upstairs and without Annie looking out for her. She pulled the cord that rang for the maid, cursing inwardly that her fashionable wardrobe required that she have someone help her dress.

"No," Melissa whispered, shaking her head. It appeared as if her long blonde hair had been pulled into a neat bun at some point during the day, but now many tendrils had escaped and hung haphazardly around her pale face. The bandages had been removed from her wrists, but long scratches were still visible and poignant reminders of that terrible night.

Frustrated and wishing for a little privacy so she could get dressed, Juliette stood uncomfortably waiting for Melissa to take her leave.

"Why don't you wait for me in the drawing room, Melissa?" Juliette suggested in as cheery a voice as she could manage. "I'll join you there as soon as I'm dressed."

"I don't want to go to the drawing room," Melissa stated calmly.

An odd sense of panic welled within Juliette's chest. "Well, where would you like to go?"

Melissa regarded her as if weighing an important decision. "I wouldn't like to go anywhere."

Juliette stared at her, at a loss as what to do.

"I would like to show you something, Juliette." Melissa gave a little smile, looking like a child. "If you would come with me."

Not even able to imagine what Melissa would like to show her, Juliette hesitated. "I need to get dressed before I can go anywhere."

"Oh, of course," Melissa laughed. "I'll help you since Lucy left."

That was not quite what Juliette had in mind. "I rang for Lucy, but she's not here yet. Melissa, would you please find her for me? I'd prefer her help."

"Is that what you are wearing?" Melissa pointed to the raspberry taffeta gown Juliette had planned to wear to the outdoor party.

Juliette nodded.

"It's very pretty," Melissa said. "You have pretty clothes."

Her nervousness growing and feeling even more vulnerable in nothing but a towel, she simply said, "Thank you."

"If I get Lucy, will you promise to come with me? I have something special I want to show you." Melissa's green eyes stared at her intently.

"Yes," Juliette agreed readily. "If you get Lucy, I will come with you." Heavens! Would the woman never leave? Juliette stepped toward the bedroom door, hoping to lead Melissa in the right direction.

There was a quick rap on the door before Lucy stuck her head in. "Did you need me, Miss Hamilton?" The plump maid's eyes widened when she saw Melissa sitting on Juliette's bed.

"Yes, Lucy," Juliette said, giving the girl a pointed look. "Would you please take Miss Fleming to wait for me in the drawing room, and then come back to me?"

At Juliette's words, Melissa quickly hopped off the bed and made her way to the door. She leaned close to Juliette. "I won't be in the drawing room," she whispered in Juliette's ear. "I'll wait for you right outside. In the hallway."

Juliette said, "All right then."

Lucy stepped aside, giving Melissa a wide berth as she allowed her to pass through the doorway and shut the door quickly.

"Please help me dress quickly," she said to the panic-stricken maid, "and then please inform Annie Morgan that Miss Fleming is up here unsupervised. I'll stay with her."

"Yes, Miss Hamilton." Understanding the urgency of the situation, Lucy bustled about, helping Juliette into her corset and gown and arranging her hair as quickly as possible.

When she was dressed, Juliette entered the hallway
to find Melissa seated on the floor just outside her door,
waiting for her, while Lucy scurried off.

Melissa stood and took Juliette's hand in hers. "At last
you are ready! Come. I have something very special to
show you."

Juliette took a deep breath and let Melissa lead her.
They continued along the hallway until they came to a
back staircase. Slowly they descended the narrow
steps, which brought them to another hallway and a
part of the house that Juliette had not been in. Still
clutching Juliette's hand tightly in her own, Melissa
glanced back and smiled wide. She seemed as excited
as a child, and Juliette could not help but smile back
at her.

Wondering where they were headed, Juliette mentally
prepared herself for anything. Finally Melissa stopped in
front of a door and looked at her expectantly.

"This is my art studio," she said, beaming with pride.
"Harrison had it made for me. This is where I paint and
I want to show you my paintings."

"Oh, that sounds lovely," Juliette murmured in relief.

Melissa released her hand and opened the door. The
room was spacious and airy, with high ceilings and
tall windows. The last vestiges of the setting sun glinted
through the windows. Various sized easels, canvases, and
tables filled the room, along with the expected pots of
paints and brushes, while the distinctive smell of oil paint
filled the air.

Juliette's eyes were immediately drawn to a large
canvas, which clearly depicted a replication of the
grounds of Fleming Farm. The detail in the architecture
of the house and landscaping was painstaking and quite
impressive. That Melissa had captured the many and

subtle shades and tones of green surprised her. All the paintings were beautiful, as if they had been painted by a professional artist. There must have been hundreds of canvases filled with seasonal landscapes and flowers and sunsets on the river. Not an art connoisseur by any means, yet Juliette could not deny that Melissa definitely possessed a rare talent.

Stunned, Juliette smiled in delight. "Oh, Melissa. I had no idea you could paint. These are so beautiful!"

"Do you truly think so?" Her jade green eyes pleaded with hers.

"Yes, I do think so," she said. Juliette continued to glance around at the staggering array of remarkable paintings in the studio. "You are quite talented."

"I'm so glad you like them." Melissa gave her a shy smile. "I wanted you to like them."

"Of course I like them. Anybody with eyes in their head could not help but like them. Have you taken lessons?"

"No." Melissa shook her head. "No. I just paint."

Impressed more than she could say, Juliette wandered about the studio, looking at the paintings resplendent with vibrant colors and realistic details. She had never seen anything like them. It amazed her that such a troubled person could create works of such stunning beauty. Juliette blinked back tears. Harrison had allowed his sister to live in this beautiful house, in this scenic and tranquil environment with people to care for her, and to have this incredible creative outlet, instead of placing her in an asylum, as the best doctors in the world advised him to do. She did not know what to think.

"Come over here, Juliette!" Melissa called to her,

waving from behind a tall easel. "This is what I wanted you to see."

Juliette made her way through more easels and paintings to reach Melissa.

"Please tell me that you like it," Melissa whispered breathlessly. "You inspired me to paint this."

Juliette stared in utter disbelief at the canvas to which Melissa pointed. This was not a lush landscape, or a cloud-filled sky, or a deer in the woods. Melissa had painted a woman seated in a rocking chair in a library. The woman wore a pale peach muslin dress. She had blue eyes and dark hair. Melissa had painted Juliette, as she had been the afternoon they first met.

"I've never painted a person before," she explained tremulously, "so I don't know if it is even any good."

Juliette could not speak, too filled with strange emotions to utter a single word.

"Do you like it?" Melissa asked in an insistence.

Slowly Juliette nodded. It *was* a beautiful painting. The colors, the light, the pose. And that she had painted it in such a short time and from nothing but a brief memory. It was quite extraordinary. That she could not deny. It was the subject of the painting that caused a slight feeling of trepidation to wash through her.

"There you are, Melissa!" Harrison entered the studio, his expression one of relief seeing the two of them together. He had obviously been alerted and searching for his sister.

Juliette met Harrison's eyes over the many easels as he made his way toward them. Juliette could not speak.

"Oh, Harrison!" Melissa cried with excitement. "Come see what I painted while all of you were away at the beach."

Harrison's expression changed from one of relief to

one of complete surprise as he came to stand beside them and saw Melissa's painting of Juliette.

"Well," Melissa urged. "What do you think of it?"

Harrison glanced nervously between the two women, his gaze resting on Juliette. "I think it's quite beautiful. It's an incredible likeness."

"I wanted to paint Juliette because she has been so nice to me," Melissa explained, her eyes darting wildly between Juliette and Harrison.

"Did you sit for her?" Harrison asked Juliette, his brows drawn together in puzzlement.

Silent, Juliette shook her head. She certainly had not posed for this portrait.

"Melissa has never painted portraits before, have you, Melissa?" he questioned his sister.

"This is my first one," she said, beaming with pride.

With his voice full of awe he asked, "And you did this from memory?"

"Yes," Melissa nodded enthusiastically.

Harrison stared at the painting. "The likeness and detail are amazing. You have captured Juliette's spirit in her eyes."

Melissa asked, "Do you like it, Harrison?"

"Yes, of course I like it," he said. "It's a beautiful painting."

"Good," she squealed, clapping her hands together, "because it's your birthday present!"

"My birthday present?" Harrison echoed.

Juliette had known that Harrison's birthday was coming up, since he mentioned it to her on the *Sea Minx*. She had purchased a gift for him at a little shop in Long Branch the day before.

"Tomorrow is July third, isn't it?" Melissa laughed excitedly.

"Well, yes," he murmured, obviously uncomfortable.

"I was waiting to give it to you tomorrow, but since you've seen it already I'll just give it to you a little early! Happy birthday, Harrison!" She threw her arms around him.

"Thank you, Melissa," he said, avoiding Juliette's eyes, and giving his sister a hug.

Juliette felt her face grow warm. Melissa had made an extremely flattering painting of her to give her brother as a gift for his birthday. She suddenly wanted to leave the room.

Melissa turned to her. "Juliette?"

"Yes?"

"Are you happy that I painted your picture for Harrison?" Melissa asked, her eyes eagerly searching hers.

Unsure how she felt about it, Juliette said, "I am honored that you find me an interesting enough subject to paint. Thank you."

"You're welcome." Melissa turned her attention back to her brother. "You can hang it in your study, Harrison. It will look lovely in there, once we have it properly framed, of course."

"Of course," Harrison mumbled, finally looking at Juliette.

Did he agree to hang a portrait of Juliette in his office just to please his sister? Or did he want the picture for another reason, Juliette wondered.

"Well, I must go and let Annie know that I am fine and haven't thrown myself off the roof or anything like that!" Melissa giggled and smiled at both of them, gave a little wave with her hand and walked to the door of the studio.

Without saying a word, Harrison and Juliette followed Melissa from the room. Annie met them in the hallway, her face pinched into a disapproving frown.

"Melissa, you were supposed to be taking a nap," Annie scolded. "I looked everywhere for you."

"I'm fine, Annie." Melissa turned and winked at Juliette, before moving to Annie's side. "I'm coming with you right this moment."

The two women continued down the corridor, leaving Harrison and Juliette alone.

"Your sister is a very talented artist," Juliette murmured.

Harrison shook his head slightly and smiled at her. "I had no idea just how talented until I saw that painting of you."

"It's sad that she is the way she is," Juliette said quietly, taking a step forward.

Harrison began to walk beside her. "Yes, it is."

Slowly they made their way to the front hall.

"Thank you again for being kind to her. She has taken quite a liking to you."

Although being with Harrison's sister filled her with a little anxiety, she said, "You're welcome."

"Have you decided to go back to London with Jeffrey?"

His question caught her by surprise. She looked up into Harrison's silver-gray eyes and unable to bear the intensity in them, she glanced away. "I shall return to New York with him, but I have not decided about London yet."

"Either way, you will be leaving Fleming Farm by the end of the week."

"Yes," she said, stating the obvious. The two of them were giving her no option but to go home.

An awkward silence settled between them and her stomach flipped.

"What will you do in New York?"

"I am not entirely sure yet." She turned to go out the

front door where a carriage was waiting to take them to the river party. His voice stopped her.

"I shall miss having you here."

Harrison's words and the meaning within them touched her, but Juliette did not look back at him, afraid she would start crying. She continued out the door.

∾ 22 ∾

Fireworks

"Captain Fleming?" Mrs. Hannah Howard tapped on Harrison's sleeve to gain his attention. "Thank you for coming to our party on such short notice."

"Thank you for inviting me and my houseguests as well," he said.

Harrison barely knew the people who were hosting the river party, but they were in effect his neighbors, so he had accepted Mr. and Mrs. Howard's friendly invitation to join them for a night of frivolity. Their sprawling house over-looked the Navesink River and their elegant lawn was lit with hundred of candles and luminaria. A bonfire was burning on the shore of the river and an orchestra played on the veranda. Their many guests milled about the grounds, dancing to the music or choosing delicious morsels from the numerous tables laden with platters of food.

Jeffrey was eagerly talking to a businessman from New York, while Juliette was engaged in a lively conversation with a young couple from town. Harrison had not taken his eyes off Juliette all evening. He had to find some way to keep her from leaving with Jeffrey on Friday. He had a feeling that once she returned to New York, she would inevitably return to London and he would never see her again. If he were completely honest with himself, he did not want such a thing to happen. If only Juliette would be sensible and just marry him, there wouldn't be a problem.

But she was entirely too stubborn.

How do you get a woman to marry you, when she does not wish to be married? Harrison had struggled to find an answer to that question for days. He knew forcing the issue with her would be an irrevocable mistake. A woman like Juliette could not be pressured into doing something she didn't wish to do. He knew that much at least.

Although Jeffrey's idea to trick her into marrying him had some merit, it was a risky bit of business. They had discussed a few strategies at great length that night on the patio and they had the makings of a rough plan in place. But it could prove disastrous if it did not work the way they wanted it to.

Meanwhile, Harrison had only a few days before Jeffrey left with her in which to change Juliette's mind about marrying him. He could just put the plan into effect tonight and be done with it. Juliette would be furious but eventually she would calm down and understand that it had been for the best. Still, he hesitated.

He had come to the conclusion that marriage to Juliette might be his responsibility, but it might be more than that. Even if he could not totally admit that to himself at this point. Aside from being beautiful and desirable, Juliette was intelligent, fearless, caring, thoughtful, and spirited. He loved that she was not afraid to try new things. He loved her sense of independence, even though it frustrated him when it concerned marriage. Life with Juliette Hamilton as his wife would never be dull.

"You are very welcome," Mrs. Howard gushed. "Are your English friends having a nice time here in America?"

Harrison forced himself to focus on the woman before him and managed to nod at her. "Yes, I believe so."

"That's wonderful. We're going to set off the fireworks display shortly. We're celebrating the Fourth of July a little early, because my husband has to leave for Boston tomorrow. So we decided to have them set off tonight."

Harrison smiled blandly. "I'm looking forward to it."

Mrs. Howard moved on to mingle with her other guests while Harrison continued to keep his eyes on Juliette. The couple she had been talking to drifted off into the throng of guests meandering the lawns. She must have sensed his gaze, because she looked up at him and smiled. Her engaging smile did strange things to him. Their eyes locked on to each other. He had to go to her.

Slowly Harrison walked through the crowd, his eyes fixed on Juliette.

"How are you enjoying the evening?" he asked when he reached her side.

"I am having a delightful time, thank you," she said, breaking their eye contact with a flutter of her long lashes. "Everyone is so friendly here."

"Would you care to walk down to the river with me?"

"That sounds like a wonderful idea." She accepted the arm he extended to her and they carefully made their way through the crowded lawn and down to the sandy beach.

"It's a lovely night. Look at all the stars," Juliette said as she looked up at the dark sky, alight with thousands of glittering stars and a glowing moon on its way to being full once again. Thick clouds were gradually moving in, however.

"Yes, it's a lovely night," he agreed, but he was not looking at the sky. He kept his eyes on Juliette. Her hand still held his arm as they traversed along the damp sand of the river's edge. She lost her footing for an instant but he righted her before she tumbled.

"Thank you," she murmured.

In silence, they continued walking further from the Howard's party until they reached a secluded alcove near an embankment lined heavily with thick shrubbery. Harrison removed his jacket and laid it upon the grass so Juliette could sit there. He sat beside her.

The familiar scent of jasmine wafted over him. Since they were on the *Sea Minx* Juliette's signature scent always had the power to arouse him and this time was no different. He steeled himself to think about something other than making love to her.

"Do you truly believe that Melissa's paintings have merit?" he managed to ask.

She turned to him, the expression on her beautiful face full of wonder. "Oh, yes! Her paintings are simply gorgeous! She captures the smallest details with such care. The landscapes are quite realistic. They make you feel as if you are there. They transport you."

Filled with pride over Melissa's ability, Harrison smiled. "You think she is talented then?"

"Absolutely," Juliette affirmed. "Your sister has a rare gift."

"I think her portrait of you is extraordinary."

"I must admit that I was surprised she chose to paint me," Juliette murmured softly.

"I'm not surprised at all by it. You have been very kind to her." Harrison explained, "Melissa hasn't seen our sister Isabella in years and she doesn't have any friends, except for Annie, and Annie is not really a friend. It's no wonder she has fixated on you."

"Fixated is a good description." Juliette hesitated before adding, "To be honest, Harrison, I still feel a little wary with Melissa."

"I know you do and that's what is so remarkable about you. Most people would avoid her or talk down to her, but you are still kind to Melissa and you treat her as if she were perfectly normal. Melissa has not painted in months, but since you've been here she has painted more than ever. It's good for her."

"I'm not sure that has anything to do with me."

"No, I think it does," Harrison insisted.

"Have you ever thought about letting her live a less isolated existence?"

"Of course," he exclaimed. "But the fact is, her unpredictable behavior prevents that from being a possibility. I cannot risk her hurting herself, let alone anyone else."

Juliette nodded in understanding. "Perhaps you could ask her what she would like? What about allowing her to have a friend or two her own age?"

He thought for a moment. "I've had Annie looking after Melissa for years now, but I never thought about getting a companion nearer to her own age. Because she has been unstable and her behavior unpredictable and at times violent, I've kept her fairly sheltered. She stays at home and only travels when absolutely necessary. I never take her to parties, like this one, or have guests over. Perhaps that was a mistake. Maybe she does need to have friends and she would be better off if she could be around people more often."

"Perhaps," she said thoughtfully. "Did the doctors ever suggest that you do that?"

"Not one of them ever suggested anything that humane,"

he said bitterly, before releasing a weary sigh. "But I stopped heeding their advice long ago."

"Doctors don't know everything there is to know," Juliette ventured.

"I even met a doctor who suggested we try changing her diet." He shook his head in disbelief. "He was under the impression that the food she ate caused her mood swings."

"She is most fortunate to have you to care for her. Aside from being utterly amazed by her talent, I am most impressed by how well you have provided for your sister, Harrison. Not many brothers would go to such lengths."

"Thank you," he whispered, deeply touched that Juliette recognized how hard he worked to make some kind of normal life for his sister.

Suddenly the quiet night air was ripped apart by the sudden blast of fireworks bursting in the dark sky. Brilliant splashes of scarlet and gold flashed across the sky, their reflections glittering vividly on the inky river. Wild shouts of excitement and applause could be heard from the lawn. Just as the sparkles receded into the clouds of smoke hugging the water, another bright explosion of color lit the sky.

"Oh, it's beautiful!" Juliette cried out, her voice filled with wonder. "I've never been so close to fireworks before!"

Harrison had no desire to watch the fireworks display while Juliette was seated so near to him. With her head tilted toward the heavens and her lips parted in wonder as she watched the colorful streams of light wash across the velvet sky, she looked more beautiful than he had ever seen her. Her angelic face cast in reflections of gold, red, and silver left him breathless and the temptation to touch her overwhelmed him.

Unable to resist kissing her, Harrison leaned in and placed his mouth over hers. Juliette's instant and welcome response thrilled him. His arms slid around her shoulders, pulling her close to him, as he continued to kiss her.

Amidst the darkness of their secluded spot, well hidden by the thick shrubbery, and with everyone's attention on the exploding fireworks, no one at Mrs. Hannah Howard's party noticed Harrison and Juliette with their arms around each other and kissing passionately on the bank of the river.

While the shimmering colors flashed above the water and the thunder of the explosions echoed around them, Harrison could only focus on Juliette and the exquisite taste of her lips. Their tongues entwined and plundered each other's mouths, taking as much as they could. His hands stroked her back, pressing her closer to him. Her body seemed to melt into his, and his heart skipped a beat or two. The heat between them intensified. He lost himself in kissing her, forgetting where they were and who was there, as his hands impulsively caressed her face, her neck, and moved lower to cup her breasts. She moaned softly as he kneaded her through the silky fabric of her red gown. He skimmed his hand to the edge of the neckline and slipped beneath, touching her bare breast. Wishing he could tear the gown from her body, he lowered his head and kissed her breast. She arched her back, and he shook with desire as Juliette's fingers massaged the back of his neck, stroking his hair.

As another burst of golden sparks exploded overhead, Harrison roughly lifted her and drew her across his lap. One hand raised the hem of her gown and layers of undergarments, and slowly slid up the length of her calf, over her knee and then up her thigh. His fingers rubbed the sleek stockings and toyed with the garters that held them in place, until he caressed the exposed, soft skin of her upper thigh. Little by little his fingers inched closer to the heated area between her legs, but did not actually touch her. He just moved his hand achingly close to the damp curls, brushing her, teasing her. With her breath coming in frantic gasps Juliette began to squirm impatiently in his lap, exciting his own body beyond rock hardness.

"Harrison," she pleaded in his ear, "please . . ." Her warm breath sent a shiver through him. "Please . . ."

He kissed her warm mouth, ignoring her plea, and continued to tantalize her with his fingers as he lightly caressed her. He knew exactly what she wanted. "Please what?"

"Please—" Juliette could barely speak. She took a deep breath and her voice trembled as she spoke. "Please do *something*."

"Do something?" he whispered, his voice thick with a burning need of his own. His teasing of her had aroused him as much as it had her. It was a dangerous game he played with her. If he didn't do something soon, they both would expire from sheer frustration.

"Yes." She buried her head against his neck, placing hot little kisses there. "Do *something*, please," she murmured breathlessly. "I can't . . . I can't take this anymore."

"Do you want me to do something . . . Something right here?" He moved his hand beneath the layers of underclothing and slid one finger into the heated slickness between her thighs.

Juliette gasped and almost collapsed against him, her body trembling. "Har–rah–son–n," she breathed, his name hissing from her mouth.

"Anyone could walk by, Juliette, and see you like

this." He whispered low as he continued to stroke her with his hand beneath her gown. "There are so many people here. Someone could be strolling along the beach and see us . . . you . . . sitting on my lap, kissing me, with my hand up your dress. What would they think to find us like this?"

"I . . . I don't—"

"Or don't you care?"

She did not answer him, so overcome with desire was she, and Harrison did not expect her to. He knew she had already surrendered to him. She closed her eyes and clung to him for support.

"My Juliette doesn't care what people think at all, does she?" Harrison's heart thudded in his chest as she melted into him. "That's it. Let it happen, my love."

His hushed and seductive words drifted around them as he continued to whisper in her ear, coaxing her, arousing her. Meanwhile his hand kept rubbing her, bringing her closer and closer to what she craved. The heat between them increased as he held her close to his heart. She pressed herself against the palm of his hand, her hips grinding against his erection.

The deep rumblings and showers of colorful embers rained around them, drowning out Harrison's low voice and Juliette's impassioned cries as she found her release.

So great was his need to possess her, it took every ounce of the willpower and self-control he possessed to not roll her off his lap, lay her on her back, shove her gown up to her waist, and bury himself deep within her, taking her right there in the grass as he wanted to. Instead, he kept his shaking arms tight around her, unable to move until her breathing returned to a somewhat normal pace and he had calmed his own body. They remained that way, recovering, until it dawned on him that the fireworks display had finally ended. Clouds of smoke drifted over the still waters of the river and typical night sounds could be heard again—voices and laughter from the party, the faint strains of the orchestra playing, crickets chirping in the bushes surrounding them.

Harrison gently smoothed Juliette's gown back into place. He pressed a gentle kiss to her warm cheek and eased her from his lap. He stood up, his legs shakier than he thought. She glanced up at him awkwardly, and he sensed her embarrassment. With his eyes fixed on hers, he held out his hand to her.

"Oh, we're not done yet, my beauty."

Her eyes widened as she stared at him, silent.

"We're going home right now."

She nodded and took his hand. He pulled her to her feet and into his arms once again.

"And into my bed," he whispered in her ear before he released her. He was finished playing games.

They walked back to the Howards' house without speaking, for there was no need for words between them. They gave their regards to Mr. and Mrs. Howard, while searching for Jeffrey to tell him that they were leaving, but could not find him. Eager to be on their way, they waited on the front porch for Harrison's carriage to be brought around. They gazed at each other, the tension between them palpable. Harrison fought the desire to touch her, to kiss her, to pull her into his arms. Their little rendezvous on the river had left him aching for her.

Finally Jeffrey strolled out on the porch, a drink in one hand and a wicked smile on his face. "If you don't mind, I'm going to stay here a little longer and enjoy the festivities." He tilted his head and gave them an assessing glance. "You two go on ahead without me."

Harrison grinned knowingly at him. "I'll send my driver back with the carriage to wait for you."

"Much appreciated." As Harrison helped Juliette into the carriage, Jeffrey asked, "Did you enjoy the fireworks, Juliette?"

Juliette, completely flustered and her face suffused with color, did not reply.

"Yes, she enjoyed the display immensely. She said they were the best she has ever seen," Harrison answered for her. "Didn't you, Juliette?"

Her eyes widened at his reference and she quickly averted her eyes. Loving the fact that he had set her off balance, he winked at her.

Harrison turned back to Jeffrey. "Have a good time."

"Oh, I will!" Jeffrey held up his glass in a silent toast to them and returned to the party.

Harrison settled himself on the seat beside her as the landau carriage lurched forward and the horses headed down the circular drive. Juliette placed her hand in his, giving him a shy smile. Not caring what his driver thought, Harrison placed his arm around Juliette. She rested her head on his shoulder and he stroked her wrist with his fingers.

After the short ride back to Fleming Farm, Harrison took Juliette's arm and hurried her up the front steps and into the house. He sent her upstairs first, the young maid Lucy following her to her room to help her change for the night. Harrison waited in the parlor a few minutes before retiring to his bedroom. There he removed his jacket, cravat, and braces and splashed cool water on his face. He paced the length of the room, ticking off the minutes until a decent interval had passed. With his ear at the door, he listened for the sound of Lucy leaving Juliette's room. As soon as he heard her footsteps, he would head down the hallway and finally make love to Juliette without any regrets, for he knew he would marry her. He had had enough of their little games and he intended to let her know it.

A soft rapping on his door startled him. Carefully he opened the door.

Juliette stood before him in nothing but a white, lawn nightgown, her long dark hair hanging loosely around her. The thin material of her nightgown hugged her curves in a most provocative manner, but it was her eyes that undid him. Her blue eyes, dark and heavy with desire, looked up at him with such longing and passion, he sucked in his breath. Fearing that someone would see her, he reached out his arm and quickly pulled her in his room, closing the door behind her.

"You took too long," she said in a throaty whisper, before he could find his own voice to utter a word in response. She stepped on her tiptoes and wrapped her arms around him.

He intended to go to her bedroom, but she had come to him instead. *She* had come to *him*. Juliette wanted him. His heart flipped over in his chest.

"Good God, Juliette," he groaned before he crushed his mouth over hers in a searing, possessive kiss and backed her up against the door.

She kissed him back fervently, her warm tongue slipping into his mouth. His hands ran the length of her, reveling in the feel of her naked body beneath the soft cotton. Her body was not bound in a corset, layers of undergarments and a gown any longer but free for him to touch. And touch her he did. He slid his hand beneath the nightgown and up one silky thigh. To his surprise and utter delight, Juliette raised her leg and wrapped it around his waist. He then lifted her off the floor and she flung her other leg around him, her nightgown hitching up along her thighs.

He broke off from kissing her to look at her face. She gave him a look full of yearning before she slid her hands down to the front of his shirt. One by one she began to undo the buttons. When the last one was unfastened, she pushed the fabric aside and ran her hands across his upper chest. As he held her, she lowered her head and kissed his chest, her lips hot on his skin.

Unable to bear her assault on his senses while standing, just as he had done aboard the *Sea Minx*, Harrison carried her to his bed. Slowly he allowed her to slide from her perch around his waist until she was on the bed. Keeling on the mattress before him as he stood on the floor, Juliette tugged the hem of his shirt. He raised his arms as she lifted the shirt over his head and tossed it to the floor. Now that he was bare-chested, Juliette focused her attention on the buttons of his pin-stripped trousers. Impressed with her determination to divest him of his clothing, he allowed her the freedom to undress him while he watched in fascination.

When her skilled fingers made short work of the buttons, with one swift movement she pushed down his pants. He gamely assisted her by stepping out of his trousers. Once again he stood before her as her nimble fingers caressed the taut planes of his abdomen to the waistband of his underclothes. With deliberate slowness she untied the strings and little by little slid the garment down his legs, revealing the rock-hard state of his arousal.

With her black hair spilling around her, she lowered her head to him. Glancing up at him through her eyelashes, she smiled before brushing the length of him with her soft lips, her heated breath sending shivers of bliss throughout his body. Harrison groaned with pleasure when her warm tongue flicked across the tip of his shaft, and he nearly exploded when she took him in her mouth. He brought his hands to her hair while she caressed him with her mouth. He let her have her way with him for sometime, before he had to stop her.

Pulling her up toward him, he wrapped his arms around her and kissed her with an unfulfilled hunger. In one smooth and swift movement he lifted her cotton nightgown up and over her head and sent it flying to join his clothes on the floor. She knelt on the bed, naked before him, her supple body begging to be touched. He eased them both down onto the bed and covered her naked body with his. He kissed her face, her throat, her neck, her chest, her breasts. His tongue burned a path down her satiny skin until he took her nipples in his mouth, making her gasp. He kissed his way back up to her mouth.

Their kisses became more intense, more heated, until Juliette broke free. She wriggled from beneath him and rolled over, straddling him. With her intense eyes set on his, she slowly lowered herself over him. He held his breath, watching as she took him inside of her. She looked so erotic, so beautiful, and so confident; he could not take his eyes off her. No longer the shy virgin she had been on the *Sea Minx*, Juliette had become more certain of what would please him and, more importantly, what would please her in bed. The sight of Juliette, uninhibited, with her silky, dark hair, her creamy white skin, and her full, round breasts, on top of him aroused him beyond belief. He reached out and placed his hands around her slender waist, guiding her as she began to move her hips, raising and lowering herself on him. Closing her eyes, she arched her back and shifted herself to seek her own pleasure and her movements became more rhythmic, more forceful.

God, but she was beautiful.

The intense sensations she caused within not just his body but also his heart, stunned him. Never before had he felt such a strong desire for one woman. It was more powerful than desire though, but he couldn't describe it.

As Juliette continued to seductively shift her hips, her movements caused untold waves of ecstasy within him. She moved faster, her eyes closed in concentration, a half-smile on her face, losing herself in feelings. He held her. Moved with her. Wanting to give her everything she needed, everything she wished for. Then her whole body tensed and he felt her climax around him even before she let out a long, rapturous cry.

When he could bear no more of this exquisite torture, he rolled her onto her back and thrust deep within her. His need to possess her fully drove him wild. Juliette cried out again and wrapped her legs around his waist. Her fingers pressed into his back and she clung to him, as he moved within her. She lifted her hips to meet his thrusts as he drove into her over and over, deeper and deeper, until he was sweaty and out of breath with exertion. Finally he called out her name and collapsed beside her, panting and too replete to move.

They lay there together for some time. Juliette snuggled next to him and Harrison wrapped his arms around her, his heart beat gradually calming to a slower pace. With Juliette in his arms, he felt a peace and contentment he had never known and it occurred to him that he wanted her with him this way always. He closed his eyes and thought, *I love her.*

While blissfully wrapped around each other, sleep overtook them both.

∽ 23 ∽

A Soft Summer Rain

Juliette awoke to find Harrison's arm around her waist and for a moment she thought she was back on the *Sea Minx*. The dim, predawn light filtered in through the long windows, confusing her as to her surroundings. It took her a moment before all of the events of the night before came rushing back to her memory. And that memory almost made her blush. *Good heavens!* Last night had been blissful, from the magical interlude during the fireworks display to their passionate lovemaking in his bed.

Her behavior last night had shocked even herself.

She had acted as a wanton or a strumpet would have done with him. Not that she hadn't enjoyed every second of it, but still it was certainly not the way she would be expected to behave. It was as if Harrison had cast some sort of spell over her. With just a smoldering look or a sensuous touch, he could extinguish all reason from her mind, and she would do anything he asked of her. What Juliette allowed him to do to her on the bank of the river was outright disgraceful. Even for her. Yet she could no more have fought against him than she could stop the rain from falling. She felt her face grow warm at the memory of sitting on his lap, yet part of her loved that he could make her feel that way.

And how very exciting it had been!

It surprised her that she had missed him so much. Missed sleeping in his arms at night. Missed kissing him. Missed spending the day with him. She had not realized how much the time they spent together on the *Sea Minx* had meant to her.

She stared at the man who lay naked next to her. This man who had this extraordinary effect upon her. She admired the masculine lines of his face. A strong chin, a straight nose, a full mouth. The features in and of themselves were unremarkable, but somehow when put together they created a classic handsomeness. Harrison was a handsome man.

With his eyes closed and deep in sleep, his face was relaxed, almost innocent looking. She could see the image of him as the little blond boy he had once been, trying so hard to take care of his family. She gently reached out her hand and smoothed down some wayward strands of his golden hair, her fingers hesitantly brushing his stubble-lined cheek. He pulled at her heart in a way that no one ever had and it confounded her.

Did she love him? She was afraid that she just might.

Harrison had accomplished so much in his life and everything he did amazed her. Especially how he treated Melissa. If it were not for him, Melissa would have been placed in one of those wretched asylums by now. His devotion and dedication to his sister touched her. She wondered what she would do if one of her sisters had the same type of ailment that afflicted Melissa. Would she care for Yvette, Paulette, Lisette, or Colette in the same manner? Of course she would, for she could not bear to think of any of them in an asylum. She loved the fact that Harrison loved his sister and refused to send her from her home.

Suddenly his eyes opened and Juliette found herself staring into Harrison's sleepy gray eyes and her heart skipped a beat.

"Good morning, beautiful." He beamed at her. "What are you doing awake so early?"

"I think I am too excited to sleep."

He held her tighter. "That is excellent news."

She smiled and placed a sweet kiss on his cheek. "Happy birthday, Harrison."

"You remembered."

"Of course I did." She explained, "Obviously I don't have it with me at the moment, but I do have a present for you."

"I think you already gave me a present." An unabashed grin lit his face, making him seem even more boyish.

"Yes." She smiled in agreement, thinking of last night. "Perhaps I did, at that."

He rolled on top of her and kissed her deeply, causing a thrill to race through her. Surrendering to his muscled arms and endless kisses, she reached her hands around his neck, her fingers splaying into his blond hair. *Good heavens, it was going to happen again!* She drew him closer to her and kissed him back. Giving in to the desires that flooded her, she let Harrison make love to her once more.

Afterward he gathered her close, as thunder rumbled in the distance. The cloudy morning cast the room in its gray dimness, but Juliette rested safely in Harrison's strong arms. She breathed deeply beside him, her legs still intertwined intimately with his. She could stay this way all day, but knew she must go soon.

She kissed his chest and whispered, "I think the rain might ruin our picnic plans today."

"We can picnic in my bed." He gazed at her suggestively.

Shaking her head with a laugh, she made a move to get up. "I should get back to my room before someone finds me here."

He drew her back into the pillows. "Stay one more minute."

"All right," she acquiesced readily. "But only because it's your birthday."

Harrison kissed her for that entire minute.

"Stay with me," he murmured seductively in her ear.

"No," she whispered with a slight shake of her head. "It would be terribly scandalous if I were caught here."

He gave her a thoughtful glance, but released her.

Feeling dreamy and satiated, Juliette left his bed with great reluctance and found her nightgown amidst his discarded clothing on the floor. She slipped the garment over her head, knowing that Harrison was watching her every move. Once she was covered, she turned to face him. He lay on the pillows with his hands behind his head, grinning at her.

"I shall see you later," she said.

"You certainly will," he promised.

Unable to resist, she ran back and surprised him with another kiss, before hurrying to the door.

Her heart pounding, she glanced down the hallway, and seeing that it was clear, she carefully made her way back to her room. Her bare feet padded quietly along the carpeted corridor. The house was beginning to come awake as sounds of morning activity downstairs could be heard. She offered a silent prayer that she would not run into Jeffrey. Idly wondering who had diverted him at the party and what time *he* finally came home if he came home at all, she opened the door to her bedroom with great care.

Slipping inside, she softly closed the door behind her. She would crawl back into bed and sleep for a little longer. Then she would bathe and dress for the picnic she had planned for Harrison's birthday. If it didn't rain that was.

"Good morning, Juliette."

Almost jumping out of her skin at the sound of a feminine voice, Juliette gave a little shriek. Then she noticed Melissa sitting cross-legged in a pink silk robe on the middle of her neatly made bed, yet again.

"Oh, Melissa, you frightened me!" Juliette exclaimed when she could find her voice. With her hand over her heart, she stared at the woman who once again had entered her bedchamber uninvited and most unexpectedly. "What are you doing in here?" she demanded rather crossly.

Melissa answered with a decided calmness. "I wished to talk to you."

Annoyed and embarrassed to be caught sneaking back into her own bedroom, Juliette snapped at Melissa. "It is rather early in the morning for a visit, don't you agree?"

Melissa eyed her nightgown suspiciously and Juliette felt her cheeks redden. "You are up and about already, so I do not think it is too early."

"Well, I consider this time of the morning entirely too early for a visit. Why don't we do something together later this afternoon?" Juliette suggested nervously.

"Where have you been all night?" Melissa asked,

twisting a long strand of her blond hair around her forefinger. "You haven't slept in your bed."

Oh good heavens! Juliette frantically searched her mind for an excuse to explain her whereabouts and her current state of undress. "I—I couldn't sleep last night. So I . . . I went downstairs to the library to get a book to read, and I fell asleep on the sofa there." That actually sounded almost plausible.

"No, you didn't." Melissa shook her head slowly and gave her a sly smile. "You are lying to me."

Juliette felt her stomach tighten and her mouth went dry. She had no words.

Then it seemed as if the very heavens themselves opened. Driving torrents of rain fell to the ground. The intense pounding noise of the violent deluge upon the house and the trees outside echoed in the strained silence between the two women.

Melissa said clearly, "You spent the night in my brother's room, didn't you?"

She knew, she knew, she knew. Somehow Melissa knew. Shame and mortification ripped through Juliette's entire body. Not once had she been ashamed while she was with Harrison on the *Sea Minx,* nor did she regret for one instance doing anything she had done with him, including last night. But somehow standing in nothing but a thin, rumpled nightgown in front of his sister, Juliette suddenly felt like a common strumpet. What on earth could she say in her own defense? Nothing. Absolutely nothing. Harrison had just made love to her again that morning. She was guilty of . . . of . . . adultery? No. Fornication? Those words did not seem to fit her situation, but surely she was guilty of something quite wicked.

In any case, she wished to God that the floor would suddenly open and swallow her up. Facing Harrison's sister this way was utterly humiliating. Her cheeks burned and her hands shook. "Melissa, I can explain—" she began softly and then stopped. She had no defense, no excuse. She could not justify her behavior at all.

Still twirling her hair, Melissa said, "You don't have to explain anything to me. I know you spent the night in Harrison's bed."

Her humiliation and degradation now complete, Juliette stared in mute horror at Harrison's sister. *Why was she in her room?* How did she know exactly where Juliette had been? It was a big enough house and Juliette could have been practically anywhere. She could have been with Jeffrey for all Melissa knew. *So how did she know?* Melissa's eerie manner unnerved her.

Melissa knew that she spent the night with Harrison. *How?* Had she spied on them? *Heaven forbid!* Just what did Melissa intend to do with this information? What was Melissa doing in her room so early in the morning in the first place? And again, where was Annie Morgan, who was supposed to be keeping an eye on her charge?

"Don't worry, Juliette." Melissa gave her a sympathetic look. "I won't tell anyone what you did."

Juliette remained motionless. An intense wave of nausea swept over her as Melissa came toward her. She could think of nothing to say that would alleviate the situation. Juliette had been caught doing exactly what Melissa suspected her of doing. She could not deny or refute the truth.

Somehow when she had been on the *Sea Minx* sleeping in Harrison's bed had not seemed wrong. It had seemed completely natural and right. But now, hearing the words from his sister's mouth . . . Juliette wanted to crawl into a hole and never come out again. She wondered if she should go back to Harrison and let him know what happened.

A flicker of lightning lit the room before a terrific clap of thunder rent the air. The rain continued to pour down in torrents.

"Did their plan work?" Melissa asked amid clamor of the ensuing downpour.

Confused, Juliette could not follow Melissa's train of thought. She could not even catch her own breath. "What plan?"

"The plan that Harrison and his friend Jeffrey Eddington came up with to trick you."

Stunned by this bit of news, Juliette could barely choke out the words to question her. "What are you talking about?"

"I heard them talking the other night, Harrison and his friend. They were out on the patio."

A sickening feeling began to blossom in Juliette's stomach. Almost afraid to know any more she felt compelled to ask anyway, "What did they say?"

"They said a lot of things." Melissa thought for a moment. "But perhaps I shouldn't tell you after all."

Her legs shaking and unable to stand any longer, Juliette woodenly sat on a nearby blue, toile-covered chair. She took a deep breath to steady her trembling limbs. This was going to take a while. "I think it may be important for me to know what they said. Were they talking about me?"

"Yes." Melissa nodded. "They think that you should marry Harrison."

"Oh, do they now?" She just bet that Melissa heard an earful that night. Juliette would have loved to have listened in on that conversation between Harrison and Jeffrey. Imagine the pair of them deciding what was best for her!

"They don't understand you."

Juliette certainly believed that. Neither one of them understood her or her reasons for not wanting to get married. "What else did they say?"

Melissa tilted her head to the side. "That they should trick you into marrying Harrison before his friend Jeffrey leaves for London."

As the rain continued to fall, lightning flashed and thunder rumbled noisily overhead.

Blinking in disbelief, Juliette was stunned by the complete and utter stupidity of the two men. Harrison and Jeffrey must have been drinking that night. Quite a lot. "How are they planning to trick me, Melissa? Did they say?"

"Yes . . ," she admitted reluctantly with a frown. "But you won't like it."

Juliette's gut instinct was that Melissa was about to tell her was the truth and she definitely would not like it. "You're more than likely right, but please tell me anyway."

Melissa actually hesitated before revealing their plan. "Well, they thought if Harrison could get you in a compromising position and someone discovered the two of you together, then you would *have* to marry him."

Dear God.

Harrison and Jeffrey had not been jesting but were serious.

Last night!

Juliette began to tremble, recalling the party on the river the night before during the fireworks. Harrison had most definitely had her in a compromising position. Any of the guests from the party could have happened upon them, and apparently that was what Harrison had counted on. *Anyone could walk by, Juliette, and see you like this. Someone could be strolling along the beach and see us . . . you . . . sitting on my lap, kissing me, with my hand up your dress.* Harrison had whispered those very words in her ear. At the time she had thought their encounter was highly erotic, now she felt sick to her stomach. She felt manipulated and used.

Was Jeffrey supposed to find them together on the bank of the river? What had happened that their plan had not worked? And what of last night in Harrison's bedroom? Was Mrs. O'Neil or one of the servants supposed to walk in on them?

What she had believed was a magical and intimate moment between her and Harrison was nothing more than a stunt to publicly humiliate her so she would be forced into marrying him to save herself. How could he think that manipulating her into a marriage would work? Filled with a deep sense of betrayal and hurt, Juliette felt hot, stinging tears spill down her cheeks.

"I knew you wouldn't like it," Melissa said softly. She rose from the canopied bed and walked over to Juliette. "I wanted to tell you last night."

Wiping distractedly at her tears, Juliette looked up at Melissa. "What do you mean?"

"That's why I came to your room before you went out. I thought I should warn you."

"Why didn't you?" Had she had that little bit of information beforehand, Juliette certainly wouldn't have allowed Harrison to lead her away from the party to a secluded spot and do the things he had done to her. However lovely they had felt.

Melissa sat on the floor at Juliette's feet, her legs curled under her.

"I am not quite sure. I felt uncomfortable and I wasn't

sure if you would believe me. I ended up showing you my paintings instead."

Juliette stated woodenly, "I believe you."

She doubted that Melissa could concoct a story this involved on her own. Melissa definitely overheard Harrison and Jeffrey discussing how to manipulate her into doing what they wanted. Juliette's stomach clenched at the idea of them talking about her as if she had no feelings, no will of her own, no say in this matter that would alter her whole life.

"I waited for you to come home last night, but you went to Harrison's room before I could tell you. And so I waited here for you to come back. I wanted to know if their plan worked."

Juliette shook her head. "It didn't." At least not in the way that they had planned.

Melissa gave her a quizzical look. "Don't you want to marry my brother?"

Juliette stood up, her blood racing in outrage. "Melissa, if I ever choose to get married and allow a man to control my life, it will be because I made that decision. Not because I was forced into a marriage by a pair of misguided idiots."

Juliette was not sure who angered her more for coming up with such a contemptible plan, Harrison or Jeffrey. How could they both think so little of her? And to add to her outrage, she was upset with herself for how dangerously close she had come to allowing it to happen! She fell in with Harrison's plans all too easily. She had lost herself completely with Harrison last night. How humiliated she would have been had they been caught by Jeffrey! Or by anyone at that party! It was bad enough that Harrison's sister had discovered her skulking back from his room after an incredible night and morning of lovemaking.

With her mind spinning and her heart aching, she began pacing back and forth the length of the room. Good fortune had been on her side her twice last night, once at the river and once in Harrison's bedroom. Anyone could have caught them together in either situation and she would have been done for. But they had not. Why they had not been found out last night, made her pause. But it also worried her. Was he planning for another time? Now that she was aware of his scheming, she could not allow Harrison near her again.

She could not risk it.

Outside, the rain continued to fall, although the intensity had lessened and the rumblings of thunder drifted further away.

"I know . . . I know my brother takes good care of me, . . . but there are times . . . when . . . sometimes . . ." Melissa began hesitantly and then faltered.

Juliette stopped pacing and turned to look at Melissa, still seated on the floor in her pink nightgown. It suddenly struck her that Melissa never wore any color but pink. "There are times that what?" she prompted.

Melissa glanced up, her eyes filled with emotion. "There are times I wish I could do what I wanted. I know Harrison is looking out for me, but he makes all the decisions and he thinks he knows what is best, but . . ."

"But what?" Juliette asked.

"He never asks me what I want or what I think would be best for me."

Juliette moved to sit on the floor beside Melissa and she took her warm hand in hers. "What do you think would be best for you?"

Melissa's jade green eyes widened and she appeared

frightened. "Oh, I . . . I don't know. I just feel very frustrated."

"I can imagine how you must feel," Juliette offered in comfort, squeezing Melissa's hand.

"I don't have any friends."

"Yes, you do." Juliette smiled, her heart breaking at the earnestness in Melissa's voice. The woman was more alone than anyone she had ever met in her life. "I am your friend."

"You are?" Melissa's expression was a mixture of disbelief and gratitude.

Juliette confirmed with a smile. "Yes, I am."

They sat in silence for some time, as the patter of the rain faded away completely.

"Thank you for helping me, Melissa. You are a good friend."

Melissa grinned and squeezed Juliette's hand back. "What are you going to do?"

What was she going to do?

Her head was spinning but Juliette knew she had to do something. And very soon. One thing was certain. She was not going to wait around until Harrison and Jeffrey put their plan to trick her into effect. It was then another one of her ideas came to her.

"Melissa," she began, "can you please help me with something?"

~ 24 ~

For He's a Jolly Good Fellow

"Since it is Harrison's birthday, he wanted me to be a part of his birthday dinner," Melissa explained, with a shy look and her green eyes wide.

Harrison cast a bright smile across the dining room table. His sister looked lovely in a pretty pink silk gown, her pale blonde hair pulled softly from her face.

"We are fortunate that you could join us, Miss Fleming," Jeffrey offered gallantly from the other side of the table.

"Why, thank you, Lord Eddington!" Melissa beamed with pleasure, her intense jade green eyes alight with happiness.

Harrison watched his sister carefully. She had not had much of an opportunity to interact with Jeffrey since he had been at Fleming Farm and Harrison felt somewhat nervous about allowing her to dine with them this evening. Melissa seemed perfectly normal and rational now, and one could not imagine she was the same hysterical person who had attempted to break windows with her hands. As always he marveled at her drastic mood shifts and prayed her calm and pleasant frame of mind would last the evening.

"Yes, I thought it would be nice to have Melissa join us since she has been feeling so much better lately." Harrison glanced across the table at Jeffrey.

"This is such fun for me to be here with you," Melissa chattered on, her excitement at joining them quite evident. "Mrs. O'Neil made all of Harrison's favorite dishes tonight. And we shall have a chocolate cake for dessert."

Jeffrey said, "It's a shame that Juliette is not feeling well enough to join us."

Juliette had remained in her room all day and Harrison had not seen her since early that morning when she left his bed. His concern for her grew when she sent word that she did not feel well enough to come downstairs for supper and he hoped she was not very ill. Every time he asked Lucy how she was doing, the maid said that Juliette was sleeping.

"Harrison loves chocolate cake. Did you know that, Lord Eddington?" Melissa questioned.

Jeffrey glanced up and smiled at Melissa. "It's my favorite as well."

"Mrs. O'Neil allowed me to help her make his birthday cake today."

"That was very thoughtful of you, Melissa," Harrison said kindly.

Even before they had his birthday cake, Harrison was impatient for the evening to conclude. Once everyone had retired, he wanted to visit Juliette's room. Aside from his concern for her well being, he needed to see her. He had fought a distinct restlessness and uneasiness all day until he came to the realization that he missed seeing Juliette.

He had relived every moment of last night in his mind a hundred times. He could not stop thinking about her. He could not stop desiring her. He did not know if he could ever get his fill of Juliette Hamilton. And once he married her, she would belong only to him. The thought filled him with satisfaction.

And he was tired of waiting for the stubborn chit to come to her senses. There was not a doubt in his mind that he was going to marry her. While he had been out earlier that day, he spoke with the reverend in town about marrying her this week. She was definitely not returning to New York and London with Jeffrey. She would not be going anywhere in the future without her husband by her side.

"Excuse me, Captain Fleming?"

Mrs. O'Neil stood in the doorway, her expression puzzled and somewhat worried.

"Yes, Mrs. O'Neil, what is it?" he asked.

"Well, I am not quite sure." The woman appeared nervous, wringing her hands together. "That is . . . It's Miss Hamilton."

The hair on the back of his neck stood on end. "What about Miss Hamilton?"

"It seems she is missing, Captain Fleming."

"What do you mean she is missing?" Harrison demanded, already rising from his chair.

"She is not in her room. When Lucy went to check on her and bring some of the broth I made, she was not there. Her bed was made up to look like she was sleeping in it, but Miss Hamilton was nowhere to be found. Lucy came to inform me right away."

Harrison could not believe it. Juliette could not have

run off again. *Could she?* "Are you sure she's not in the library or the drawing room or some place?" He walked toward the doorway, but not before he caught the look on Jeffrey's face. Jeffrey knew it as well as he did.

Juliette had fled.

"Most of her things are gone, Captain Fleming." Mrs. O'Neil looked as if she might cry.

Rushing from the dining room, Harrison ran up the stairs, taking the steps two at a time, and raced along the corridor to Juliette's room to see for himself. He swung the door open and stepped inside. The sight of her empty room confirmed what he already knew in his heart. He stood there in disbelief. Was the idea of marrying him so repellent to her that she had to sneak away from him a *second time*?

He sighed heavily, yet an intense anger began to grow. Glancing around, there was not even a note from her.

"She's gone."

Startled, Harrison turned to see Melissa standing behind him. Knowing how attached his sister had become to Juliette, he fervently hoped that Juliette's abrupt departure would not upset her too much. "Yes, it seems that way."

"I know where she went."

Deflated, he said, "Where else would she go but to New York."

"Yes, that is where she went. She left on the ferry this afternoon. She had one of the stable boys drive her to the dock while you were out."

"How do you know that?" Harrison asked, perplexed by his sister's knowledge of Juliette's actions.

"Oh, we had quite a long talk about it this morning before she left," Melissa explained softly. "I wasn't going to tell you, but you look so sad now."

Harrison's eyes narrowed at her and his chest filled with a sudden unease. "What happened this morning?"

Melissa stared at him oddly. "Do you know *why* she left you, Harrison?"

"I think I have a pretty good idea, yes," he remarked bitterly. She did not want to marry him that was why she fled from him once again. But then again with Juliette he could never be one hundred percent sure of anything.

"Well, I know exactly why."

"You do?" What had the two of them been up to this morning? When he had last seen Juliette she had given him no inkling that she was about to pack up and return to New York. They had just made love in his bed yet again, after an incredible night. How could she just leave him without a word of explanation? Or even a good-bye? On his birthday, for God's sake!

"Yes." Melissa nodded emphatically. She seemed angry with him. "It's because of what you and Lord Eddington were planning to do to her."

"What Jeffrey and I were planning to do . . . ?" Harrison suddenly had a very bad feeling.

"Yes. I heard you both talking and plotting that night on the patio about how you could get her to marry you."

"You heard us that night?" *Oh wonderful.* This was all he needed.

"Yes. And I told Juliette because I didn't think it was very nice of you to treat her that way. When I knew she spent last night in your bedroom—"

"Melissa!" Harrison exclaimed, in shock that he was even having this conversation with her. She should not know what happened in his bedroom. She shouldn't even mention it. "That's enough!"

Good lord! His sister knew more than was appropriate about his relationship with Juliette. But worst of all was that Juliette thought he had planned to trick her into marrying him. Yes, he and Jeffrey had discussed it while they were both well on their way to being more than inebriated, and it had seemed like a very good idea at the time. But now, Juliette knew what they had planned to do but never actually got around to doing. After last night on the river, she must have assumed the worst of him. Harrison groaned inwardly, angry with himself. No wonder she left!

Melissa gazed at him thoughtfully. "Harrison, you think because you're the captain of a ship that you can order everyone around all the time, but you cannot just give orders to people you love and expect them to obey. Do you know that you never *asked* Juliette to marry you?"

"That's ridiculous!" he exclaimed hotly in defense. "Of course I asked her. More than once!"

"Did you?" Melissa asked softly, her green eyes intent. "Or did you simply tell her that she had to marry you?"

Dumbfounded, Harrison stared at his sister as the dim light of realization dawned. He had been a complete idiot. Melissa had finally given him the key to handling Juliette and the information left him reeling.

Looking frazzled, Jeffrey entered the room, glancing nervously in Melissa's direction before speaking. "I checked with the stable and one of the boys drove her to the dock this afternoon. Juliette has gone to New York."

"I know." Harrison nodded woodenly. That was exactly where he would have expected her to go.

"We'll go after her in the morning," Jeffrey continued reassuringly. "The only logical conclusion is that Juliette must have gone to the Dunbars. We'll catch up with her soon enough. We'll find her."

Harrison stood there in mute silence, with Melissa and Jeffrey staring at him. Juliette was gone from him. Torn between an overwhelming sense of outrage and a profound hurt at Juliette's betrayal, he wondered just how far he would have to go before he reached her and made her see that they were perfect for each other.

And if it would even be worth his effort.

～25～

You Reap What You Sow

"Juliette!" Christina Dunbar exclaimed when Juliette, for the second time in a matter of weeks, unexpectedly knocked on the door of Christina's Fifth Avenue townhouse later that day. "I thought you were still traveling with Lord Eddington."

"I need to return home," Juliette explained briefly.

Leaving Fleming Farm had been her only option after Melissa revealed the extent that Harrison would go to coerce her into marriage. With nowhere else to go, she went to the only place she knew. That she had managed to get to New York on her own was a small miracle in and of itself. She had to move quickly that morning and luckily the rain had subsided as she took the *Sea Bird* to New York. She packed lightly, bringing only the most necessary things with her, and left most of her clothes with Melissa, who had been thrilled with the gift.

"You are more than welcome to stay here with us for as long as you like," Christina offered kindly, her searching brown eyes filled with compassion. "I would love to have you here. You know that, do you not?"

"Thank you for your generous offer, but I don't think that I can stay." Juliette shook her head, full of determination. Not only could she not stay with Christina because of the inappropriateness of her husband's behavior, she needed desperately to be with her family again. "It is time for me to return home."

Christina gave her a questioning glance. "What happened to your English lord?"

Juliette laughed lightly, but felt a sharp tightness within her chest. "Lord Jeffrey Eddington is not, nor has he ever been, *my* English lord. He is merely a very good friend." She sighed in weariness. "But I suppose he will be here looking for me soon enough."

She knew without a shadow of a doubt that Jeffrey would come after her, if only to make sure that she was safe. Part of her wanted to wait for him, but she feared that Harrison would more than likely be with him. She was angry enough with Jeffrey, but she did not know if she could ever forgive Harrison for attempting to manipulate her into marriage with him. She wanted to scream at the top of her lungs every time she thought about what had happened.

As soon as Melissa revealed all that she had overheard, Juliette knew she had to get away immediately before Harrison's plan had a chance to succeed. And considering how she lost all sense of lady-like decorum, reasonable composure, and any semblance of good judgment when she was with Harrison, she had best leave immediately. She could no longer trust herself with him.

"I need to book passage on a ship to London as soon as possible," Juliette said to her friend as they sat in her private sitting room, having tea.

"Well, we shall see what we can do about that," Christina said brightly. "Maxwell will be home soon. I am sure he can see that you are booked on a ship for England."

At the mention of Maxwell Dunbar, Juliette cringed. His leering eyes and loose hands made her skin crawl. That man had caused her the only moment of hesitation she had at returning to New York. She definitely could not stay any longer than absolutely necessary at the Dunbar residence.

"Thank you. I appreciate your help on my behalf." Juliette thought for a moment. "Christina . . ." she began hesitantly. "Are you happy in your marriage?"

Christina stared at her oddly. "What on earth do you mean?"

"I meant just what I said. Are you happy being married to Maxwell?"

"Yes, of course," Christina murmured, her hand instinctively covering her swollen belly. "Why do you ask?"

"You and I talked about our futures and marriage a great deal when we were younger." Juliette shrugged. "Since I am not married myself, I simply wondered if marriage was what you thought it would be and if you were happy with your life now. That is all."

Christina continued to stroke the curve of her stomach unconsciously and she did not smile. "I have a very wealthy husband, a baby on the way, and I live in the most fashionable neighborhood in New York City. My parents made an excellent choice for me. What more could I possibly wish for, Juliette? Of course, I'm happy in my marriage. Who would not be happy with all of this?"

"Yes, of course," Juliette responded woodenly. "How silly of me to think otherwise." A wealthy husband and a baby. Why wouldn't any woman be happy? And why wasn't the thought of that enough for Juliette? Why did she crave something different when every woman she knew found a husband and children to be more than satisfying enough?

That was the question that had kept her tossing and turning for many a night.

And searching for that elusive something was what lured her to all of her quite interesting, yet unconventional, choices in her life.

"If you don't mind my saying, Juliette, it probably is for the best that you return home."

Surprised into silence, Juliette said nothing as her friend continued.

"Not that I have not enjoyed having you here to visit," Christina explained hurriedly, with a little wave of her hand. "I am only saying this to you because I am your friend and I think it needs to be said. I am sure that once you are back in London, your sister can help you find the perfect husband. Now that Colette is married to an earl and future marquis, she and her husband must have only the most eligible prospects in mind for you. You could marry as well if not better than your sister, if you would put a little joy and effort into it. Don't you see? Your family's circumstances have changed drastically since I first met you. A whole new level of society has been opened for you. Last year, your uncle put you on the market for your beauty. But now you have a dowry *and* your beauty. You could be quite the catch of the Season."

Christina paused to catch her breath for a moment and still Juliette said nothing, for she was rendered speechless.

Her friend persisted in a rather serious tone, "I would have given anything to have such an opportunity! Oh, you claim that you don't wish to be married, but that is stuff and nonsense and you know it! Be realistic, Juliette!

What else can any woman aspire to in this life but to marry well? So you might as well marry as successfully as you can. Do you really believe you can continue traipsing about by yourself? Having adventures? Aside from being ridiculous, it is unseemly and terribly dangerous. And if you are not very careful your behavior could damage your reputation forever. You are restless and unhappy now only because you have no one to take care of you properly. But once you are suitably married, as I am, and you are settled down in a lovely home with a husband you can care for and even a precious baby on the way, you shall see just how nice and comforting a marriage can be."

Taken aback by Christina's condescending speech, Juliette counted to twenty before she opened her mouth. With every fiber of her being, she resisted the urge to contradict her friend's conventional beliefs. Suddenly she felt indescribably sorry for Christina.

They had become friends long ago, when they were young girls and they both shared the same vision of their future. Now it seemed they had nothing in common, for Christina had changed over the years. Her parents had arranged a marriage for her with a man who did not love or care for her, or even respect her. What other choice did Christina have but to accept her irreversible situation and put forth a happy façade? How else could she bear it? And who was Juliette to tell her differently, when she still had options available to her in life?

Juliette would rather be alone for the rest of her life than to be trapped forever in a marriage to someone as unappealing and offensive as Maxwell Dunbar. The thought of having a man like that in control of her life was unbearable and only perpetuated the stultifying and demeaning rules of society for women. She was more resolved than ever to not get married and let a man control her life.

"I daresay you are correct, Christina," Juliette lied, feeling slightly nauseated. "Once I have a husband and I am properly settled, I am sure I shall be as happy as you are." The words stuck oddly in her throat, and she wished with all her heart that she were home already.

"You shall see that I am right one day." Christina smiled knowingly at her, a satisfied smile on her face. "Hopefully sooner rather than later."

Just as Juliette predicted, Jeffrey Eddington showed up at the Dunbars' townhouse early the next afternoon. By that time she was more than ready to give him a piece of her mind. Once again Christina and Maxwell Dunbar, eyeing Juliette suspiciously, allowed her and Jeffrey some privacy in their lavish parlor.

"I must say I am becoming a little tired of chasing after you, Juliette," he quipped the moment they were alone.

"I never asked you to come after me," she responded heatedly.

"What you did, yet again, was irresponsible and dangerous! You cannot continue to simply go off on your own like that. Anything could have happened to you!"

"Oh, spare me the details on how a woman cannot travel safely by herself!" She retorted angrily, rising from her seat on the divan. "As you can plainly see, I am fine. I have traveled about on my own many times now. I was not accosted. I did not get lost. There is not a scratch on me. I am perfectly capable of getting from one place to another on my own. I know what I am doing."

"You have just been exceedingly lucky!" he exclaimed,

his voice growing louder. "Do you honestly think you know what you are doing?

"Yes, I do!" She said in a furious whisper, well aware that he was referring to more than just her travels. "And keep your voice down or Christina and Maxwell will overhear everything!"

Glancing quickly to the door, he turned back to face her. When he spoke his voice was softer but no less irate. "Do you ever consider, for one single moment, anyone's feelings other than your own?"

She nodded, yet her stomach flipped over. "Of course I do!"

"No you don't!" Jeffrey spat out. "Do you even realize what you've put your sisters through? What you have put Harrison through? What you've put *me* through?"

Juliette fumed in silence, biting back a stinging remark.

Jeffrey continued to berate her. "You cannot continue to just take off running from place to place with complete disregard for everyone—"

"We've already discussed this topic!" she interrupted furiously. "But while we're on the subject of considering the feeling of others, what about you?"

"What about me?" He echoed in disbelief. "What have I done but travel from one continent to another to make sure you were safe?"

Juliette's cheeks flushed scarlet and her hands clenched tightly at her sides. "Oh, don't play the martyr to me! I know all about how you and Harrison were planning to trick me into marrying him!"

"What of it?" he retorted.

Juliette gasped. She had not expected this response from him. "So you do not deny that you and Harrison planned to compromise me to force me to marry him?"

"No, I don't deny it," he stated flatly. "It was for your own good!"

"How dare you?" Juliette fought to contain an enraged scream. "Are you both so great a pair of fools that you think I can be so easily manipulated? How could you possibly think something like that would work?"

Juliette had never seen Jeffrey look so angry. He glowered at her and his jaw was set. For even as furious as she was, she took a step back from him.

"Oh, I see," he said, his words dripping with disdain. "I see now. You have a double standard. One set of rules for others to adhere to and another set for you."

"What is that supposed to mean?" she scoffed.

"It was perfectly acceptable for you to trap an unsuspecting Colette and Lucien into marriage last year, because *you* thought it was for the best, but when you are the object of manipulation, when somebody does something they think is in your best interest, it is suddenly not allowed. *You*, Juliette Hamilton, are the worst kind of hypocrite!"

"Be quiet!" she hissed between clenched teeth, while furtively glancing at the door. "I am not a hypocrite, because they are not the same matters in the least! Why you cannot even compare the two situations at all! Our little deception of Lucien was well intended and harmless!"

"Harmless?" Jeffrey cried in indignation. "He gave me a black eye!"

"Shh!" She commanded with a sharp look and then continued as if he not spoken. "What you and Harrison proposed to do to me was despicable! You were planning to publicly humiliate me!"

"As if you ever gave a damn for what the public thought of you! You don't care about anyone but yourself!" Jeffrey blasted her in a low tone. "And you certainly didn't care when you arranged for Lucien to be embarrassed publicly! Your ideals were not quite so high then, now were they?"

"You have no idea what you are talking about!" She found her own voice becoming shriller by the moment.

"I have a better idea than you give me credit for. You give yourself airs about your independence and freedom, yet you turn tail and run from situations and people you cannot control because you are scared!"

"I am not scared of anything or anyone!" Juliette trembled, unnerved by their outbursts. She and Jeffrey had never been this angry with each other.

He pinned her with a scathing look. "Then explain why you ran from Harrison a second time?"

Her chin went up. "I ran because I didn't want to be forced into a marriage and because I never wish to see Harrison Fleming again as long as I live!"

"Well, I've got good news for you then," he flung the words at her. "You just got your wish!"

She paused then, taking a deep breath at Jeffrey's words, trying to ignore the growing tightness in her chest. "What do you mean, I got my wish?"

Jeffrey folded his arms across his chest, satisfied that he had taken the wind from her sails. "I mean just that. You never have to see Harrison Fleming again, because you have finally managed to drive him away for good!"

"That suits me perfectly!" Juliette snapped. Her stomach rolled at Jeffrey's news. In spite of all she said, she had expected Harrison to come in search of her. She wondered what Harrison had said or done when he discovered that she had left, but she refused to ask Jeffrey. She feigned indifference.

"You can be terribly cold, Juliette," Jeffrey shook his head in disdain.

The door to the parlor opened unexpectedly and both

Jeffrey and Juliette froze. Maxwell Dunbar poked his gray-haired head in the room. His beady eyes moved quickly between Juliette and Jeffrey, attempting to assess their situation. "Christina and I thought we heard voices raised. Is everything all right in here?"

Juliette pasted a bright smile on her face, "Oh, we were simply disagreeing about when to return to England. We are absolutely fine. I am terribly sorry if we disturbed you."

"Yes, I'm afraid I possess rather a loud voice." Jeffrey smiled as well. "May we have another moment, please?"

Maxwell considered them both suspiciously before nodding his head in agreement. "I shall be directly outside the door if you have need of me, Miss Hamilton."

"Thank you." She cast him a brilliant smile. When the door was closed once again, Juliette rolled her eyes in frustration.

Turning his back on her, Jeffrey walked to the window. A long and tense silence grew between them.

"Melissa was also quite saddened by your sudden departure," Jeffrey said in a considerably softer voice.

Juliette's heart began to race wildly at the thought of Harrison's sister. "She isn't, that is—she hasn't done anything—"

He turned from the window and faced her again. "No, she has not done anything dangerous," Jeffrey informed her. "At least as far as I know. When I left, she was still in her calm mood." He shuddered. "Eerie girl, that one."

Melissa definitely had her problems, but Juliette had found a sympathetic friend in her. Almost a kindred spirit. Oddly enough, Melissa, in her own tortured inner world, understood Juliette as no one ever had. Meeting Harrison's sister had been an eye-opening experience for Juliette. Relieved to hear that Melissa had not done anything to hurt herself, Juliette relaxed somewhat.

"Judging from your rather sudden departure from Fleming Farm, I take it that you are ready to have your little adventures come to an end?"

"For now," she murmured resentfully. Yes, she would be returning home, and yes, it was more than likely a wise decision, only because she needed to get as far away from Harrison Fleming as she possibly could. However, she would never cease to give up her dreams to seek adventure and freedom in her life. She just needed to go in a different direction was all. Yet on some level, she could not help but feel that she was returning home to her family in failure and disgrace.

Jeffrey's voice was clipped and cold. "Then I shall take the liberty of booking passage for us both on the first ship for London." He gave her a sharp look. "Unless, of course, you plan to stay here in New York and allow Maxwell Dunbar to fondle you."

"I shall leave with you," she murmured low, somewhat subdued by their fierce encounter. Even as angry as she was with him, she did not like the tension between her and Jeffrey. She managed to choke out, "Thank you."

"Just remember, Juliette," Jeffrey cautioned her before he left. "Not everything in this world revolves around you."

Juliette watched him leave with a heavy heart.

Jeffrey had not visited her at the Dunbars' house again nor had they repaired their friendship by the time they left New York a few days later. After a tearful good-bye from Christina, Juliette found herself aboard the *Oceanic*, the White Star Line's newest, fastest, and most modern steamship on her way back to England. Matters between Jeffrey and her still felt awkward when they boarded the steamship. Unusually quiet and withdrawn, Jeffrey immediately retired to his cabin.

An unexpected pang of homesickness washed over her as they sailed away from New York and America. Somehow she felt defeated and sadder than she had ever been in her life. Juliette spent most of the first day in her cabin, not in the mood to socialize with the other passengers. She would be back in England in no time. In some ways it felt as if she had been gone for years instead of only weeks.

The ship was quite elegant and she had a lovely cabin, but the *Oceanic* was not as exciting and special as the *Sea Minx*. It lacked the grace and beauty that only a clipper ship possessed. Granted, this was only her second transatlantic crossing, and Juliette had more nautical knowledge after having sailed with Harrison, but on this journey she did not have free rein of the ship. She was simply another one of the many passengers.

The next morning Juliette awoke quite early. She dressed and went above deck to get some fresh air. Not many people were up at that time of the morning, aside from the crew. As she strolled and watched the sunrise, she spied Jeffrey, leaning over the railing in an odd manner.

"Are you all right?" she asked him, concerned.

He turned to face her and she paused in shock. She had never seen Lord Jeffrey Eddington looking so disheveled and unkempt. With his tie undone and his clothes wrinkled, he was unshaven and his eyes were red-rimmed. "Why, Jeffrey!" she exclaimed in astonishment. "You are seasick!"

"Thank you for the diagnosis. I had no idea what was wrong with me," he muttered miserably.

Juliette stifled a giggle. "I'm terribly sorry. I had no idea sea travel affected you this way."

"Unfortunately, it does," he moaned. "I shall remain this sickly shade of green until my feet are on solid ground once again." He closed his eyes for a moment, then took a deep breath of air and focused his attention on the horizon.

"Can I get you anything?"

"Unless you can get me off this ship, no there is nothing you can get me. And do not, I repeat, do not even *mention* food. I cannot bear it."

She could not get over the change in him. And she felt terribly guilty that she now knew that this was the second time he had endured this agony for her. "I'm sorry to see you this way."

He looked at her with something akin to awe. "Do you mean tell me that the horrendous swaying of this ship has no effect on you?"

Juliette shrugged helplessly, feeling a tiny bit guilty at her natural born sea worthiness, as unexpected as it was. "Not in the slightest."

Jeffrey gave her a pathetic glance. "It figures," he mumbled.

"I am sorry."

He continued to stare off in the distance. "It's not your fault."

"No not that," Juliette began, "I'm sorry for all the trouble I've caused you."

Jeffrey turned to look at her. "Go on."

Seeing him this way, put into perspective all that he had done to see that she was safe. He dropped everything in his life to come after her and she had not taken any of that into consideration.

"I've been thinking that perhaps you are right," she murmured low. "I am deeply sorry for behaving so recklessly and causing everyone, including you, to worry"—she gave him a sympathetic glance—"and suffer needlessly on my account."

He said nothing.

"I don't like for us to not get along, Jeffrey. We may not always agree, but I do value your opinion. You mean too much to me, and I'd hate to think that my behavior has been the cause of ruining our friendship."

"You haven't ruined it," he said.

"Haven't I?"

"No." He closed his eyes and breathed deeply. He looked at her, his blue eyes intent on hers. "We are still friends, Juliette. I cannot stay angry with you either."

"You accept my apology?"

"Yes."

"Thank you," she whispered, feeling more relieved than she would have expected by his forgiveness. She reached up and hugged him. He hugged her back, holding her tightly.

Jeffrey released her. "I'm going to lie down now. If I die, toss my body overboard quickly and say a sweet prayer for me."

"I take it I won't see you in the dining salon then?" she asked with a teasing smile.

Jeffrey did not even attempt an answer. He glared at her before shuffling back to his cabin, leaving Juliette standing on the deck. She nodded politely at an older couple who strolled by, feeling incredibly lonely.

It felt strange to be on a ship without Harrison. She did not know what to do with herself. She could not very well join the crew and sing bawdy songs. She did not think the captain would appreciate her help with the sextant or chronometer. And she did not dare climb one of the masts!

She sighed, holding tight to the railing, and stared fixedly at the blue line of the horizon. The soft gleam of morning light stretched across the sky as the glowing sun climbed higher and higher. A new day was beginning. A new chapter of her life was beginning; the part of her life after meeting Captain Harrison Fleming. She would never be the same for having known him.

Knowing now that she might very well never see him again caused a sudden and heavy aching sadness in her heart.

~ 26 ~

Adrift at Sea

Harrison could not stop thinking about Juliette Hamilton. Even though he sure as hell had tried.

From Jeffrey's note, which arrived at Fleming Farm that morning, he knew that the two of them had sailed for England on the *Oceanic* only the day before. That had been the final straw. He had secretly hoped against hope that Juliette would change her mind and return to him. That little dream was now just that. A dream.

He had never had a woman flee from him. Never.

At first he had been so angry he decided that he would be quite happy if he never saw the infuriating, stubborn, reckless woman again. If she wanted to leave, then so be it. He had offered to marry her and she had rejected him. More than once. When Jeffrey left for New York to find her, Harrison refused to go along with him. He was done with her. He had had enough of Juliette Hamilton causing turmoil in his life. If she had wanted to be with him, she would have stayed at Fleming Farm and married him.

But she had not.

As the days slipped by with Juliette no longer in his life, Harrison had come to realize that something Melissa said to him was more than likely right. He had never *asked* Juliette to marry him. He simply told her that she would be his wife. Not that that excused her childish refusal, but it did explain her balking at the idea. He knew he could have handled Juliette better. She was too free-spirited and independent to succumb to someone else's wishes so easily, let alone if she were ordered or tricked into it.

He did feel badly that she had found out about his and Jeffrey's plan to coerce her into marrying him. Even though he had been desperate, he should never have made that an option.

All he had to do was ask her.

But he hadn't and now she was gone.

And, God, he missed her.

He missed the sound of her laughter, the flashing of her blue eyes, her quick wit and untamed spirit. He missed the comfort she gave him, the feel of her body beside him in bed. He missed all of Juliette.

For the first time that he could recall he was at a loss of how to handle his emotions. He found himself moping around Fleming Farm, feeling like a fool and too restless to do anything of any substance.

"Captain Fleming?"

Harrison turned away from the window he had been staring out of. Annie stood in the doorway of his study. With a wave of his hand, he motioned for the nurse to come in. "Good afternoon, Annie."

She smiled at him. "Melissa has a new painting that she would like you to see."

His sister had been quieter since Juliette's departure

but had thankfully remained calm. She had spent most of her time painting, which he figured was therapeutic for her. He had feared that Melissa would fall apart after Juliette left. Much to his own surprise and chagrin, he was the one who fell apart. "Thank you. I'll go to the studio now."

"Her lunch will be ready shortly."

"I'll bring her back with me," Harrison assured Annie.

Harrison made his way to his sister's art studio, thinking about Melissa. He feared for her future and wished he knew what to do to help her. He opened the door to the studio and in the bright summer sun, the large, window-lined room was filled with light, which displayed her many paintings in brilliant color.

"Harrison! Over here!" Melissa called to him from behind a tall easel holding a rather large canvas.

"Annie tells me you've been painting quite a lot and you have something new to show me," he said when he reached her side.

"Yes," Melissa said, wearing a paint-spattered smock. "This is the one."

With a flick of her hand, she gave a last touch of the brush to the painting of two men sitting on the patio. His patio. The men were depicted in silhouette, from the back. The rich detail of the star-filled sky, the gleam of their white shirts, and the faint smoke of their cigars illuminated the velvety darkness of the night scene. Her talent was nothing short of stunning.

Undoubtedly the two men were he and Jeffrey, the night Melissa overheard them planning to trick Juliette into marrying him.

"I gather you are no longer interested in painting landscapes?" Harrison quipped, unable to ignore her recent subject matter.

Melissa suppressed a giggle. "I've decided people are so much more interesting to paint than trees."

"You are more than likely right about that." Although he did not like to be reminded so vividly of that fateful evening, he could not deny the beauty of the painting.

"Do you like it?" she asked, her voice eager.

"It's a wonderful painting, Melissa." He paused for a moment, deep in thought. "Perhaps we should do something with your paintings."

"Like what?" Her delicate brows furrowed in puzzlement.

He shrugged. "I don't know that much about the art world, but maybe we could display them somewhere, even sell some."

"Oh, no. I could never sell them!" she cried in a panic, her cheeks coloring. "They would laugh at me. No one would want to buy my silly paintings!"

"No one would laugh at you." He glanced around the studio, at the myriad gorgeous canvases she had painted. "In fact, I am quite sure many people would want to decorate their homes with these beautiful paintings of yours."

"Oh, Harrison, do you truly think so?"

The hope and excitement on his sister's pretty face, now smudged with paint, made Harrison vow to have her paintings sold. If that would make her happy, then he would see to it that it was done. "Yes, I think so."

"That would be lovely!" she whispered.

Again Harrison looked at the paintings surrounding him. They were quite remarkable, and he wondered why he had never noticed before. Then he realized that it was Juliette who brought the beauty and talent of Melissa's work to his attention.

"I think your paintings would be in such high demand that—" Harrison suddenly froze at the sight before him.

Melissa's exquisitely detailed painting of Juliette rested on the table beside him.

Seeing the portrait almost brought him to his knees. The ache and longing at the sight of Juliette's beautiful face overwhelmed his rather raw emotions. Unconsciously he reached out his hand and touched the canvas. She had been gone only a few days, yet it felt longer. Much longer. He could think of nothing but Juliette.

"You miss her," Melissa whispered, standing next to him.

Harrison could not deny his sister's simple statement. "Yes, I do," he admitted.

"I thought you were going to marry her from the first minute I met her."

Puzzled by her declaration, he looked sharply at his sister. "You did?"

"Yes. That first afternoon, I even asked her if she was going to marry you."

Harrison held his breath for a moment. "What did Juliette say?"

Melissa sighed. "She said no, but I knew she did not mean it."

"Why would you think that?"

"I just sensed that the two of you belonged together and that you would marry."

He had believed he would marry her also. He cleared his throat. "Well, it seems you were wrong." He pulled his eyes away from Juliette's painted face.

"Go after her, Harrison."

He turned to his sister. "She ran from me, Melissa. Twice." He could not help but add, "With no thanks to you."

Melissa laughed lightly at him. "Oh, she didn't leave

here because of anything I did, Harrison. Oh, no! You have no one to blame but yourself that she is gone."

His sister was right, but Harrison did not want to admit that. He said, "She has made it painfully obvious that she does not want me."

"She's in love with you."

Harrison's heart began to race. "Did she tell you that?"

"She didn't have to. I could see it in her eyes when I met her."

He stood motionless, taking in that bit of information. *Juliette was in love with him?* If that were true then . . . Then what? What would he do? *Would he go after her?*

"If she has gone home to London," Melissa said, "then you should go get her. You will never find anyone who is more perfect for you than Juliette."

He knew that Juliette was perfect for him. It had been all he had been able to think about since she left. "I wasn't planning to leave you or the farm so soon. I just got home."

"I will be all right if you go."

He stared at his beautiful, tormented sister. Usually she hated when he traveled or was away from her for any great length of time, and his absences frequently coincided with her darker moods. Now here she stood, suggesting he leave! Had Juliette truly made such an impact on both of them? He paused. "I don't want to leave you alone, Melissa. Why don't you come to London with me?"

Melissa looked aghast at his suggestion. "Oh, I couldn't. I couldn't possibly."

"Yes, you could," he insisted, taking her hand in his.

"No, not now." She shook her blonde head and smiled sweetly at him. "Perhaps I'll go another time. I would only slow you down. I shall still be here when you return with Juliette."

He hesitated.

"You could lose Juliette for good if you don't go after her now, Harrison."

He had the strangest feeling that Melissa was right in her prediction and he wondered how and when his sister became so insightful.

"Go get her," she urged with a smile, her jade green eyes alight with excitement. "If you don't, you will never know for sure and it will haunt you forever."

Less than two days later, Harrison had his crew assembled again and was sailing the *Sea Minx* back to England. Filled with a sense of well being that only the sea could give him, Harrison stood at the wheel, feeling better than he had since before Juliette left.

"What are we headed to England for this time, Captain?" Robbie asked, a cheery grin on his face.

Harrison gave him a cryptic smile. "I need to retrieve something very important to me."

"So are we in a hurry?"

"Yes," Harrison admitted freely. "I want to make the trip to London in record time."

∼ 27 ∼

There's No Place Like Home

"I know my apology is woefully inadequate for what I have put you all through, but I am very sorry."

Colette continued to stare helplessly at her sister. Although relieved at Juliette's unexpected return to London the day before, Colette could not help but still be somewhat angry with her. They had talked briefly last night when Juliette arrived at Devon House escorted by Jeffrey Eddington, but this was the first opportunity they had had to talk privately together. After breakfast her first morning home, Juliette had joined Colette in her sitting room.

"Be careful of his head," she admonished, sitting on a chair near the window.

Juliette looked up at her, carefully but awkwardly cradling Colette's infant son in her arms. "My nephew truly is a handsome little boy. I think he looks like you."

"Lucien's mother thinks he looks like me and Mother thinks he looks like Lucien." Colette shook her head slightly. "I think he looks like Lucien."

"The name Phillip suits him."

Colette smiled, thinking of their mother, and how she had named him. "Yes, it does, doesn't it?"

"How did Mother react to my leaving?" Juliette asked.

"Why she was thrilled with pride and joy!" Colette muttered sarcastically. "What did you expect, Juliette? Of course, she was furious and blamed you for breaking her heart and disappointing her. You are quite fortunate she returned to Brighton just before you got back or you would have had to face her wrath first thing. We shall have to send word to her that you are safely home again. The only bright spot for her during her visit was meeting Phillip."

"I'm most sorry I wasn't here when he was born." Juliette sighed heavily. "I know leaving the way I did was wrong and that I worried you—"

"Worried is an extreme understatement." Colette recalled the unrelenting anxiety she had experienced constantly until they received Captain Fleming's message via telegraph that Juliette was safe in New York. She had imagined horrors of all sorts happening to her sister.

"How could you just disappear without telling me?" Colette could not hide the note of hurt in her voice. "We always tell each other everything!"

"Because you would have tried to stop me."

"Of course I would have!" Colette cried in indignation. "What sane person wouldn't have tried to stop you? What you did was utter madness!"

Juliette laughed ruefully. "Yes, it was." She paused for a moment, staring down at the baby sleeping peacefully in her arms, then glancing back at her with her eyes sparkling. "But do you know something, Colette? I enjoyed every moment of that madness."

Knowing her sister, Colette suspected something more

had happened on that little journey than the tame story with which Juliette had regaled the family the night before. She told of an uneventful sailing on the *Sea Minx*, a lovely time in New York with Christina Dunbar and her husband, and a visit with Jeffrey to Captain Fleming's country home.

"I half expected to never see you again." Colette murmured, trying to keep her anger in check. "If you were enjoying yourself so much in America, then why did you come home with Jeffrey?"

"Because of Harrison."

"Ah, I note he is no longer Captain Fleming." She also noted that Juliette's cheeks had reddened slightly.

"Oh, Colette, I have so wished I could talk to you."

Colette tilted her head toward her sister. "I may still be slightly hurt and angry with you, but I'm here now."

"I don't even know where to begin, so much has happened."

"Well, you had better begin somewhere."

Juliette took a deep breath. "I came home because he wanted to marry me."

"Oh." Colette leaned back in her chair, surprised by this bit of news.

She had liked Captain Fleming when she met him. The American sea captain had been a polite and charming houseguest although he had struck her as somewhat reserved. While he had been staying at Devon House, she had not detected any sort of attraction or romantic interest between him and Juliette at all. She knew the man was handsome enough, but every man paled in comparison to Lucien for her. So a romance had blossomed aboard ship between Captain Fleming and her sister? "And you apparently did not wish to marry him?"

"Yes . . . No . . ." Juliette murmured slowly. "I did

not want to marry him at first, but now I am not sure anymore. It's so complicated and now I'm here and he's in America and . . ."

Her sister's voice trailed off. Colette eyed her carefully. "What happened?"

In a halting voice and still holding the baby, Juliette began to describe the series of events that occurred after she left home and Colette listened, pausing to ask a question from time to time, such as, "What in heaven's name would possess you to climb the mast of a ship?" "He locked you in his cabin?" When Juliette attempted to share some of the more intimate details of her relationship with Captain Fleming, Colette suddenly interrupted.

"Wait a moment," she explained with a giggle. "I don't think Phillip should hear any of this."

Juliette waited while Colette carried the baby to the adjoining nursery and placed him gently in his cradle. She then hurried back to the sitting room and settled herself in her chair. She urged, "Go on."

"You were absolutely right," Juliette confessed. "That medical book doesn't even begin to describe what things are really like between a man and woman in bed."

Colette smiled knowingly, recalling when she had discovered that same wonderful secret with Lucien. Although concerned by Juliette's serious involvement with the American sea captain, she was somehow not surprised.

She continued to listen to Juliette's story with interest until she asked, "Just how unbalanced is Captain Fleming's sister?"

"That's the saddest part, Colette. I don't think anyone truly knows. She seems to be fine and then . . . and then suddenly and inexplicably, she's not."

When Juliette finally revealed the reason she fled from Harrison's farm and decided to come home, Colette said, "Well, I think that Jeffrey and Harrison made their plan, however misguided, with good intentions and not to do something terrible to you." She gave Juliette a pointed look. "And I do seem to recall a certain sister of mine concocting an outrageous plan last year to trick Lucien into admitting he was in love with me."

"Yes," Juliette admitted reluctantly. "Jeffrey reminded me of that as well."

"Well, there you are." Colette shrugged. "But the true question here, the only one that matters, is, do you love him?"

"It doesn't matter now. I shall never see him again," Juliette whispered.

"You are not answering the question."

Juliette almost squirmed under the pressure. Colette had never seen her sister this uncomfortable before. Someone had finally captured Juliette's heart! She would have laughed aloud if her sister did not look so distraught about it.

"I'm not answering it because I don't know the answer. I wish I did. Besides he does not love me."

"But you said he wanted to marry you?" Colette asked, somewhat confused.

"He only wanted to marry me because after what we did together, he felt it was the right thing to do. It was his responsibility, his duty, to marry me."

"Did he say that?"

"Yes."

"I see." Colette asked, "How do you feel about never seeing him again?"

"At first, I was so angry with him, I truly didn't care if I ever saw him again or not. But then . . ."

"Then what?"

"The more I thought about him, the more I missed

him," Juliette said with a note of surprise in her voice. "And during the whole voyage back home, I could only think about how sad I was without him and how I ached to be with him."

"Can you imagine being with anyone else?"

"No."

"Then you are in love with him," Colette explained. "That's how it was with me and Lucien."

"Colette, for the first time in my life, I don't know what to do about anything anymore. I went seeking adventure and what I've only just realized is that the greatest adventures I had were when I was with Harrison." Juliette paused thoughtfully. "And nothing has been the same for me without him."

"You are definitely in love with him." Colette stared at her sister. She saw that her eyes had begun to fill with tears. Juliette had changed while she was away. In spite of her melancholy, there was a new calmness about her that had not been there before.

"Yes, I think I am in love with him," she sniffled in despair. "But I have made a dreadful mess of things and now I shall never see him again. Even if I did see him, he would never forgive me for running off on him the way I did."

Before Colette could respond to her teary confession, the door to the sitting room swung open and her husband entered. Juliette hastily stood up and wiped her eyes as Lucien looked askance at her. Juliette and Lucien never had the easiest of relationships. She thought he was too rigid and he thought she was too reckless.

Colette smiled at Lucien as he came and gave her a kiss.

"If you both would excuse me," Juliette said as she made her way to the door. "I should go spend some time with Lisette and the girls."

"There is no need to leave on my account," Lucien said easily. "I stopped in only to say good-bye. I'm on my way out for the day."

Juliette shook her head. "Lucien, I want to apologize to you for all the worry and trouble I caused you as well." She hurried out of the room.

Sitting on the arm of her chair, Lucien took Colette's hand in his. "What was that all about?"

"She didn't want you to see her crying."

"That doesn't surprise me," he said. "Did you find out anything more from her?"

Colette nodded silently, thinking that her sister had created a fine mess, indeed. "Yes, I did."

"Well, are you going to tell me?" he coaxed.

She gave her husband a funny smile. "It seems our Juliette is in love."

"Ha!" Lucien laughed out loud. "I don't believe it!"

"Well, you had better believe it, because Juliette is in love with none other than your friend Captain Fleming."

Shock registered on Lucien's handsome face. "You are not serious!"

"I am not jesting."

Her husband stared at her in disbelief. "I just never would have put those two together. Poor Harrison!" He shook his head.

"Poor Juliette!" Colette added.

"You might be right at that. Harrison is not the marrying type."

Colette gave him an arch look. "Well, he proposed to Juliette."

With a surprised expression on his face, Lucien stammered, "Harrison wants to marry Juliette? Then why did she come home without him?"

Amused by his obtuseness, she grinned at him. "You have a very short memory, Lucien."

"What do you mean?" he asked.

"Love is not always an easy path," she explained patiently. "They are both in love with each other, but both are too stubborn to admit it."

"Is he aware of Juliette's feelings?"

"I don't know."

Finally catching on, he said, "Ahh . . . And now he's in New York and she is here."

"Yes. I'm not sure how they will solve this one."

Lucien shook his head again. "Juliette and Harrison? Who would have thought? It's funny. Even though they both denied any feelings for each other, I had always expected to see Juliette and Jeffrey end up together."

Colette had thought that as well. She loved Jeffrey dearly and would have been thrilled to have him as her brother-in-law.

His dark green eyes intent, Lucien said thoughtfully, "Now that I think about it, Harrison and Juliette are perfect for each other. He is a good man and strong enough to handle her. And she could never complain of being bored while she was with him."

Colette squeezed his hand. "Oddly enough, I was thinking the same thing. I don't know why I didn't notice it while Captain Fleming was staying with us. It seems so obvious now."

"Well," Lucien said, "what will they do?"

"I think it would help if we brought the two of them together."

Lucien raised his brows. "Are you suggesting that we send your sister back to New York?"

She shrugged her shoulders. "At least we could send her there properly this time, with our blessings and an appropriate chaperone. The alternative is that she is miserable and remains here pining over him."

Lucien grimaced. "I don't believe I could bear a miserable Juliette pining away. I'll see what I can do. I think I'll have a little chat with our friend Jeffrey as well. I'm sure he knows more to this story."

"He must. He saw the two of them together." Colette paused. "You don't think . . . You don't think Jeffrey is hurt by this do you?"

"I couldn't say and if he were, I doubt he'd tell me. He is rather tight-lipped about matters of the heart. But I will talk with him," Lucien continued, "if only to see what he has to say on the matter of Harrison and Juliette."

"Thank you," Colette whispered tilting her head up to kiss him. "I love you."

"I love you too."

∼ 28 ∼

Ships in the Night

"It is so wonderful to have you back home. I know I've said it before, but we did miss you terribly, Juliette," Lisette said, as the last of the customers left Hamilton's Book Shoppe.

"I missed you most of all," Yvette said, with an emphatic toss of her blonde head.

Paulette nodded in agreement, "Even *I* missed you."

"Because you had no one to annoy you?" Juliette responded with a laugh.

"No, I missed annoying *you!*" Paulette said gleefully, as she returned a book to its rightful place on the shelf.

The five sisters had spent the day together working at the bookshop, something they had not done for some time. Juliette made a special point of visiting the family store. She had detested working there while she was growing up and had wanted nothing more than to leave and never see the infernal shop again.

She had left and now that she was home she wanted desperately to see it once more.

Since Colette had married Lucien, and certainly since she had her baby, she did not work in the store every day, but had hired a manager to operate the day-to-day business, while she oversaw everything. The book shop had continued to thrive, becoming more successful under Colette's supervision and guidance than any of them had ever dared to dream. The beautifully arranged bookstore allowed costumers to browse easily and comfortably, with elegant signs hung with dark green ribbon demarking each section of books. With her unflagging customer service and attention to even the smallest of details, Colette had developed a steady and loyal clientele and a side business selling fine stationery. The women's reading circle that Colette had begun had grown to over forty members and met bimonthly. It had become one of the most successful book shops in London next to Hatchard's.

Colette and Paulette still spent more time than any of the sisters at the store, as was always the case. Once they had moved to Devon House, Juliette had rarely set foot inside the shop again, while Lisette and Yvette did so only from time to time. As for the upstairs rooms above the shop, which had been their childhood home, they had all decided to keep their newly redecorated rooms for their private use.

In the shop that afternoon, Juliette looked at everything with a new perspective. She helped customers and wrapped packages. She organized displays and reshelved books. Instead of resenting her unconventional upbringing, she now appreciated all that she had had. After learning the horrific details of Harrison and Melissa's childhood, Juliette realized just how blessed she was with her life and her family, in spite of all their imperfections. She had grown up safe and well cared for and always knowing she was loved. She had never thought about it that way before.

"And I actually missed hearing you both bicker," Colette added with a laugh.

"I seriously doubt that!" Paulette retorted pertly.

"New York must have been exciting," Yvette said with a dreamy air.

"It was," Juliette readily agreed. "I had quite a wonderful time there."

"We thought you would be gone for ages, if you came back at all. Why did you return so soon?" Paulette eyed her carefully.

"Because I missed you," Juliette responded without missing a beat.

"Are you going to go back to New York?" Lisette asked.

Juliette hesitated a moment before answering, "I would like to someday."

"Yes, but next time you will travel with an appropriate companion and with our consent and knowledge." Colette declared in a tone that brooked no argument.

Juliette cast her an amused look. "Of course." *Would there be a next time? Could she bear to return to New York and know she would not see Harrison Fleming?* Juliette did not wish to consider such a possibility. It hurt too much.

"Perhaps you may return sooner than you expect," Colette said with a sly smile.

Juliette stared at her older sister, wondering what she meant.

"Did you meet any dashing and handsome gentlemen on your trip?" Yvette, the baby of the family, sat upon a stool behind the counter resting her chin on her hand.

"Only you would ask such question!" Lisette said with a laugh.

"Well it is a perfectly reasonable question, Lisette!" Yvette cried hotly in her own defense. "Just because you are practically married to Henry Brooks doesn't mean the rest of us cannot think about dashing and handsome gentlemen!"

"That's all you think about, Yvette!" Paulette teased.

Lisette's face turned a deep shade of pink. "I am not practically married to Henry Brooks! And I would greatly appreciate it if everyone would stop making the assumption that I am."

"Well, he has been courting you for a year now," Paulette offered sagely from her perch atop a bookshelf ladder. "What other conclusion are we supposed to draw from that other than an intended marriage?"

"Leave Lisette out of this," Colette said in a calming tone.

"Yes, we were discussing dashing and handsome gentlemen," Yvette agreed with an injured air. "*Not* Henry Brooks."

"Yvette!" Lisette exclaimed indignantly. "That was not very nice!"

Yvette's eyes grew round as she realized her blunder. "I did not mean that to signify that Henry Brooks was not dashing or handsome, because he is!"

Juliette laughed. *This* was what she missed the most while she was away, the familiar and easy banter between her sisters and the bonds that only they shared. Being with them again lightened the aching heaviness in heart.

"Now, let's hurry up, girls. I need to get home to Phillip," Colette announced, and no one argued.

"But Juliette did not tell us if she met any dashing gentlemen or not!" complained Yvette.

"I shall tell you all about it later," Juliette whispered confidentially to her.

Juliette walked to the front door to turn the "Open" sign to the "Closed" side. Just as she was about to lock the door, a man appeared on the other side of the glass, startling her.

"Jeffrey!" she cried, opening the door for him. The bells jingled as he entered the shop. "You gave me a fright."

He grinned charmingly, looking his usual handsome self. It seemed he had fully recovered from his miserable bout of seasickness. "It was not my intention to startle you. I just stopped by Devon House and was informed by Granger that all five of the lovely Hamilton sisters were here at the shop. So of course, I hurried right over."

"We were just speaking of dashing and handsome gentlemen . . . And here you are." Juliette laughed lightly for she was truly happy to see him again. After some intense conversations on board the *Oceanic*, they had mended their temporary rift and now things were as they should be between them. And for that she was profoundly grateful. "Well, we are delighted that you decided to join us!"

Colette hugged him warmly. "It's so good to have you home again, Jeffrey."

"It's very good to be here, I must admit," he said. He greeted each sister in turn, lavishing them with his winning smile. "Ah, here is my sweet Lisette. She has not changed a bit. Oh, but I think my thoughtful little Paulette has grown taller. And, of course, I could never forget the most beautiful of all, Yvette, who has become even prettier in my absence."

Paulette and Lisette cast him indulgent looks, more than used to Jeffrey's effusive compliments, but Yvette stared at him with adoring eyes.

"Why, thank you, Lord Eddington," Yvette whispered softly, her fourteen-year-old face awash in admiration.

"You are most welcome," he bowed gallantly.

"We were just closing up the shop and going to return home for supper," Colette explained. "Would you please join us at Devon House this evening?"

"Yes, of course," he said with his usual charm. "How could I refuse an invitation to dine with all five of my favorite women?"

Jeffrey gamely offered to allow the younger girls to ride with him in his carriage and was rewarded by their squeals of delight at being given such a rare treat, while Colette, Lisette, and Juliette rode home in their usual coach emblazoned with the Sinclair family crest.

At Devon House that evening, supper was an informal affair with just the family gathered.

While they sat at the long dining room table, Juliette thoughtfully observed the faces of the people she loved: her four sisters of course, Jeffrey, Lucien, and his parents, Simon and Lenora, whom she had grown incredibly fond of over the past year. Lenora Sinclair had been the most sympathetic to Juliette upon her return.

Juliette only hoped her own mother would be as understanding when she finally saw her again, but knowing Genevieve all too well, she doubted it. She had written her mother a long letter that very morning, explaining her actions as best she could. Whether her mother would forgive her or not was now out of her hands.

But this group seated around the table, she loved with all her heart.

In spite of her longing for Harrison, Juliette felt surprisingly calm. That urgent sense of suffocation and restlessness she had experienced for as long as she could remember no longer plagued her. She was happy to be home and happy to be with her family again, even though she wanted to cry for missing Harrison. It was the strangest sensation and she could not explain it.

"Juliette is unusually quiet this evening," Lucien remarked as their food was served.

She glanced up at the sound of her name and caught her brother-in-law's green eyes. He smiled at her. Juliette said nothing.

"What is this?" Arching one brow, Lucien teased her. "No witty reply?"

"She has only been home a few days. Perhaps she is still tired from traveling," Lenora Sinclair suggested in a soothing manner.

"No," Paulette added pensively. "Juliette seems rather sad to me."

Staring at her sister, Juliette did not know what to say. She *was* sad. Incredibly sad. Sadder than she had ever been. As they cavalierly discussed her mood as if she were not there, it occurred to her that she had not missed *this* particular aspect of family life.

"Maybe she would like to take another trip to New York." Colette gave her a pointed look, her eyes dancing.

"Yes, I daresay that might cheer her up," Lucien agreed in a rather jovial tone.

Narrowing her eyes in suspicion, she shot an accusatory glance at Jeffrey for good measure. Juliette finally spoke up. "What is going on here?"

"Nothing," Colette said innocently. "Nothing at all. We were just thinking that you might like to return to America for a while."

"Sss–sounds like you are trying to g–get rid of her," Simon Sinclair, the Marquis of Stancliff and Lucien's father, declared loudly from the opposite end of the table. He had somewhat recovered from a paralyzing illness that had ravaged his ability to speak and move freely two years ago, but he was still weak. All the women in the house doted on him, especially Juliette.

"Yes, it does, does it not?" Juliette asked, grateful for the elderly man's bluntness.

"Oh, Juliette cannot leave again!" Yvette cried in dismay from her highly prized seat beside Jeffrey. "She only just came back home and we are finally all together again."

"We are not trying to send her away," Lucien explained calmly. "We are simply offering her an opportunity to return if she so desires."

"Well, she does not wish to return to New York. She is home for good, are you not, Juliette?" asked Yvette.

Juliette, her stomach tied up in a knot, looked between Lucien and Colette and knew her sister had told her husband all about her romantic involvement with Harrison Fleming. *Were they suggesting that she return to Harrison?* And more importantly, did she wish to go to him?

"Juliette does wish to go back to America." Once again her sister Paulette summed up her situation with her keen insight. Either that or she had been listening in on her conversation with Colette the other day. One could never be entirely sure with Paulette.

The door to the dining room opened.

Granger, the Devon House butler, entered the room. "Excuse me, Lord Waverly?"

"What is it, Granger?" Lucien asked.

"I apologize for the intrusion, but a visitor has just arrived and wishes to speak to you privately," Granger explained with a meaningful look. "He says it is an urgent matter."

"Please excuse me for a moment," Lucien said to

them, as he rose from his chair. "I shall see what the problem is."

Juliette's head spun wildly with the knowledge that Colette and Lucien were providing her with an opportunity to return to New York. In actuality she would not be just returning to New York, but to Captain Harrison Fleming, and they knew that. Her heart raced at the idea of being with him again. If she could leave tonight, she would! It all seemed so simple now. She would just go back to him.

"You are going to go, aren't you?" Lisette said softly.

Juliette nodded hesitantly, knowing her decision would sadden her sisters. She looked at Colette as she said, "Yes, I might be going at that."

A sudden seed of hope blossomed within her. If she went back to New York, to New Jersey, to Fleming Farm just to be with Harrison, perhaps he would forgive her for refusing to marry him and running away. Even if he were not pleased with her return, she had to make the effort. She could not spend the rest of her life knowing she did not at least take the chance to find out. If she could be with Harrison again, all would be worthwhile.

"Oh, no, Juliette," Yvette wailed. "You cannot leave us again."

Lenora suggested kindly, "She is not leaving you, Yvette. You must not look at it that way. However, you must allow your sister to live her life the way she sees fit."

"Maybe we could all go with her?" Paulette suggested, always looking at the positive side of things.

Jeffrey remarked, "That's good thinking, Paulette."

"I just don't understand why she has to go anywhere when it's perfectly lovely right here." Yvette pouted, stabbing at the food on her plate with her fork.

"You will understand some day," Jeffrey consoled her with a charming smile. Yvette beamed in adoration.

The door to the dining room opened again and Lucien walked in. He had an odd expression on his face and looked directly at Juliette. "It seems we have an unexpected visitor joining us for dinner this evening."

Lucien stepped aside, allowing the tall figure of Captain Harrison Fleming to enter the room.

Juliette dropped her fork on the table with a clatter as her heart slammed into her chest. For a minute she could not breathe at the sight of him. His presence absorbed all her focus in an instant.

Harrison looked impossibly tall and handsome, the masculine lines of his face tanned from the sun and his golden hair gleaming in the candlelight. Wearing only a crisp white shirt and dark, form fitting trousers with black boots, his tall and muscular presence overwhelmed her. He was not dressed appropriately for dinner, which told her that he must have come immediately from the *Sea Minx*. His intense, silver-gray eyes met hers immediately, and her mouth went dry.

What was he doing here? Had he come to London just to see her? Dared she hope that much? What other reason would bring him back to Devon House so soon, except her?

"Why, Captain Fleming! What a lovely surprise to see you again!" Colette said, her face registering her astonishment at his presence at Devon House, yet she smiled warmly. "Won't you please have a seat and join us?"

Harrison pulled his eyes from Juliette to answer. "I would be honored to join you. Thank you very much, Lady Waverly," he said taking the vacant seat on the other side of Yvette across the table from Juliette. He nodded with a smile. "Good evening, everyone."

"Harrison!" Jeffrey called to him. "You must have set sail shortly after we did. Are you here on business or pleasure?"

Wishing she sat closer to Jeffrey so she could give him a swift kick under the table for that question, Juliette settled for glaring at him instead. He ignored her.

As a footman brought him a place setting, Harrison paused before answering Jeffrey. "I am here on business, as a matter of fact. Urgent, personal business."

"I see," Lucien said, resuming his seat at the head of the table. "Is it anything we can assist you with?"

"That remains to be seen, but I shall let you know."

"Well, I must say it is a pleasure to see you again, Captain Fleming," Lenora Sinclair began in a gracious manner. "Did you have a smooth crossing?"

He nodded. "Yes, and the *Sea Minx* made it here in record time."

"So the weather was good?" Lucien asked.

"Yes, it was perfect," Harrison said. Once again his eyes flicked briefly in Juliette's direction. "It could not have been better if I had planned it."

"Thank you for taking such good care of our sister," Colette said. "She had us all quite worried until we received your telegram."

"I am pleased I was able to see her safely to her destination."

"We were quite glad as well," Colette commented. "Juliette mentioned you have a sister, Captain Fleming."

Harrison's eyes brightened. "Yes, she met my sister Melissa. She is a remarkable artist. In fact, I brought some of her paintings with me this time to show you. I almost convinced her to come to England with me on this trip, but she has a fear of ships."

"It is a shame that your sister has a fear of ships for

Juliette has told us wonderful things about the *Sea Minx*," Lisette remarked amiably.

"Has she now?" Harrison's silvery eyes met Juliette's again.

Her pulse raced erratically and she forced herself to look away from him. She wanted to craw under the table and hide. She simply could not grasp that Harrison was really there. In her home. Conversing easily and naturally with her family, acting cool and calm as if Juliette were not seated across from him. As if they had not shared the most extraordinary intimacies together. As if there were not an ocean of feelings between them that they needed to address. As if he did not sense the agonizing anticipation between them. How could he simply sit there and act as if everything were normal? Could no one else sense the unbearable tension that stretched out between them? Could they not see it? She felt Harrison's physical presence with every fiber of her being. Juliette wanted to scream in frustration.

Paulette eagerly volunteered, "Yes, all she could talk about is how exciting sailing with you was."

"Perhaps we could visit your ship one afternoon?" Yvette asked.

"That is a wonderful idea. I would be more than happy to show it to you." Harrison smiled conspiratorially at her younger sister and his voice dropped. "I shall even show you where your sister tried to stow away."

Juliette's jaw clenched tightly as the tension seethed within her.

"Juliette also told us all about your farm in the country," Lisette continued blithely. "She described your house as beautiful and very modern."

"It is quite modern," Harrison explained. "I had all

the latest plumbing conveniences installed when it was constructed."

Jeffrey commented, "And he has a very talented cook. The seafood there was absolutely delicious. Wasn't it, Juliette?"

She nodded slightly and gripped the edge of her chair so tightly she was beginning to lose feeling in her fingertips. How could they expect her to participate in this mundane conversation? Could they not see that her heart was about to burst with excitement?

"Isn't your house on the shore as well, Captain Fleming?" Lisette questioned.

"Yes, and also near two rivers," he responded. "Which is why there is an abundance of seafood."

"The location is quite beautiful and only a short trip from New York City," Jeffrey added brightly.

Paulette spoke up. "Juliette was just informing us that she plans to return to America, because she liked it so much."

"Stop it! Just stop it!" Juliette cried out in frustration. She slammed her palms on the table as she stood up.

Amid the surprised gasps, nine pairs of eyes turned wide and stared at her in shock. No one uttered a single word. Juliette glanced around the table. Lucien, Colette and Jeffrey looked slightly amused. Paulette looked suspicious while Yvette, Lenora and Simon appeared confused. Harrison remained expressionless. Juliette did not care what they thought for she could take no more of this charade.

"Would you please excuse us for a moment while I speak with Captain Fleming in private?" she asked through clenched teeth.

Nine pairs of eyes turned to Harrison for his response.

"Well, I am under the distinct impression that Miss

Hamilton wishes to speak to me privately, do you not?" Grinning, he too stood up. "Would you please excuse us both?"

"Yes, of course," Lucien said, watching them carefully.

Without a backward glance, Juliette strode hurriedly from the dining room.

∾ 29 ∾

Face to Face

His heart pounding with high expectations, Harrison followed Juliette as she stalked determinedly through the elegant rooms of Devon House and made her way out to the immaculately manicured gardens behind the townhouse. The sun had set and the grounds were illuminated by flickering gaslights. After he conferred privately with Lucien earlier, Harrison was confident that Juliette would welcome his arrival, but with a woman like Juliette one could never be sure of anything. Her outburst in the dining room surprised him for he had never seen her react in quite that manner before.

When she reached a spot in the garden that could not be easily seen from the house, but still had enough semblance of light for them to be able to see, Juliette spun around and faced him. Her chest heaved in breathless anticipation and she gazed at him with her gorgeous blue eyes, her dark hair swept up and arranged prettily around her angelic face. She wore a filmy gown of pale lavender that displayed her cleavage in a most tempting manner. He fought the desire to touch her, to kiss her, to crush her to his chest and never let her go.

They stared at each other for a long moment, neither moving, neither speaking. Time seemed to melt away as they stood in the garden, looking into each other's eyes.

"Did you come here for me?" she whispered so low that he almost imagined that she said it.

"I would follow you to the ends of the earth, Juliette Hamilton."

She gasped at his words and closed her eyes, placing her hand over her heart. He reached out a hand to steady her. Instinctively her blue eyes flew open and she took a step back from him.

"If you touch me now, I shall cry." Her voice trembled.

Puzzled by her reaction, he drew his hand back to his side. He stared at her and simply said, "I need you."

It was as if his words opened a floodgate for her. "Oh, Harrison, I need you too. More than you can imagine. The moment I set foot on the *Oceanic* I knew I was making a dreadful mistake and I feared I would never see you again. I was a fool to leave you the way I did. I thought about you constantly and wanted only to be with you. Why just this evening at supper, I was discussing plans to travel back to New York to see you."

Confirming what he heard in the dining room, he said, "So it is true?"

"Yes." She took a deep breath. "I wanted to see you again, because . . . I realized something very important after I left you."

"What was that?"

She stared up at him, her eyes sparkling in the light. "*You* are my adventure, Harrison."

"Your adventure?" he questioned.

"All my life I wanted to have adventures; to go places and see things and meet people. But the most adventurous, most thrilling, most wonderful experiences I've ever had, have been when I was with you, Harrison."

Deeply touched he reached his hand out to her again. This time she placed her hand in his, interlocking her fingers with his. He stepped toward her.

"I'm sorry for leaving you the way I did," she continued. "I think I was more afraid of my own feelings than anything else. I was angry and hurt and it was wrong of me to sneak away in such a manner."

"Yes, it was," he concluded. "You left without a word of explanation to me, aside from the fact that while traveling alone you could have been lost or accosted or—"

"I was *fine,*" she interrupted him impatiently.

"You were extremely lucky."

Juliette rolled her eyes heavenward.

He continued. "While we are on the subject of apologies, it seems I owe you one as well. My little plan with Jeffrey, although we never had the chance to actually carry it out, was reprehensible. I am sorry and I am ashamed that I even considered it. You were right to be angry with me."

"I know I was," she said indignantly. "I cannot believe the two of you thought something like that would work when—"

"All right now," he said with a laugh. "I admitted it was foolish and apologized. Let it go."

"Very well," she murmured, giving his hand a light squeeze.

They stared into each other's eyes again for some time. His heart pounded so loudly, Harrison was sure Juliette could hear it from where she was standing. Flooded with feelings for her, he took a deep breath. He whispered, "I love you, Juliette."

Her eyes widened slightly before she said, "I love you, too."

She loved him too. Knowing all she knew about him, about his childhood, about his mother and father, and about his sister, Juliette still loved him. This beautiful, intelligent, brave, spirited woman loved him. Unable to speak, he pulled her to him, wrapping his arms tightly around her slim waist and holding her against his chest. The heady scent of jasmine washed over him. He lowered his head to hers and kissed her, deeply, thoroughly. She clung to him, kissing him ravenously in return.

The weeks without her melted away as he breathed in the familiar fragrance of her hair, felt the softness of her breasts pressed against him, caressed the silky skin of her arms, and tasted the sweetness of her mouth and tongue. Juliette loved him and he loved her. Nothing else in the world mattered.

She whispered, "I was so afraid that I would never see you again."

"I couldn't let that happen to us, which is why I came to London to get you."

"When I saw you walk in the room tonight I thought you were a dream."

Again he kissed her, the inherent passion between them rising instantly. For days he had dreamed of holding her this way again. It was where she belonged.

With great reluctance Harrison slowly released her. He had to before he did something reckless with her right there in the Sinclairs' stately garden. Besides, there was still another matter he needed to resolve with her.

"There is something else I wish to apologize for," he said softly.

"What could that be?" she asked, brushing her lips close to his cheek.

"I apologize for not doing this properly the first time."

Her brows drew together in puzzlement as she looked up at him.

His voiced choked a little. "Will you marry me, Juliette?"

Suddenly she stiffened in his arms and attempted to break free from his embrace.

"What is it now?" he asked, releasing her as if scalded.

"I don't know . . ." She became rather flustered and reached for his hand, but he pulled away. "It's just that . . ."

"It's just that what?" he demanded, growing impatient with her. Honestly, how many times could a gentleman's offer of marriage be refused before he got the message? "It's just that you don't want to marry me?"

She grabbed his hand quickly. "No, it's just that . . . It's just that the very idea of marriage scares me." Her voice faltered.

"What do you mean?" He held her hand tightly in his, feeling the smoothness of her skin. He brought her hand to his lips and pressed a soft kiss to it. "You are not afraid of anything."

"Yes, I am," she confessed in a very serious tone. "I am afraid that you will control my life and make my decisions for me."

Harrison said, "I would expect us to make decisions about our life together."

"You are too used to being a captain and giving orders."

"I can promise to try not to order you about." For Juliette he would try anything.

She eyed him with suspicion. "I'm still afraid."

"Of what?" he asked.

"I am afraid that I won't be the kind of wife that you

cxpect me to be, and I will disappoint you and we will both end up regretting it."

Harrison looked deeply into her eyes. "And just what kind of wife do you think I expect you to be?"

"A respectable, traditional wife. I think you want one who will obey you and would not argue with you about anything, and one who can properly manage your house. You want a wife who waits for you at home while you sail around the world."

Her tender confession touched him and he suddenly understood. "What kind of wife do you think you would be, Juliette?"

"One who would most likely not obey you, nor even always listen to you. One who would argue with you and probably infuriate you." She continued in a hesitant voice, "But I would also be one who would be honest and loyal. One who would want to travel with you and sail away with you. One who would love you and make you laugh, and hopefully make you proud."

Harrison's heart flipped over in his chest. He leaned down and kissed her lips tenderly, the taste of her leaving him wanting more. He then whispered in her ear, "That sounds like the only wife I could ever want, Juliette."

She gazed up at him in wonder. "Are you quite positive about that?"

He could not imagine sharing his life with anyone else but Juliette. She was the only woman for him. "You are perfect for me just as you are."

"Harrison," she whispered as she rose on her tiptoes and wrapped her arms around his neck, pressing her soft lips to his.

Her sweet kiss almost undid him. "So is it yes?"

"I suppose so," she answered slowly.

"You suppose so?" he echoed in disbelief. "I've asked

you so many times now that I deserve a definite yes at this point."

"You have only *asked* me once," she argued. "The other times you *told* me that you had to marry me because it was your responsibility. Consequently, I did not think you truly *wanted* to marry me. So, I actually have not refused your offer at all. I only disobeyed your orders. Does that surprise you?"

"Not at all," he admitted. He laughed and pressed her closer to him. Life with Juliette would be exactly the way she described it. She would infuriate him and delight him. She would love him and gamely follow him wherever he sailed. And he wouldn't have it any other way.

"Where would we live if we were to be married?" she asked him. "Here or in America?"

"Anywhere you want." The answer came so easily he surprised himself with his response. He honestly did not care where he lived, as long as Juliette was in his arms each and every night.

"Could we sail around the world together?"

He reached out to brush a stray tendril of hair from her face. Traveling with Juliette had already proven to be an experience like none other. Showing her the world would be a dream come true. "Of course. China. India. Africa. Fiji."

"What about children?" she questioned, her eyes narrowing.

His heart almost stopped at the prospect of having children with Juliette. What beautiful, spirited offspring they would have. "If we are fortunate enough to be blessed with children, we shall bring them with us."

"What about Melissa and my sisters? When would we be able see them?"

"We can visit them or they can visit us as often as you

like. They can even travel around the world with us, if that is what you wish."

She finally paused in her questioning and gave him an assessing glance. "You are making this very difficult for me to say no."

"Then say yes."

The silent pause lengthened as he waited anxiously for her response.

"Yes." She smiled at him, a smile that lit her beautiful face from within. Her eyes never left his. "Yes, Harrison Fleming, I will marry you."

Overwhelmed with happiness at her words, he leaned down and kissed her soft lips, sinking into the warmth of her. He held her in the circle of his arms, this amazing woman he loved more than he ever could have imagined.

This woman who would be his wife.

A young female voice called from the house. "Are you two ever coming back inside? We are holding dessert for you, and it is ice cream so you had better hurry!"

Harrison and Juliette looked at each other helplessly, both wishing they could be alone for a while longer.

"That would be Yvette," she murmured with regret in her tone.

"I suppose we should go back in and face your family," he suggested.

Juliette nodded. He took her hand in his and led her through the garden and into Devon House.

Yvette waited for them just inside the doorway, eyeing them curiously. "I was supposed to find out if you wanted to have dessert with us."

"Thank you, Yvette," Harrison said with an amused grin. He was sure the young girl was sent as a not so subtle hint to let the two of them know that they had been outside alone for long enough. "We would love to have dessert."

They followed her back to the dining room, where everyone was still seated at the table chatting amiably. Surprised to see that Juliette was blushing, he squeezed her hand in silent encouragement. His love for her flooded him with happiness. They remained standing near the table as Harrison declared, "We have an announcement to make."

A dramatic hush fell over the dining room and all eyes focused expectantly on them.

Harrison could not help but smile as he said, "I have asked Juliette to be my wife and she has agreed."

The room came alive with a chorus of excited shouts and cries.

"That's wonderful news!" Colette exclaimed, jumping up from her chair.

Suddenly Juliette was surrounded by Yvette, Paulette, Lisette, and Colette, who excitedly hugged her. A bit of pandemonium ensued for a moment or two while they hugged him as well. It occurred to Harrison that he had just gained four more sisters, and oddly enough that thought pleased him. He now had an even larger family.

Lucien's parents offered their good wishes, as Lucien shook his hand.

"Congratulations, my friend," Lucien offered affably. "Welcome to the family."

"I knew she would eventually come around and see the wisdom in marrying you," Jeffrey said to him in a low tone, after shaking his hand as well. "You are a lucky man, Harrison Fleming."

"Don't I know it!" Harrison winked.

Then Jeffrey said to the room in general, "What we

need now is to celebrate with some champagne! I think even Yvette should be allowed to have some!"

As footmen hurried to fill crystal flutes with champagne, congratulatory toasts were made in their honor. Harrison took Juliette's hand in his once again, happier than he had ever been in his life.

∽ 30 ∽

Smooth Sailing

Harrison and Juliette were married within the week. Juliette had not wanted a grand and traditional wedding and saw no reason to wait, for they both wanted to return to Fleming Farm and see Melissa again as soon as possible. Lucien managed to quickly procure a special license for them and they were legally wed in a brief and intimate ceremony in a small chapel.

They day they were to sail to America, Juliette bid a tearful good-bye to her sisters, with heartfelt promises of plans to visit as frequently as possible.

"You must come visit at Christmas," Colette pleaded, her eyes red from crying.

"Oh, Juliette will probably be in China by then!" Paulette quipped while sniffling.

Juliette nodded, her heart filled with emotion, giving each of them one last hug good-bye. Leaving them this time had a finality about it that she had not felt before. She would never come home to live with her sisters again in the way that they had always done. She was highly aware of that fact. And so were they. "But you will have to come and visit us too," Juliette said. "There is so much I want to share with you and show you there."

Jeffrey saved a special hug for her, holding her tight before whispering, "You found your highwayman, Juliette, and I am happier than anyone for you."

She smiled inwardly as he referred to her ideal man. Leave it to Jeffrey to say something unexpectedly sentimental that completely melted her. She would miss her friendship with him, and again she knew instinctively, that it would never be quite the same between them now that she was married. "You will find someone perfect for you. I know you will. And no one will be happier for you than I will," she whispered back before he released her.

As the biggest adventure of her life was about to begin, Juliette waved good-bye to her family. Once again aboard the *Sea Minx*, this time as Harrison's wife, Juliette greeted the crew with a delighted smile. The sailors applauded the newly wed couple with whoops and hollers.

Robbie shyly congratulated her. "It is good to see you again, Mrs. Fleming."

Yes, she was now Mrs. Harrison Fleming. She had resisted becoming his wife, anybody's wife for that matter, for so long. Now that she was married to Harrison she could not imagine her life any other way.

"It's good to see you too, Robbie," she said.

Being on the *Sea Minx* again, she felt a sense of homecoming. She loved the ship that had given her her very first taste of freedom and independence and adventure. Or had that more to do with Harrison? It was difficult to say because the two were forever linked in her heart.

Gazing at her handsome husband who stood behind the wheel of his beautiful ship, his blond hair glinting in the sunlight and his powerful arms turning the wheel, Juliette knew she would never be bored being married to this amazing man. She loved him more than she realized.

. As the great ship made its way forward, Juliette stood beside Harrison behind the wheel.

"Anywhere in particular you would like to visit first, Mrs. Fleming?" he asked her playfully, his eyes dancing.

"After we go home," and how good it felt to refer to Fleming Farm as home, "it does not matter where we go as long as I go with you, Mr. Fleming," Juliette replied, her heart brimming with happiness. Harrison had come for her and she never wanted to be without him again.

"That can easily be arranged," he whispered.

"I love you, Harrison."

"I love you, Juliette."

The sadness she felt at leaving her sisters began to fade as she looked out to sea and looked forward to her new life of adventure. With Harrison by her side.

Dear Readers,

I hope you enjoyed reading *Desire in His Eyes* and following Juliette's little adventure into the world outside Hamilton's Book Shoppe.

I think the best part about reading a series is that the stories don't end, and I can continue following the characters I've grown to love. It's great knowing I can read more about their lives and don't have to say good-bye just yet. Writing my own series is special in that same way. I can keep writing characters that I love, while still introducing new ones.

So if you are interested in knowing how the lives of the other Hamilton sisters turn out, read on to get a little preview of my next book, which, of course, is about the third sister. Sweet, unassuming, and dependable, Lisette Hamilton is so busy caring for others, she rarely thinks of herself. But what happens when Lisette's neat and orderly plans for her life are thrown into turmoil when she accidentally meets a very handsome stranger?

Thanks for reading!
Kaitlin O'Riley
www.KaitlinORiley.com

Lisette Hamilton never saw him coming.

Later on she supposed that because she was rushing it was her own fault. But still he was just as much to blame. A man should always be mindful of where he is going and should take more care when rounding a corner and not throw himself about like a cannon out of a barrel. None of it would have happened at all if she had simply stayed in the carriage. But no, she had stopped for a moment to visit with Mrs. Brooks. Since Lisette was planning to marry the woman's son, of course she had to stop and speak with her. It was Henry's mother, after all. Yvette had already been complaining of a headache, so Lisette had instructed their carriage driver to take her younger sister home while she remained. She chatted with Mrs. Brooks longer than she intended before realizing how late she was. Lisette detested being late. Hated to think that anyone was waiting for her or inconvenienced in any way by her tardiness. It was the height of rudeness.

Consequently she was walking as fast as she could, her little black boots clicking along the cobblestones of the neat alley behind Devon House. The alleyway was empty of people except for Lisette that chilly November afternoon, and the sky was heavy with dark clouds. She pulled her muff closer to her for warmth. Just as she reached the corner, bordered by a high brick wall covered in a thick blanket of ivy—BAM—she ran smack into a wall of another kind.

Knocked flat on her back with an impossibly tall man on top of her, she could not breathe.

When Lisette opened her eyes, she found herself drowning. Drowning in a pair of the bluest eyes she had ever seen. Not just a regular, ordinary blue, but the clearest, purest sky blue. The word cerulean came to mind. The color of the sky on a clear spring morning. At first they were wide with surprise but then they narrowed their focus on her. Her heart seemed to stop and the world faded around her. Neither she nor the man spoke or moved for a full minute.

They simply stared in mute fascination of each other.

Oh, but the rest of him was fine also. His face was arresting in its perfection. A strong jaw. An aquiline nose with just the slightest tilt at the end. A mouth that looked as if it smiled easily. He was not smiling now though. No, but his lips were close enough for her to feel his breath on her cheek. A lock of his light blond hair fell across his forehead in a boyish way.

She wondered if she knew this gentleman. The familiarity of him called to her, but she could not place him. Had she met him recently? At the book shop perhaps? No. No, Lisette had never met this man. She certainly would have remembered him. And how wonderful he smelled, like spices and bayberry.

As she lay with this handsome stranger, Lisette completely forgot where she was going and why she was in such a hurry to get there. She lost herself in the feel and the weight of the length of his muscular body pressed against hers, barely noticing the cold cobblestones beneath her. His long legs nestled intimately between hers.

The heat and strength emanating from him kept her quite warm. A strange lethargy crept over her as her body melted with his.

The gentleman gently touched his gloved hand to her face in a soft caress.

"Are you all right?" His voice fell in a silky whisper around her, as he traced the side of her cheek.

Even speaking could not break the strange spell she was suddenly under. Lisette only nodded her head in response to him. Her heart pounded wildly.

He leaned even closer to her, placing the lightest of kisses on her cheek. The brush of his warm lips on her skin sent a shaft of pleasure coursing through her entire being. Lisette thought she would faint. This was mad! She did not even know this man, yet here he was. . . . His lips moved closer to her own, and she held her breath, hoping against hope that he *would* kiss her. Heaven help her, she desperately wanted this man to kiss her. Wanted to feel his lips pressed against hers. She yearned to kiss him.

The barking of a dog in a nearby yard pierced the air around them, breaking their intimate reverie.

Suddenly aware of their awkward position, they both roused themselves in a fluster. The gentleman made a move to stand up. Lisette, her cheeks burning, took a shaky breath as she rose on her elbows. Taking her gloved hand in his, he helped her to her feet. As she stood, he did not release her hand. Nor did she pull away from him. Something about him holding her hand felt natural and she did not want to let go.

"Are you quite sure you are all right?"

"Yes," Lisette murmured in a whisper, but she was not all right. Far from it. She had never felt less like herself.

"I am terribly sorry," he began again. "Forgive me. I did not see you."

She had to tilt her head back to look up at him. Again she felt lost in those blue eyes. Was it a figment of her imagination that he had kissed her cheek? Had she dreamed that he almost kissed her lips a moment ago? "I did not see you either."

He still held her hand, and he pulled her slightly closer. "Oh, but we have seen each other now."

"Yes," she breathed. The sound of his voice, low and husky, made her shiver with delight. "Now what?"

He smiled at her. It was as if the sun suddenly burst through the clouds. Lisette could do nothing but smile back helplessly in response.

"Now I believe we ought to introduce ourselves. I am Quinton Roxbury."

Quinton Roxbury. His name repeated over and over in her mind. Who was he? And why should this man have such a tremendous effect on her? *Quinton Roxbury.* She suddenly had butterflies in her stomach. "I . . ." She had to pause a moment to recall her own name. "I am Lisette Hamilton."

"Well, Miss Hamilton, please forgive my clumsiness. In my haste I seemed to have knocked us both off our feet. Are you sure you are not hurt?"

Lisette shook her head. No, hurt would not be the word to describe how she felt. Mesmerized. Enchanted. Awestruck. Those were better words.

"May I escort you home?"

Again, she shook her head. A strange sense of loss surged through her realizing that their astonishing encounter was coming to an end. She did not want him to leave. She glanced across at her hand, still clasped firmly in his. That reassured her somewhat.

He looked disappointed by her refusal. "No?"

"I am already home." Lisette gestured to the tall white house just beyond the brick wall.

"Devon House?" he questioned, his brows raised. "You live here?"

"Yes."

He smiled and then explained, "I was just there, meeting with Lord Waverly."

"He's my brother-in-law." She felt a little better that Lucien knew him. He did not seem like such a stranger to her now. Not that he had right from the start.

"Well, I can at least escort you to the door."

He released her hand and took her arm. As long as he was touching her Lisette did not care what he did. At this moment she would have followed him across London if he wanted. Instead she walked with him to the front of Devon House. Her heart fluttered against her chest at the feel of his strong hand on her arm. Good heavens! What was wrong with her?

"Once again, I offer my sincerest apologies for knocking you down, Miss Hamilton."

"It's quite all right," she murmured, as they stood in front of the gate, noting with some satisfaction that he did not apologize for kissing her cheek. She stared into his eyes.

"I must be on my way," he said.

"Yes, of course."

"It was a pleasure running into you." He laughed, deep and throaty, and her heart skipped a beat at the sound. He released her arm. "Good afternoon, Miss Hamilton."

"Good afternoon," she whispered while her eyes followed him as he walked away. She stood outside the gate, immobile. She did not even hear the footsteps coming up behind her.

"Lisette!"

She turned around at the sound of her name. Henry Brooks stood beside her. *Henry.* "Henry!"

"Who was that gentleman you were talking to?" His kind face stared at her in obvious concern.

Lisette blinked. "I don't really know. I just met him."

But she had the strongest feeling that this man had just changed her life.

ABOUT THE AUTHOR

Kaitlin O'Riley is the author of *Secrets of a Duchess, One Sinful Night, When His Kiss Is Wicked,* and *Desire in His Eyes.* She first fell in love with historical romance novels when she was just fourteen years old, and shortly thereafter she began writing her own stories in spiral notebooks. (Fortunately for her none of those early efforts survive today.) She is still an avid reader and can actually boast that she has read thousands of romance novels. Kaitlin grew up in New Jersey in a family of girls, the inspiration for her Hamilton series, but now she lives in sunny southern California, where she is busy working on her next project, which happens to be a vampire novella! Please visit her at www.KaitlinORiley.com.